BRIDGET WALSH

Daughters of The Famine Road

First edition

Cover art by Latte Goldstein

This book was professionally typeset on Reedsy. Find out more at reedsy.com

With love and thanks:

To my team:
Nancy Carnell, copy editor and daughter.
Charlotte Walsh, marketing editor and daughter-in-law.

To my readers:
Nancy, Fran, Con, Paul, and my sister, Trish Bland.

To my supporters:
My husband, Michael Walsh and son-in-law, Ash Carnell.

This book is written in memory of all those who suffered in the Irish Famine,
and in all the other Famines around the globe.

All mistakes are mine.

the familiar smell, earthy and loamy.

Yes, the soil smelt good - the potatoes might be sound. She shook a potato free and felt it to test for any softness. 'They are sound, thank God. So why is our crop rotten in the ground and this lot fine? God's punishment, some say. For what?' Jane asked of no-one in particular.

She dug some more and her body grew warm from the exertion; her arms ached and the muscles in her back stiffened. 'I'm like an old granny, of no use to no-one.' Nevertheless, she carried on digging; she'd dig all day and all night if she could take home a bucket of potatoes for the supper.

* * *

After a while, Jane called across the field. 'Brendan, come and see what I've got.'

Brendan left his spade in the ground and walked over to her.

'What do you think of these?' She held up three large 'lumper' potatoes. The cousins stood close together and examined the freshly dug potatoes. They rubbed the earth from each cool handful and smelled them to check for the blight.

'Thanks be to God, Janey, they're sound,' Brendan said. 'You've brought us luck this morning, girl. Let's get them stored here and covered with straw.'

Brendan took a couple of the potatoes and headed across to show Aoife and the neighbours. He moved briskly and Jane smiled to think she had brought good luck to the family that day. She whispered a prayer of thanks and continued to dig her corner of the field.

3

She bent down to check each potato and piled them against the stone wall, then brushed her hair back from her face. 'Yes, plenty of food here for the rest of the winter. Maybe some to spare for me to bring home to mam and dad and the boys? We'll cook them and eat them this evening.' Saliva rushed into her mouth at the thought of the taste of hot, salty potatoes. 'Please God, let it be so.' It was months since she'd eaten a potato; months since she'd had a full stomach.

* * *

Later, Jane glanced across to the top of the field and saw the men falter and stop their digging, so she set off over to them. The sound of the children's voices as they played was a counterpoint to the serious faces of the diggers.

She got nearer, slowed, then tasted the sharp, sour tang of something off on the breeze. 'Surely not. Not the blight, no.' Brendan's face told the answer, head down, eyes closed. The potatoes appeared fine – but the smell told a different story. Jane brushed her sudden tears away. 'If it's in part of the field, then . . .'

Jane saw Fahy and O'Sullivan standing by the low wall at the edge of the field, heads down, not talking. Will they dig the rest of the crop to see if they could save any? Or leave it in the ground? Fahy, the younger man, didn't have the worry of a family. O'Sullivan was a widower whose children were grown. Brendan though, with his little family . . . Jesus, Mary and Joseph! Jane forced herself to join them, but didn't speak, as she blinked away her tears.

Brendan was leaning on his spade, his fingers clenched around the wooden handle as if to stop himself from falling to the ground. Aoife dug her spade into the earth and joined him as Jane reached them. Aoife's bare hands and arms were muddied and cold from the work, her skirt and apron were stained with the dark earth of the field. Dirt clung to her as if to wrap her in the disease that had rotted their food for the winter. She put her arms around her husband to hold him. Her face, gaunt and worn with worry, belied her words.

'Brendan, *a mhuirnín*. It's not so bad. I've still got a sack of oats in the cabin and some turnips so we'll manage for a while for food. But we'll have to spend the rest of the rent money to see us through the winter.' The couple looked at each other without speaking. The children, Sorcha and Jamie, walked slowly up to their parents who bent down to gather them into their arms.

Brendan stood and put his arm around Aoife's shoulders. His wife leaned into him and they stood silently together holding their children. The high clouds had filled in and darkened, and now moved relentlessly across the sky, covering the azure beyond. The Atlantic Ocean lay hidden in the distance by a dark mist. In those few minutes the day turned from bright sunshine to grey and the temperature dropped. A few moments later, misty fog settled on the plants in the fields and enclosed the bitter smell from the land like a damp Galway cloak that covered the earth and trapped Jane and her cousin's family in their own little piece of hell.

On her way home, Jane thought about the winter ahead. She and her family; her mother, father and younger brothers, had been hungry for weeks now. Clothes and coats had been pawned. What was to come?

County Waterford, the south-east coast of Ireland, 1845

The light sound of a tin whistle and the solid beat of a *bodráhn* reached them on the evening air as they walked towards the Butlers' cabin on the Ashling estate.

'I wish those two would put their shoes on and not run around barefoot.' Annie Power said, as Finn and Katty, her brother and sister, ran on ahead, impatient to reach the dance.

'Sure, they don't want to get them all dirty before they get there, do they now?' Pat Power, her father, asked.

Single-room cabins, home to the estate tenants, were strung out along a narrow lane. To the south-east, the broad estuary of the River Suir opened into the Irish Sea. All around, the land belonged to Lord Ashling, the local Member of Parliament. This year, it was now October, the land was blighted, the potato crop had failed and his tenants were hungry.

Annie pulled her cloak tight to keep warm against a chill easterly wind that blew in off the river. It was still early in the evening and the sun was just visible over the hills to the west; an orange ball whose flames of red and gold leached away across the sky. At the same time, the full moon stood clear and bright, high above their heads.

'The whole family, Da! I just can't believe it,' Annie said.

'I think they're being too hasty about the whole thing,' her Da replied, 'but I hear the last ships will be sailing next week, so if they don't go now, they'll have to stay here till the spring.'

'How can they afford the price of tickets to America?' Annie stopped and turned to look at her father, her brow creasing with puzzlement. 'Sure they're like us; they can't have that kind of money.'

Da linked her arm and they walked on. 'You know Davey's wife has family already in Boston. They went over around the same time as your aunt Bridie. I'd say they helped with the tickets.' Pat lifted his black felt hat, scratched his head and sat the cap back down on his wiry auburn hair. He was a stocky man in his early forties, a widower these past eight years.

'Well then, we should ask auntie Bridie to lend us the fare and go too,' Annie said.

'Don't start on that again, girl. You know we're not going anywhere. Now, off with you, go and find Eileen and see if your young man is here, too. I've not seen him for weeks. Find out what he's been up to.'

Annie bit her lip but obeyed her father and walked on ahead to the cabin. Brín had said he'd be along later. In the meantime, she'd have some time with her best friend, Eileen.

Finn and Katty were with their friends. The seven and eight year-old children, like Katty, raced around and through the adult dancers. Doting parents laughed to see their children causing mischief. Thirteen-year old Finn stood with the older boys and watched. Soon enough, they'd be dancing with their sweethearts.

* * *

Inside the small cabin, the family's bags had been packed and placed by the door, for the Butlers were to leave early the next morning. Annie waited by the door for Eileen to come over. She saw Eileen's father pour tiny amounts of *poitín* into a cup that would be passed around the men in the room and offer the cup to Annie's own Da first.

'Ah, God bless you, Davey,' Pat said, 'and here's to a safe crossing.' He lifted the cup, took a sip of the spirit and passed it to the next man.

The air was thick with smoke from the fire and from the men's pipes, for there must have been ten or twelve men standing around the turf fire. The open door allowed some of the firelight to spill outside where Eileen's mother was watching the dancers with the rest of the women. Eileen came then and the two girls hugged and Annie turned to greet her friend's mother.

'*Dhia is Mhuire dhuit,* God and Mary be with you, Annie,' Orla replied. 'But bless you girl, you get more and more like your poor mother, God rest her.'

'*Go raibh maith agat,*' Annie thanked her for the compliment. Caitrín, Annie's mother, had died eight years ago and Annie, only a child herself, had stepped in to help raise her younger brother and new-born sister.

Eileen, a slight, dark-haired girl, was already in her best dress for the journey the next day. The two girls had started school together and had stayed good friends. That was ten years ago, and to this day they had shared everything. Annie grabbed Eileen's hand. 'Let's dance.'

They both slipped their shoes off and joined the dancers.

8

Bare feet allowed for a lighter spring to the step in the dance. The earth was hard and dry, just right.

The two girls loved to dance reels and jigs and soon their friends stood aside for them to show off their steps. The musicians played faster and faster and the girls jumped and whirled, almost as if in flight. Annie felt her hair fly around her as she moved; while Eileen's fine black hair seemed turned to silver in the moonlight. After some minutes, the drummer slowed the music and they stopped and took a bow. The watching crowd clapped and cheered both girls, as they tried to catch their breath and laughed and hugged each other.

'Ah, Eileen. Sure, I'll miss you,' Annie said.

'I can't wait for tomorrow. I want to be on the ship and in Boston as soon as I can,' Eileen replied. 'It'll be wonderful, Annie.'

'But won't you miss us all here?'

'For sure! You're my best friend. But it's the right time, so mammy and daddy say.' Eileen smiled. 'Mammy's brother's doing really well for himself and he said we're welcome to stay with them until we get settled.'

Annie saw her friend glance over to the cabin she was born in, at the light and the open doorway. Annie caught her hand. 'Come on, let's dance again.'

'I'll just go and say goodbye to the others. Be back in a minute.'

* * *

Annie had seen the tears in her friend's eyes and stood by the side of the side of the cabin door to wait for Eileen to come back. She overheard her father's voice and peeped around the doorway.

'I just don't understand why they're going, Larry,' her Da said to his neighbour, an older man who chewed on the end of his empty clay pipe.

'Well, this potato blight has hit them hard,' the neighbour said. 'If I had a family, I'm sure I'd think about going. Sooner than go hungry here for the winter.'

She saw her Da frown. 'We'll not be going anywhere. My family have lived on this land, going back years. We have a good landlord and he'll see us right, until this crop failure is over.'

Annie pressed her lips together. Why would her Da think that, when all around were leaving? It didn't make any sense to her. She peeped around the edge of the door again and saw Davey go over and put his arm around her father. 'Pat, my friend, our dear old Mother Ireland is beaten by this new potato disease. I hear it's all over the country. In my opinion, our days of living on potatoes are finished. Even if the next crop is sound, we'll just wait for the next blight to destroy all our hard work and go hungry again.'

She saw some nods of agreement, while others, her father included, stayed stony-faced and silent.

'And, if that's not enough, we have a government in London who think we're all ungrateful rebels. It's for certain that view is not going to change,' Davey added.

'Well, Davey, I hope you're wrong, because what'll become of us if you're right?' Annie's father laughed and clapped Davey on the shoulder.

Annie saw the parish priest heading towards the door of the cabin and stepped back into the shadows.

Annie's Da and Davey came out to greet the priest.

Davey knelt and bowed his head for the priest's blessing, then stood. 'Thank you for coming, Father. Will you have a drop of *poitín* with me?'

'Sure, I don't mind if I do, Davey,' the priest replied. He took the cup and sipped the alcohol. 'Very good it is too,' he murmured. The music stopped and he turned to the gathered neighbours, raised his hand and made the sign of the cross and addressed them.

'My dear brothers and sisters, as you know, Davey and Orla and their children are off on a long and difficult journey. They'll be making a new life with their family in Boston. It's right that we join together to give them a good send-off. Let us pray to the Blessed Lord and his Holy Mother to keep them safe in their new life in America.'

The assembled friends and neighbours knelt before the priest and joined in the Latin prayer. *'Ave Maria, grazia plena . . .'* When they had finished reciting a decade of the rosary, the priest gave them a final blessing and took his leave of the family.

* * *

This was the signal for the musicians to resume their playing. Annie caught up with Eileen and joined in the dancing. After a while, Annie saw Brín, at the edge of the crowd. He'd come. Giving Eileen a little wave and pointing to Brín, she stepped away from the dancers.

'It's so good to see you,' she said. The two of them stood together, their hands almost touching. Friends since childhood, both now seventeen and sweethearts.

'Sorry I'm late, Annie. You look lovely.' He reached out to

11

lift a long, auburn curl.

'Where've you been? I've not seen you for a while.'

'Off, looking for work. But it's scarce around here. Phh!' Brín blew in frustration. 'Anyhow, let's enjoy this party. You know they call it a wake in Cork, they've had so many leaving. And these two,' he pointed to the girl playing the tin whistle and her partner drumming the *bodhrán*, 'are making a fine few shillings going to all the leaving parties in the county.'

'Brín, would you go to America?'

'Not at all. Sure, we're better off here I think. At least we know where we are and we've got our family and neighbours around us.'

'But what about the potatoes? The blight?'

'The early crop will come through fine next spring, I'd say.' Then he paused. 'It'll mean a hard winter, but we've had them before.' Brín echoed her father's words and took her hand. 'What do you say we go and dance?'

'What if the priest comes back?' she teased him.

'He won't come back, he's off home to his bed. Here, give me your hand.'

They soon forgot their troubles as they danced and reeled to the music.

* * *

Later that evening, the musicians slowed the tempo of the music. The girl with the tin whistle held it by her side while she sang songs of leaving Ireland. She was a few years older than Annie, a slim, fair girl, dressed in a plaid woollen skirt and white blouse. The golden tones of her voice seemed full of tears and the night air lifted her song and silenced those gathered around. At the end of the verse she raised her hands and everyone joined their voices in the chorus. Annie saw Eileen standing alone at the edge of the crowd, eyes closed as she swayed to the music. Annie went over to embrace her friend and stood with her until the song ended and everyone clapped and shouted for the family they'd likely never see again.

Annie watched Eileen, her mother and father and sisters, as they said their goodbyes. Annie yearned to go with them. Why could they not all go together, the two families? When Eileen reached Annie, they both smiled through tears and hugged each other so tightly Annie could hardly breathe and she found it hard to let go. Eileen, her best friend since childhood, the one she had shared all her secrets with, was leaving her behind.

'Annie, when we get settled, I'll write and let you know where we are,' her friend said.

'Take me with you.' Annie whispered. They both knew it was an impossible dream. Annie could never leave her father and her brother and sister.

'We'll see each other again. I'll write, and you'll come out to me.' Eileen said.

The leaving wake drew to a close and the Power family walked slowly back home. Night had drawn in. The sky was now a dense black, but there was a brilliant full moon overhead to illuminate their way. The wind had picked up and rattled through the bare branches of scrubby trees along the lane and fluttered the fringe Annie's shawl. She pulled it tighter around her waist.

'There's a change in the weather coming, I'd say,' her Da said, as they entered their tiny cabin. He closed the door and put the shutter to the window against the coming storm.

* * *

In the weeks after the leaving wake, Annie felt the absence of her childhood friend as a hollow loneliness in her heart. Somehow, she promised herself, they'd meet again. Annie would get on a ship when this was all over and visit Eileen. She knew Brín would never go with her. Well then, she'd just go have to go without him.

Ashling, November 1845

By the end of November, the weather had changed from bright autumn days to winter storms, bringing wind and rain. When they got home from school, Annie, Finn and Katty remained in the cabin. The constantly burning turf fire kept them warm, but food began to run low; the same meal every day, oats and more oats, began to pall. Annie's mouth watered at the thought of a potato. Just the one potato would do, even one to share.

The lanes around the cabins soon filled with rain water and turned into a mud-choked mess. Annie stood at the cabin door and looked out across the fields to the river beyond. The water was flowing fast; there would be no boats out fishing that day. She was sure that Eileen must be in Boston by now, thank God, and there'd be a letter from her soon. The wind tore the waves into the air and smashed them into white spray while broken water stretched right across even the deepest part of the river. She blessed herself and prayed. 'Dear Lord, protect us from the storm.'

As if in answer to her prayer, the rain began to ease a little and she waved when she saw Brín coming to the house. He waved back as he approached, his lithe body moving easily over the ground.

'Come on girl, let's go for a walk and get some air,' he said. While he greeted her family, she grabbed her cloak, wrapped it around her, slipped her feet into her boots and joined him. They walked together along the lane and cut through onto the strand and met the force of the wind as it blew in from the Irish Sea straight up the river towards Waterford.

The beach in the bay was all churned up with large stones and driftwood washed in by the strength of the water. Pebbles rattled against each other as waves crashed onto the shore. Sea gulls screeched as they flew into the air to avoid the churn. There was nowhere to walk on the strand as the water came right in, almost up to the verge where the sea-grass grew and was now flattened by the wind. Annie and Brín walked along it, their boots squelched in the soft wet ground.

Brín spoke, she could see his lips moving. 'I can't hear you.' Annie shook her head and gestured to the wind and waves.

The sky was full of low clouds, the sun was hidden behind charcoal thunder clouds, and evening was approaching fast. She looked up and saw a brief flash of lightning, a jagged silver line, cut through the clouds to touch the surface of the water. She glanced at Brín, but he looked straight ahead along the beach and hadn't seen it.

They walked hand in hand, and she looked at his face. She had tried so many times to count his freckles; she knew she would never tire of looking at him. He held her hand, and she could almost feel their pulses in rhythm with one another. They continued to the point where the cliff edge came vertically down to the foreshore and took shelter there from the wind. Brín put his arm around her and kissed her. Wisps of her hair had blown out from under her shawl and caught in his mouth; he laughed and pulled the gleaming strands away, but Annie didn't join in with his laughter.

'What's wrong, Annie?' he asked.

'Brín, I'm so afraid, all the time. Everything is getting worse for us. We seem to be all on our own here. No-one sees the trouble we're in. Only me.' She looked down at the flattened sea-grass and out at the river racing past them. It felt as if she was stranded on an island in the middle of a raging sea, with no way out and no-one to rescue her.

Brín squeezed her hand. 'We're all worried, Annie, but your father is right, we've just got to sit tight and see this through. This will pass. Sure, what else can we do?'

'We can starve, that's what. I'm only thankful we have our cow to give us some milk, but she's getting old now, bless her. I'm sick of looking at oats, morning and evening, then when they're gone, I worry we won't have anything.' Annie brushed the rain away from her face.

Brín nodded. 'I read in the paper there's some people in serious trouble in the west of Ireland. Please God, it's a false tale. At least I hope it is.' He was silent for a moment then swung her hand. 'Come on, let's turn back before the tide rises any higher. Then we'll be know all about trouble.'

They linked arms and walked quickly back to the break in the dunes, from there out onto the mud-filled lane and found a little respite from the gales.

* * *

When they got near to Annie's cabin, there was a crowd of people at the doorway. Annie saw that some of them were crying and holding onto each other. Some seemed to be praying. She looked at Brín and broke into a run.

17

'What is it? What's happened?' she called out. 'Da, Da!' Her heart was beating so fast, she couldn't breathe. Had something happened to her father, or Finn or Katty?

Then she saw her father wave to her as he came out to meet her. 'Annie, it's not us. We're all right.' He held a newspaper in one hand.

'What is it then?' she paused and looked around. Not her family, then who? 'Who is it?' She looked at all her neighbours, some were crying, keening in grief. Others stood just looking at each other, with stunned expressions on their faces.

She heard her Da speak. 'The ship. It sank three weeks ago, in sight of land.'

She looked at him for a second, then held her hand up in front of her and shook her head. 'No, don't say it!'

But he continued. 'It struck an ice-berg and sank in the Saint Lawrence River. They saved some of the passengers. The Butlers were lost, all of them, the whole family.' Da held out the newspaper to her. 'It's all in here.'

She saw the headline, on the front page "Emigrant ship, the Saint Edward, flounders in sight of land" and turned away.

* * *

She pushed through the crowds of neighbours, all trying to see the newspaper, and raced out, back along the lane towards the river. In her mind's eye, she could see Eileen's excited face, so eager to start her new life and ran and ran, not hearing the calls from Brín and Da. Then she was back at the beach and saw the tide was now full in, right up to the sand dunes.

'Dear God! God! No!' She screamed into the wind blowing off the river, and the wind whipped her words away. Spray from the river and the rain mingled with her salty tears, the same water came in from the Atlantic Ocean. The same water that Eileen had drowned in only a few weeks ago. 'No!' She raged at the sea, and the sea crashed and battered the shoreline.

Later, she sat on the wet grass and watched her father walk along the dunes towards her, his head bent, one hand holding his hat on against the wind.

'Come home, *a chroí*, sweetheart. It's too cold and wet here. You'll make yourself sick.' He held out his hand to her. She took it and stood. He pulled her to him into an embrace, smoothed her drenched curls and pulled her hood up around her head.

'My girl.' Her father kept his arm around her, 'Come.' They walked slowly up off the darkening shore and away from the crashing waves and screaming gulls.

* * *

By the time they reached their cabin, the neighbours had left. Brín nodded to them both, but didn't speak, before he too left.

Inside, she saw Katty and Finn sitting in their father's chair by the fire. Their eyes were swollen almost shut from crying. They were both nearly asleep with exhaustion and Annie lifted Katty and took her over to the bed in the corner. Finn woke and crept in to his father's bed.

'Sleep, my darlings,' she whispered. They didn't stir as she made the sign of the cross in blessing on their foreheads.

Annie used the privy out by the back of the cabin, kissed her Da goodnight, kicked off her drenched boots, skirt and blouse and lay down on the bed next to Katty. Her mind shut down instantly, and she fell into a dead sleep.

* * *

The next morning, all the neighbours from estate and from the nearby village gathered at the chapel to hear Father Corcoran say mass for the dead family. The high altar was bathed in light from the candles, and the sun shone in through the long, narrow windows on the back wall. Two altar boys swung incense burners and a rich sweet scent filled the chapel. Annie inhaled and felt the smoky fumes choke her throat and lungs. Already hungry from fasting before mass, she saw black dots in front of her eyes and bent over on the bench, as if praying. At the consecration, an altar boy rang the bells and the congregation stood in line to kneel before the altar and receive the Host onto their tongues. Annie stayed seated and felt her Da touch her shoulder.

'Go ahead, Da.' she whispered. 'I'm feeling a bit dizzy. I'll stay sitting.' Her father, and Katty and Finn, went with the others to the altar to receive communion then returned, knelt and prayed. Annie tucked a stray curl under the edge of her cap and prayed 'Dear Lord, why have you abandoned us? Turn your gaze upon your faithful servants.' She knew that it was too late to pray for the Lord to save Eileen. Was it too late for the Lord to save the rest of them? She shook her head. No, there must be a way for them to get through this. She hid her face in her hands and wept for her friend and herself.

The congregation gathered outside the church speaking quietly about the Butlers. 'God rest their poor souls. They had such great hopes for Boston,' said one. Annie couldn't bear to listen to them talk about Eileen and her family, she walked to the edge of the path and waited for the others to join her.

The church bell in the tower began its slow funeral toll. A harsh clang followed by a silence then another clang, and another. The tolling of the bell followed them as Pat Power and his children made their way out past the cemetery to the road. There would be no burial, and no marker for the Butlers. The Power family walked home in silence and arrived back to a hungry cabin.

Galway, December 1845

Brendan, Jane's cousin, had come to tell them his news. He sat by the fire with her mother and father while Jane sat on the low stool and listened.

'We didn't have the money for the quarter's rent, we had to spend it on food. I had gone into town to try and get work, but there's nothing at all. Nothing. When I got home, Aoife said the bailiff had just walked straight in, threw the notice on the floor, then turned and left without a word.'

Brendan then went to seek out the bailiff. 'I explained to him that we had nowhere to go, but he just said we're to get out of the cabin and off the land. And we're not the only ones. This dirty work has been going on for the last month.' Brendan's face tightened and his lips thinned as he spoke. 'I tell you this, I'm not leaving here. We've had this land for years and no-one will drive me off it.'

Jane's mother handed Brendan a cup of tea. Her father offered him a pipe of tobacco. Brendan, the poor man, knew that his relatives were not much better off than he was, but what little they had, they shared.

'They can't do that to you, Brendan,' Jane said. 'They'll think again, don't worry.'

She saw a look pass between Brendan and her father and

mother. 'When is it to be?' Jane's father asked. 'We'll come over.'

'The first of January.'

Jane was the only one who believed the bailiff would not evict the family.

Waterford, December 1845

The days after the news of the sinking passed slowly. Annie focused on her work at the school. She prayed every day for Eileen and her family. Then she would pray to her guardian angel for protection. 'O, Angel of God, my guardian dear, . . .'

At night she often dreamed that she stood on the shore of the Saint Lawrence River and watched the ship sink. In her dream she could hear Eileen's voice calling through the darkness. Annie called back to her friend, then she woke, her heart thumping in her chest and had to stand out of the bed and lean on the mantle to catch her breath.

One night, after a particularly vivid nightmare, Annie had seen Eileen in the water and called out to her. Annie's father heard her and they knelt together and prayed to Saint Michael, the Archangel, to bring the souls of Eileen, her mother and father and sisters to their eternal rest in heaven. Annie felt her father's reassuring hand touch her hair at the end of the prayer and he sat with her until she fell back asleep.

* * *

On Christmas Eve, Annie started to clean the cabin for the

Holy Day, the birth of Christ. She swept the floor and carefully laid the clean straw she had saved, it would keep the floor underfoot warm and dry.

The day before, she and the two children had taken the donkey and cart up into the hills and made slow going along the lanes covered in hard snow. Then they got out and walked in the search for holly and ivy and finally found some in the woods alongside the Landlord's mansion. Tenants were allowed to gather some of the holly and ivy to decorate their cabins, but not to sell, of course.

Back at home, she placed the dark green holly boughs, with their gleaming red berries, along the mantel above the fire. Then she lay long streams of ivy over the holly and let some of the paler green pointed leaves hang down where their cream veins gleamed in the firelight. She stroked the curling tendrils of the ivy, felt the sharp points of the holly and the smooth berries with her fingertips, and closed her eyes. 'Blessed Mother, keep us all safe from harm, as you kept your new-born son.'

Later that evening, she sent Finn and Katty to fetch water from the spring. When they arrived back with a bucketful each, Annie heated the water on the fire and they took turns to wash themselves, ready for Christmas Day.

* * *

The next morning, Annie, her father, and Katty and Finn, set off for the chapel to hear Mass. They all wore their best clothes and loaded into the small cart pulled by their ancient donkey. They made their way along the snowy roadway towards the chapel of St John the Baptist in the neighbouring village of

Passage East. The chapel overlooked the river, and that day the water was dark iron in colour and flowed sluggishly between the hills on either side of the wide expanse of water. Snow crunched under foot as the family approached the chapel. They greeted other parishioners. *'Dhia dhuit',* 'God be with you,' and received the reply, *'Dhia is Mhuire dhuit,'* 'God and Mary be with you'. On past Christmases, the chapel would be full with local people, all dressed in their best clothes to celebrate the birth of their Lord, Jesus Christ.

Today was different. Annie saw it straight away as they took their seats at the back of the chapel.

She turned to her father and spoke in a low voice. 'Da, where is everyone? Sure, there's almost no-one here.'

'Hush, daughter. We're early, maybe they're just not here yet.' He looked puzzled all the same, and looked over his shoulder to the door more than once.

The priest entered at the top of the church and turned to face the altar and genuflected. *'In nomine patris et filius et spiritus sanctus.'* 'In the name of the Father, the Son and the Holy Ghost.' He began the Latin Mass they had all been brought up to love and cherish then switched to English for the sermon.

'Our Lord and Saviour was born in a humble stable in Bethlehem. He knew hardship and poverty. We offer this Mass to Him and His Blessed Mother, and beg them to come to our aid in these hard times. God bless you all.'

The Mass continued in Latin until they came to the Our Father. This was the only prayer that Annie knew in all three languages; English, Latin and Gaelic. She joined the congregation and spoke the Latin words, *'Pater nostrum, qui es in caelis,'* as the English words, 'Our Father, who art in heaven,' ran through her mind. She smiled to herself, as the prayer ended and whispered the Gaelic words her mother had taught her. 'Ar n'athair'.

The congregation then left their seats and moved towards the altar. When she reached the altar rail, Annie knelt with her hands joined in prayer. The priest held up the sacred Host, the Body of Christ, in the form of a tiny sliver of bread. Annie closed her eyes and opened her mouth for the priest to place the host on her tongue. She blessed herself, stood and returned to her place where she knelt again and prayed for her dead mother, her friend Eileen, her own hungry family, and her neighbours around her, all struggling. 'Are you there, Lord? Can you hear me?' she prayed.

Brín caught up with them on their way home from the chapel.

'Nollag shona, Annie!' She returned the greeting. 'Happy Christmas to you, Brín. It's good to see you home.' He walked along the lane with them and caught and swung Annie's hand in his as they walked.

'Where's your mother, Brín?' she asked. 'I didn't see her in the church.'

'Ah sure, she was at Midnight Mass. You know my mam, she's not one for Christmas Mass in the day.'

'She likes to get going early!'

'Will you be home later?' he asked. 'I'll come round for a visit.'

'I'll be there, and you'll be welcome.' They squeezed hands lightly. Brín saluted Da and the children and turned off towards his home.

* * *

They arrived back at the cabin and Annie took out the gifts she had bought for Katty and Finn at the market the week before. Katty held up her gift, two lengths of bright yellow satin ribbon. 'Oh Annie! This is lovely, the best present.'

'Come here to me, *acushla*, my darling, we'll see what it looks like. Finn, open your present too.' She sat Katty on her knee while Finn opened his gift of a neckerchief made of a dark green checked cotton. 'Thank you, Annie. I love it,' he said.

'I thought you would. You'll be very grown up now.'

While Da tied Finn's neckerchief, Annie brushed and plaited Katty's long dark curls. Then she tied them off with the ribbons, the bows hanging silkily down her back.

'Now you're beautiful, sweetheart,' Annie said. She put the plaits over Katty's shoulder so she could see and admire her satin bows.

'And I've bought us a treat for the day that's in it,' their father said. He took a small parcel down from the mantel over the fire and handed it to Annie. 'You open it, Annie.'

She opened it carefully and found a small twist of paper with an ounce of black tea leaves and another twist of sugar. The last wrapped package, when opened, let out the scent of spices that filled the room. 'Cake!' she said. 'Da, where did you get this?'

'While you were off looking for ribbons for this one here, I called into the baker in Waterford. She had a Christmas cake that was broken and was selling off the last pieces. This was the best of it.'

The dark cake showed flecks of chopped almonds and red cherries, and was bursting with raisins and sultanas. The sharp and sweet aromas of treacle, cinnamon and nutmeg made their mouths water.

'Well, I'll get the tea on then. Oh, sugar for the tea! Da, this is lovely!' Annie said. They sat around their turf fire and enjoyed the cake with tea. They ate well that day. Before bed, the three children knelt with their father and recited the rosary in memory of their mother and their lost neighbours.

Eviction. Galway, January 1846

T he date of the eviction was upon them. That morning, Jane, with her father, Dara, and the neighbours, O'Sullivan and Fahy, had come to support Brendan and his family. Somehow, they would try to stop this eviction.

'There's no-one on this earth who would evict a young family, and if there is such a one today, then we'll fight them,' her father said. Although Jane had never seen him raise his hand to a soul.

That morning in January, the empty potato fields were covered with a foot of snow. It lay in drifts against the stone walls and filled the laneway between the fields and the family's cabin. Puddles had turned into patches of ice, sleet fell and the Atlantic roiled its dark grey sullen waves in the coves below.

They heard the bailiff, his men, and the constable, approach on horseback. The horses stepped carefully through the deep snow and ice-crusted puddles. On they came, almost right up to the cabin door, where they halted. The riders stayed mounted. The wind had dropped, although sleet continued to patter over the breathy sounds of the horses and the rattle of bridles.

Jane watched Brendan walk slowly over towards the mounted men. His hair was wet, and the icy rain ran through it, down his face and onto his jacket. Brendan's winter coat had long since been pawned and he shivered in the cold air. His wife and children waited outside the cabin, as if already dispossessed. Aoife's black cloak covered herself and the two little ones; her cloak the only thing to prevent the sleety rain from drenching them all.

Jane, with her father and the neighbours, stepped up behind Brendan. Each carried the spade they used for digging potatoes. They stood silently together, as Brendan started to speak, but the bailiff held his hand up for silence.

The bailiff's small black eyes glittered as he observed the family. His pink face and neck seemed rolled into one, very much like a piglet fattened for the table. He sat there, warmly wrapped in a black oiled top-coat, with serge knee breeches tucked into stout leather boots. Jane thought that his top hat, if pawned, would have easily fed Brendan's children for a month.

Jane recognised the constable, Niall Smullen, a local man and neighbour. He sat there high on his horse, too. Jane caught his eye but he glanced away. Would he speak up for Brendan? But he stayed silent.

The bailiff read slowly from a piece of paper. 'Brendan Keating, you have not paid the rent due on this plot of land, so by law you will be evicted today. The cabin will be repossessed by me, on behalf of the landowner, and the roof removed. Your possessions will be confiscated to pay the outstanding debt. You must leave this place by the end of today.'

Brendan, the big man, strained upwards to speak to the bailiff on his horse. 'Mr Burke, I beg you, have mercy on my family. Don't evict us. Give me a few months for this blight to pass. We'll either pay the back-rent or we'll go. Don't throw us out in the middle of winter. In the name of God, have pity on my children.'

* * *

At this point, Jane's father and the two men, had planned to support Brendan and speak as one, but only Jane heard the bailiff lower his voice and reply.

'By the end of today, Keating, and take your shit family with you.'

Brendan shouted at the bailiff. 'No, you'll not do this. I'll not let you. By God, I'll not allow it. You'll not throw us onto the road.' He reached up to catch the reins of the bailiff's horse. At the same moment, the constable held his pistol high in the air and let off a warning shot. The sudden gunshot set crows clattering off into the sky.

Jane heard Sorcha scream. 'Daddy, daddy.'

'Don't threaten me, Brendan Keating.' The bailiff then drew his own pistol and pointed it at Brendan. 'Stand back and let us conclude our business here.'

Jane reached out to her cousin. 'Brendan, come away.'

Brendan took no notice, he caught the bridle and the horse reared in fright. In the same instant, Jane saw the whites of the horse's eyes, then she heard an explosion that seemed to stop the earth moving.

The bailiff had fired his gun, and the bullet went straight into Brendan's eye. He collapsed backwards on to Jane. Together, they fell onto the snow-covered ground. Jane was deafened by the gunshot and instantly drenched in slippery, hot blood that pulsed across her face and down her neck. She coughed and choked on blood in her mouth and could hardly breath from the weight of Brendan's body on her. When she caught her breath, the smell was overpowering, like raw meat, and her stomach churned. Brendan's destroyed face was turned towards her and almost touched her cheek.

Jane's father pulled Brendan's body off her and laid him on the ground. Aoife reached Brendan, held him in her arms and kissed his face, all bloody, but stilled now. Aoife's screams pierced the sky like a lightning strike.

Jane felt herself pulled into her father's arms and heard his voice hoarse with emotion.

'What have you done, man? In the name of God, what have you done?'

Jane tried to move but her body was rigid with fear, her eyes were blinded by blood and she could still hardly breathe, for the choking smells of death and gunpowder.

She looked over at Brendan's bloodied face and body in Aoife's embrace. Jane willed him to open his eyes and push himself off the ground. She looked at her hands and the front of her jacket and felt his spilled blood thicken on her own skin. It seemed as if an hour passed and Jane still felt her father's arms around her and waited for Brendan to wake up. She looked at her father. 'Daddy?'

Her father tightened his arm around her. 'I have you, daughter,' he said, then called to Niall Smullen. 'This is murder, Niall. We all saw it. Arrest him for Christ's sake.'

The constable shook his head. 'There's nothing I can do. Mr Burke defended himself.'

Jane saw the bailiff glance at the constable, then put his pistol back in its holster. 'We'll be back in an hour to take possession.' He pointed to Aoife and her children. 'I don't want to see you or those children again. Do you understand?'

The eviction gang rode off, leaving the men, Jane and Aoife and children, with Brendan's body, in front of the small cabin that had once been a home.

* * *

Jane heard her father's voice, but couldn't understand his words. She felt as if she had left her body and stood above the little scene by the cabin.

'Janey, are you hurt? Janey! You're all covered in blood, girl.'

Finally, she understood what he said. 'I'm not hurt, daddy.' She looked at her hands; they were crimson and sticky. 'What have they done to him?'

'It happened so fast,' her father whispered as he wiped the rain and tears off his face. 'They shot Brendan right in front of us.'

Aoife still sat on the ground next to her husband's body. Little Sorcha clung on to her mother, while her older brother, Jamie, just stood and stared, as if transfixed, at his father's ruined face.

Jane tried to get up, but her knees crumpled beneath her. Her father helped her stand and she leaned on her spade while Fahy spoke to her father. 'We need to get a move on here, Dara.'

There was no time to lose. Aoife and the children had to be gone before the bailiff and his men came back, and they'd be back soon.

'We'll bury him here. Brendan belongs here on his bit of land. What do you say, Aoife?' Jane's father said.

Aoife nodded her assent but seemed to have lost the power of speech. She just sat on flattened snow beside the body of her husband and held his hand and scarcely heeded her children. Her hands were covered in Brendan's blood.

Fahy and O'Sullivan began to dig beside the hedge, between the field and the cabin. Jane's father picked up his spade and joined them. Jane walked over to Aoife and hugged her, then went to help dig Brendan's grave.

Aoife sat with her dead husband and bedraggled children and watched them dig. After a while she went into the cabin and brought out a basin of water. She washed Brendan's face and covered it with a small cloth, hiding the ragged gunshot wound in his eye.

The snow of the last few weeks had cocooned the earth and prevented it from freezing. It was easy to dig. A cool, scented aroma rose up as they worked in silence, deeper and deeper. Jane's face streamed with tears and sweat, her muscles ached from the constant shovelling, her breath strained from the effort, and she glanced every so often at Brendan's body lying on the ground.

* * *

Finally, the grave was ready. Jane's father spoke quietly. 'Gently now. Fahy and Jane, you take the feet. O'Sullivan, we'll take his shoulders.'

They took the weight of him and stepped down into the grave. They paused as they held the body of a young man, father, husband, friend and cousin. They lowered him to lie alone in the cold ground and crossed his arms across his chest in a final prayer.

By that time, evening was drawing in and the air had turned to mist and the mist back to sleet. It slanted into the grave, and icy arrows drenched the body in a frozen shroud. The sleet fell harder and harder and spattered on the body, washing Brendan's blood into the dark earth. There was silence, apart from the clatter of sleet, as if the heavens tried to clean away all signs of this murder.

Jane and her father picked up their spades and stood with Aoife and the children in silence at the edge of the pit.

Aoife knelt at the edge of the grave and murmured, 'Brendan, Brendan, *a mhuirnín*, my darling.' Aoife wept, her children beside her, clutched their mother's cloak while she whispered a final prayer. 'Eternal rest grant unto him, O Lord, and let perpetual light shine upon him . . .'

Then the four of them; Jane, her father, Fahy and O'Sullivan began to fill in the grave. Jane dug a spadeful of the earth beside the grave and threw it onto Brendan's body. It was only then, that she knew in her heart, her cousin was truly dead. Her tears fell as she helped fill in the grave until just a dark mound stood proud at the edge of the snow-filled field. They covered off the top with snow to disguise it, so that from a distance it looked no more interesting than a patch of raised earth. There had been no priest to send Brendan on his final journey and there would be no stone to mark his final place of rest.

* * *

Jane followed Aoife into the cabin. The two women washed themselves clean. Jane's mind still seemed to be somewhere out of her body. She could see and hear herself in the cabin as she spoke to Aoife, but felt as if she were apart from her body in some way, like a bird soaring over the earth, unable to land.

'Are you ready, Aoife?' Fahy asked. 'We'll find you and the children shelter in town.'

Aoife put a few bits of clothes into a bag, gathered her two children to her, and they set off on the four-mile walk to Galway town. Fahy held Jamie's hand and Dara carried Sorcha. Jane walked with Aoife and tried to imagine her feelings on this day and those of the poor children who had witnessed the murder of their father. God help them, no good could come of this journey. Jane's head reeled and she stumbled; Aoife put her hand out to steady her. Rain and sleet flowed over the edge of Aoife's hood and into her eyes. Jane looked up at the sky to see the heavens had still not relented, she was drenched and freezing.

Jane stopped and watched as the constable and his gang of men rode past on their way back to the cabin.

'Aoife, I need to do something, I'll catch you up,' she said. Her father was up ahead with the children and didn't see her turn and run back to the cabin.

* * *

Rows of thick turf formed the sturdy roof of Brendan and Aoife's low cabin. Niall Smullen rode up to the cabin, stood in his stirrups, and reached across to the roof. He had a long spike in his hand and used it to lift the edge of the lowest piece of turf. The piece came away and dropped to the ground. He sat back in his saddle and looked at the three men with him.

'Right,' he said. 'Go to it. Check inside, then get the roof off.'

One of the men searched the cabin for any valuables but came away empty-handed, then they began to dismantle the roof piece by piece with their metal spikes. Some of the drier sods landed on the embers of the turf fire inside and sparks flew around the interior of the cabin.

Jane picked up her shovel and ran over to the men. They were like a gang of rats up to mischief.

'Get away from there, leave it,' she lifted her shovel and brought it down on one of the men's metal spikes. The men stepped back and looked at Smullen. He moved his horse towards Jane.

'You've no business here, Keating. Get on your way,' he said.

'You're a coward, Niall Smullen. I saw what you did. You'll pay for this!' Jane put her hand on the bridle to stop the horse and glanced through the door of the cabin. The fallen sods of turf burst into flames and fed on the few bits of furniture left in the single room. The fire's energy grew, and in seconds the entire cabin was in flames; scarlet, crackling and hungry for more things to burn through.

She turned back to face him square on. 'You looked on, while Brendan was murdered. God will punish you, if the British Government won't. You'll rue this day, Niall Smullen.'

The constable jumped down from his horse, grabbed Jane's arm and pulled her to him. His other hand caught her neck and squeezed hard.

'I didn't kill him, but I won't forget you either, Jane Keating. Your lot are next.' His breath was hot and rancid against her mouth, his yellow teeth bared.

Jane dropped her shovel, lifted her hand and slapped him hard in the face. He staggered back, then stepped forward and pushed her. 'Get away from here, bitch! This is your last warning.'

Jane's feet slipped in the mud and she put her hand out to

catch the stone wall beside her. Its rough edges bit into her skin, stinging and drawing spots of blood from the tips of her fingers.

She picked up her shovel, turned and walked quickly away to catch up with her father and the others. Her hands stung and her heart hammered in her chest. She wept to think of her beautiful cousin lying alone in the cold earth, but she didn't look back.

The Schoolroom at Ashling, County Waterford.

Annie set the fire with twigs and kindling, then lit it with a spark from the flint. She left the door to the cast-iron stove open to catch a draught. When the kindling started to crackle and flame, she laid some broken pieces of turf on top and waited for them to catch light. The earthy, warm scent from the turf soon spread around the cold barn. She turned and looked at the school room. There were five long tables made of planed wood, each with a matching bench big enough for five or six pupils to sit on.

At the front of the classroom there was a teacher's table and chair, with a stool for Annie. The school-room had been set up ten years previously when Miss Margaret Nagel, the daughter of His Lordship's solicitor in Waterford, had offered to run a school for the children on the estate.

His Lordship had agreed and loaned out a small barn and furnished it with the tables and benches and a stove. Annie had been one of the first pupils to attend when she was just six years old. She had graduated three years ago, and now worked as a teaching assistant to Miss Nagel.

Annie smiled to see the Phelan twins, Roisin and Jemmy, had arrived first, as usual. They were the only twins in the class and, at ten years old, were Annie's favourites, apart from her own brother and sister, of course.

'Here you are, Miss Annie,' Roisin said. 'Daddy says this'll keep us warm for the week.' It was the Phelan family's turn to provide the fuel this week.

'Sure, you're just the best. We're down to the last few pieces of turf for the fire. Empty it into the bucket. You'll be wanting to take your basket home.'

More children arrived until there were thirty boys and girls aged from five to twelve years old.

Their teacher pulled up outside in her pony and trap. Padraig, one of the older boys ran outside to see to the pony.

The pupils stood by their desks while their teacher walked to the front of the classroom and greeted them. 'Good morning, everyone. Please sit down.'

Once the children were sitting quietly, from left to right according to their age, Miss Nagel turned to Annie.

'I think today we'll concentrate on reading, geography and mathematics. I'll take the older children and, let me see, how many younger ones do we have today?' She counted them. 'Ah, ten for you, Annie. You can have the maps first and do geography, then I'll use them later.' The teacher opened the bag on her desk. 'I've brought some new reading books in, so you may try them out.'

Annie smiled with delight at the new books. She turned the books over in her hands and felt the soft paper and scanned the titles. Even though they were already well-used, there were quite a few of them. Her pupils would enjoy reading these stories.

'Ah, that's good to see, Miss Nagel. You're great at getting us new books!'

The teacher nodded. 'Let's get started, shall we?'

Annie gathered her pupils around a table at the back of the class.

'Today we'll be looking at a map of the world and learning about America. It's a great big country and we'll find its capital city on the map. Now who knows the name of the capital city of North America?'

She brought out the precious map of the world and the battered globe donated by Miss Nagel's father and began the lesson.

* * *

Later that morning, as they were working on mathematics, Padraig, the tall boy who had taken care of Miss Nagel's pony, came over to Annie and sat down heavily on the bench near her.

'Miss Annie, I feel strange. My head's not right and I can't see properly.' Annie looked at him, his face was ashen and grey.

'Do you want to get a drink of water?' she asked.

Before he could reply, his eyes rolled up as he fell forward and his head banged on the table.

'My God! Miss Nagel, Miss Nagel!' she called. 'Come quickly.'

The teacher rushed over. 'Dear Lord! Is that Padraig? What on earth is the matter with the boy?'

Annie fetched a cup of water from the bucket by the door and rubbed the boy's cold hands in hers. 'He's as pale as a ghost,' she said, 'and he's freezing with the cold.'

The boy's eyes fluttered and he tried to lift his head.

'Padraig, what ails you? Are you sick?' Miss Nagel asked.

He shook his head, as if to shake off the dizziness. 'I'm alright now. I'm sorry, I don't know what happened.' He sat up and sipped at the water and looked up at the children surrounding him, all staring silently.

'Now then, children let's get back to our work,' their teacher said and clapped her hands. She pulled her shawl across her ample bosom and tucked the ends in at the waist ready to resume her teaching. She turned to Annie. 'Keep Padraig with you until he feels better.'

Annie's pupils got on with their sums and, after a few minutes, Annie called over to Miss Nagel. 'Can I borrow Finn to help me for a few minutes, please?'

'Of course. Finn, go and help your sister.'

'Will you stay with the children, Finn? They've got adding and subtracting to do. I just want to take Padraig out to get some fresh air.'

Her brother smiled and nodded to Annie. 'Yes, Miss.'

Annie motioned to Padraig to walk outside with her. She closed the door behind them and looked along the road towards the cabins and at the gleaming, limestone mansion of His Lordship up on the hill, and the land around, and this barn, their schoolroom. She felt an understanding come over her. All this, including the people here, were his property in some way, to be disposed of as His Lordship saw fit.

'Padraig, you're still poorly.' She reached up and felt his forehead, 'and you're still cold. Why haven't you got your jacket on today? Sure it's the middle of winter.'

The boy looked at Annie, he'd stretched up lately and was taller than her, then he looked away. 'I forgot my jacket, Miss Annie. It's at home. I'll get off now, if that's alright. Will you tell my brother and sister that I've gone home?'

'I will to be sure, Padraig, and I'll call in on my way past later, to say hello to your mother.'

'No, don't do that,' he replied. 'Mam's not well and she won't want you calling in.' He still didn't look at her and gave a wave as he turned to walk away.

Annie watched his long, skinny legs as he walked slowly along the laneway. Well, you'd think he'd want someone to call in, she thought.

* * *

When school ended, Annie walked back to the cabin with Katty and Finn.

'Go on ahead home, my darlings. I'm just calling in to see if Padraig is feeling better.' She stopped at the first small cabin in the row and saw her brother and sister wave to her and race on home.

The door to Padraig's cabin was ajar, and she knocked and peeped inside. '*Dia dhuit!*' Hello!' she called.

'Ah, come in and *Dhia is Mhuire dhuit,* God and Mary be with you.' A low voice from the cabin answered. 'Is it Annie?'

'It is. Did Padraig tell you I'd call by?' Annie asked, as she stepped into the room. She hid her shock at the state of the place. There was no fire, the air was freezing and the floor was filthy. Padraig's mother, Jean, sat beside the empty grate. Padraig was right, his mother was ill. Her head drooped and her face was pinched and a browny-yellow in colour, like the smoke stains from the fire on the cabin wall.

Annie went to Jean and knelt beside her. 'Padraig said you're not well. And where are the children?' She held Jean's thin hand and felt the lightness of her bones through the papery skin.

'They've gone to my sister in Passage. She'll give them a bit of supper. Not that she has much to spare, God bless her.'

'Do you have no food in the house?' Annie asked.

'We ran out of oats last week. I don't know how we're supposed to live with no potatoes in the ground.' Jean's eyes filled with tears as she spoke. 'Their father has gone to England to earn money, but I've not heard from him for weeks now. I'm so worried about him. I've even had to pawn our coats to get a few shillings for food. We've nothing left.'

The woman's ragged dress hung loosely on her and Annie could smell the stale odour of her unwashed body.

'There's soup at home. I'll go and fetch you a bowl, then we'll talk.' Annie stood and lightly touched Jean's shoulder. 'I won't be long.' Annie left Jean and rushed home.

* * *

Her father was sitting in his chair by the fire, with Katty on his knee. Annie smelt the soup on the pot over the fire. Finn was at the table doing his homework by the light of a candle. The only sound was the whisper of the red heart of the turf as it broke apart in the fire.

She turned to her father and Katty. 'Da, did they tell you where I was?' She picked up a wooden spoon, lifted the lid from the pot to stir the soup, and steam billowed out into the room. She had managed to get hold of a small bag of barley and a few vegetables at the market the week before. Some grains of the barley, together with an onion, a swede and a few carrots had been cooking in the pot for the afternoon. It

45

was a thankful change to the oats and they were all looking forward to their supper.

'I told Jean I'd bring her a bowl of soup. She's sitting there with not a bite to eat, poor thing.'

Annie spooned out some of the broth into a bowl then covered it with a cloth and set it down on the table. She went to the water bucket and dipped a cup in, filled it with water, brought it to the pot and stirred it into the remaining soup, then replaced the lid.

Da stood and sat Katty on his chair while he walked Annie to the door and held the door open for her.

'Annie, you're a kind-hearted girl, but you mustn't do this again.'

She looked at her father's solemn face. He didn't seem angry with her but she could see he was troubled.

'Finn and Katty are our main job now.' Her father said. 'We have to keep them safe. We all have to be safe and well. Don't you see, daughter, we don't have anything to spare?'

She certainly did see. But at the same time, her neighbour was starving.

'Tell Jean, she needs to get herself into the workhouse in Waterford. They'll feed her and the children. There's no point in her sitting there while they all starve.'

She nodded. 'I'll tell her. Oh Da, it's so sad.'

* * *

The next day, Annie went early to the school-house and started the fire. She heard Miss Nagel arrive and went out to meet her and unhitch the pony from the trap.

'I went to see Padraig's mother yesterday. You remember,

46

he fainted?'

'I surely do. How is the boy?' the teacher asked as they walked into the schoolroom.

Annie lowered her voice and pulled the barn door closed. 'He fainted from hunger, I think. His mother's in a bad way in the cabin, no fire and no food for her or the children. The father is away and they've not heard from him for weeks.'

Miss Nagel's large blue eyes opened even wider as she turned to Annie. 'But that is awful to hear. What on earth are they going to do?'

'My Da said they're to go to the workhouse in Waterford. At least they'll be fed. He's giving her and the children a lift there today.'

'Ah, in a way it is the best thing for them, I suppose. But it is so sad to hear.' The teacher paused and a frown appeared on her broad forehead. 'And we'll be losing three of our pupils.' She glanced briefly at Annie. 'Although they haven't paid their fees for months now, along with most of the others in the class,' another pause. 'We'll talk about this later. Let's get on with teaching the scholars we have, why don't we?' With that, she moved past Annie, opened the door, and called the waiting pupils in to begin their day.

After setting their work, Annie looked at her small pupils bent over their slates to copy out grammar sentences. They all looked tired and dirty. Many were barefoot, but most went barefoot, even in winter, and yet none of the boys wore their jackets. Some girls had shawls, but not all of them. Had their jackets and shawls been pawned, like Annie's cloak? How many of them had been fed today, apart from Finn and Katty? And what did Miss Nagel want to speak about later?

At the end of the school day as they tidied up the classroom,

Annie spoke to again to the teacher.

'Have you noticed that these children are all hungry?'

'I have seen that they can't concentrate on their work as they used to,' the teacher replied. 'Is hunger the reason do you think, Annie?'

Annie sat down, leaned on the table and rested her head on her hand. 'If the truth be told, we're all going hungry, Miss Nagel.'

'Oh, my dear girl, I had no idea this was happening.' The teacher's eyes, magnified behind her spectacles, looked around the classroom. 'But what can we do?' She sat down next to Annie. After a few moments, Miss Nagel tapped Annie on the back of her hand. 'I know! There's a committee in Waterford. They give out grants for charitable work to relieve distress. I'll think of the name in a minute. My father is on the committee. What is it?'

The two women sat together in silence, until Miss Nagel remembered. 'It's the Central Relief Committee. They have money from the government to alleviate rural poverty. I'll speak to my father when I get home and see if he can get us a grant to buy some food.'

Annie looked at Miss Nagel. 'Do you really think they'll help us?'

'They might. But that's not all though, my dear Annie.' The teacher paused before continuing. 'Do you recall I mentioned earlier, that many of the families have not paid their fees in the last few months?'

'I do. But any money they've had has been spent on food, now there are no potatoes to dig. You can see that, surely?' Annie breathed hard to stop her tears. 'And it seems they now have no money left to buy bread.'

'That fee money pays your wages, and it pays the rent on this barn to His Lordship.' Miss Nagel explained. 'I don't have any money of my own. I give my work for free here, because I believe I'm doing the Lord's work. But now I can't pay you. I'm not even sure if I can keep the school going for much longer, if we can't pay the rent.' The teacher's eyes filled with tears behind her glasses. Annie put her arm across Miss Nagel's plump shoulders and found herself comforting the Anglo-Irish lady who had never seen a hungry day in her life.

Miss Nagel dried her eyes and stood and hugged Annie. 'I'll go home now and talk to my father about the grant. That'll keep us going for a while, if we can get it.'

The two women walked out to the pony and trap, Annie waited as the teacher got up onto the seat and clicked for the pony to walk on.

Annie made her way slowly back home. The day was still bright. Along the road she passed a couple of red squirrels running along the stone wall beside the roadway, their tails waving in the breeze as they whipped past her. She heard the usual song of blackbirds on their nests in the scrubby trees by the road. But still, she felt there was something not right. It was the absence of sound. No children's voices as they played their games or ran and skipped; no-one walking to the spring for water, or chatting on the corner. She reached the cabins. The place felt abandoned and lonely, as if all the life has been drained out of it.

* * *

The following week, Miss Nagel arrived unusually early on the Monday morning and bustled into the schoolroom. Her pale cheeks were flushed, and her fringe, normally curled across her forehead to cover the expanse of it, was swept to one side revealing her sparse eyebrows and receding hairline.

'I got a grant,' Miss Nagel said. 'The committee met last Friday and Papa put my request before them. They've granted ten pounds. Papa sent out straight away for some supplies for us. I have them here.'

Annie clapped her hands. 'That's wonderful! We're blessed. Thank God for you and your committee.' She leaned forward to hug Miss Nagel, then thought the better of it and shook her hand instead.

The teacher continued. 'The money must be spent on food, but they have allowed us to pay for the rent on the schoolhouse for another month. Then we'll see. We must pray the Lord will provide.

'I'm afraid it is not all good news though, Annie. I can't use the money to pay your wages and I don't have any fee money coming in.' Miss Nagel paused. 'I am sorry to ask this of you. Will you be able to work for nothing, like I do?'

Annie closed her eyes; her small wages helped to keep them fed at home. She nodded.

'I must ask my father. I think he'll say yes. But if there's any food left over at the end of the day, can I take it home for our supper?'

'Of course you may. Now, come outside with me and help me bring it in.' The teacher stood and smoothed her fringe back into place.

Children were arriving for their lessons as Annie and Miss Nagel walked out to the pony and trap. They passed two of the bigger boys.

'Anthony and Ciaran,' Miss Nagel said. 'I have jobs for you

both. Anthony, you unhitch the pony, and then the two of you carry in the sack of oats there. Thank you.'

Annie picked up the milk pail and Miss Nagel took the large cooking pot and the bag of bowls and spoons and they carried them into the schoolroom.

'Now we're ready for the day. Annie, I must confess, I have no idea how to cook porridge, do you?'

'I'll cook it gladly, Miss Nagel. You're a saint, so you are.' Annie replied.

Later that morning, Annie stood the pot on the stove and added oats and water, then let the pot heat and stirred it a few times. She left the porridge to cook for an hour while the pupils did their lessons. The aroma of oats cooking brought smiles to the faces of the scholars. At noon, everyone had a bowl of porridge, with a drink of milk to wash it down. She saw colour come back into the faces of her pupils and thanked God. There was some left in the bottom of the pot for Annie to take home, too.

Annie and Miss Nagel. Waterford, 1846

That hardest of winter months slid into February with no let up. The weather was the worst in many years and snow piled high in the fields and ditches around the small village. But the children still managed to get to school and they were thriving as a result of their porridge and milk for dinner. Annie cooked a little bit extra and took it home with her, to reheat for breakfast the next day.

As the new month began, Annie saw their last sack of oats was almost empty and at the end of the day, she showed the sack to Miss Nagel. 'Can you buy us more food?'

The teacher shook her head. 'I'm afraid it's all gone, Annie. I paid the rent up to the end of January and the arrears. Most of the rest went on food and milk. Money doesn't go far with thirty mouths to feed every day.' Miss Nagel pulled her shawl around her, tightened it at her waist and continued. 'I asked my father to request another grant for us, and he did. They turned us down. Well, in fact, the committee don't have any more money left. Sit down here with me for a minute.' Miss Nagel sat opposite Annie and held her hand. 'I'm so sorry, I just couldn't tell you, but now I have to. I must close the school at the end of this week, we can't continue.'

Annie saw Miss Nagel's tears, but she herself had no tears left. This day felt so inevitable. There had been a small flicker of hope when the oats arrived on the back of Miss Nagel's trap and she could pour milk into the mugs for the children, but it was still winter, and the wind and snow continued to pummel the barn sheltering the two women and their pupils.

'When do we tell them?' Annie asked.

* * *

At the end of lessons that day, Miss Nagel made an announcement. 'Dear children,' she said, 'I have urgent news to impart to your parents. Please ask them to come here tomorrow, when school finishes. I won't keep them long but I must speak to them.'

On the way home, Finn asked, 'Annie do you know what Miss Nagel wants to tell everyone?'

'I do know, Finn,' she replied, 'but I can't say anything about it,' then she paused. 'I'll tell Da.'

* * *

The next day, when lessons had ended, all the children and their parents squeezed on to the benches in the barn. Miss Nagel stood by her desk, with Annie beside her, while the remaining parents arrived, shuffled in and found a seat. Both women looked sombre and the parents sat quietly, expecting bad news. For what other sort was there?

'Good evening to you,' said Miss Nagel. 'Thank you for coming.'

The men had removed their hats, the women's heads

remained covered by their thin shawls or cloak hoods. Miss Nagel adjusted her own finely woven shawl across her bosom and continued. 'It has been my privilege to teach your children these last ten years. Indeed I have taught some of you adults.'

There was a low murmur of agreement and a few of the parents nodded.

'As you know, we have been loaned this barn by His Lordship. What you may not know is that he charged rent for the use of this place.'

The teacher's wire-rimmed glasses glinted as she paused to take a breath and glanced at Annie, as if for strength, and continued.

'The school fees you have paid. They go to pay the rent on this barn, this schoolroom. I know that for many of you, this has been a sacrifice, and you've paid willingly for your children to be educated. I also understand, since the potatoes failed last autumn, that many of you have not been able to pay the fees. As a result, for the last three months I have not been in a position to remit the full rent to His Lordship. I asked for and received a grant from the Local Relief Committee and that paid the arrears and the rent up to the end of this week, as well as the oatmeal and milk we've provided.' Miss Nagel paused to compose herself.

'His Lordship has informed me that he can offer no further credit and he plans to repossess the barn. It pains me greatly to say that I must close the school at the end of this week.' Miss Nagel took out her handkerchief and blew her nose.

Annie looked at her Da sitting on the front row with Katty and Finn. Both children looked stunned at hearing this news. Annie stepped forward to speak. She held her hand up to quieten the low sounds of dismay in the room.

'*Dia daoibh, a chairde*, God be with you, friends.' Annie greeted her neighbours and friends. 'This is hard news to take for all of us. I know Miss Nagel has worked tirelessly to try to find an answer to this.' Annie took a deep breath. 'But it appears there is no answer. She has repeatedly asked His Lordship to allow us to have the barn free of rent until the potato crops recover, but the answer is always no.'

Annie looked at Katty and Finn. 'My brother and sister and all your children love coming to school here, as I did when I was a child, and many of you too. I've loved working for Miss Nagel as her assistant and I'll be heartbroken when the school closes. I know that some of you may be able to get your children into the National school in Waterford, but I also know that won't be possible for many in these hard times. I want to thank Miss Nagel for her generosity in coming here, every day for the last ten years, to teach us and our children.'

Annie turned to the teacher and clapped her hands. Finn, Katty, Da and the rest of the parents and children stood and joined in. The loud clapping continued for several minutes and reverberated off the wooden walls of the barn and around the rafters. Miss Nagel's tears flowed freely and she was soon surrounded by her pupils as she shook hands with their parents and wished everyone well.

* * *

The walk home from the school was a silent journey as the Powers made their way, with their neighbours, back along the lane towards the cabins. Night had drawn in and a full moon lit up the lane and illuminated the bare branches of elm trees beside the stone walls of the fields. It was cold but there was no wind, just a sheen of frost along the top of the walls. Annie kicked at some loose stones on the ground and sighed. Her father put his arm around her. 'Be calm, daughter, anger won't help.'

'Oh Da, he could have let us keep the barn. What does he need it for? This whole estate has gone to rack and ruin these last few years. He's not here to care for it, off away in London and Dublin in his fine houses.' Annie kept her voice low, but her words carried in the quiet night air.

'It's his to do with as he wishes, Annie.' Her father let her go as Katty and Finn caught up and held his hands. The children turned from one to the other as they listened to Annie disagree with their Da.

'And our cabins, what about them?' Tears shone in her eyes. 'They're his to do with as he wishes, too. Aren't they?' She swept away the tears before they fell.

'Ah now, Annie, don't upset yourself girl. Let's just be thankful we have a roof over our heads and a fire to sit by. Please God, the next potato crop will be sound and we'll get back to how we were.'

She looked at her father, he looked so tired; his eyes were dark and troubled.

Before she could speak, Brín, who had been at the meeting, caught up with them. He linked her arm in his. 'Annie, sure it's terrible, this news. Are you alright, girl?'

She shook off his arm and refused to look at him, for she didn't want sympathy. 'What does it matter if I'm not alright, Brín, or the children, or any of us? There's nothing you can do, anyway.'

* * *

Annie lengthened her stride and walked off along the lane leaving Brín, her father, Katty and Finn to stand and stare after her. She overtook a few of the neighbours and her boots crunched on stones as she walked on and kicked out again in frustration. She had blamed Brín, but he was as hamstrung as the rest of them. There was no way round this.

She looked up at the stars and saw an owl perched on one of the branches above her. His white face shone in the moonlight; he tilted his head to look at Annie, then spread his wings. He had no need to pay rent for his nest in the barn, only His Lordship's poor tenants had to keep on paying.

But what if their landlord truly didn't know how badly off they were? It might be that his Agent was making these decisions. Her father always insisted His Lordship was a good man. Maybe their landlord didn't know about all this.

'That's it! I'll write to him! That's what I'll do. What do you say, Mr Owl? Can we save our school?' Annie's delighted voice travelled through the night air.

The bird took off and flew away over the fields, towards the barn they had just locked up.

* * *

Once back at the cabin, Annie began the letter.

Dear Lord Ashling

My father is one of your tenants. He is Patrick Power and has been a tenant on the Ashling estate for the last twenty years.

You must know we had a problem with potato blight last autumn. However, I am not writing to you about this.

You also know that Miss Nagel, our teacher, runs a school for the children of the estate in one of the barns on the estate. I work in the school as her assistant.

Annie stopped writing. What would persuade His Lordship? The gratitude of the families on the estate? Maybe not. The benefit to the children living on the estate? Possibly. His good name? Probably. She picked up her pen, dipped it in the ink and wrote again.

In the last few months, many families on the estate have not been able to pay the school fees due to not having any money to spare. All their money has been spent on food since the potato blight and most now have nothing left.

Annie stood up and went to the door. She looked out over the dark fields towards the river. Will he be generous? A small voice in her head asked. 'Why should he?'

'Because he's a Christian man and we're his loyal workers and tenants,' she said aloud.

She went back to her writing.

I know you are a good Christian and will not want the children on the estate to suffer in any way. For now, we cannot afford to pay the rent on the barn. As soon as the next potato crop comes in we'll be in a better position to catch up with the payments.

Please allow us to continue our little school. You will be forever in our prayers for this great generosity.

Annie's father knew His Lordship's address in Dublin. She signed the letter and put it in her bag to show to Miss Nagel the next morning, then she'd post it after school. His Lordship would help them save their school; he was a good man, he'd understand.

* * *

The next morning, Miss Nagel read the letter and shook her

head. 'Annie, I've written to him several times. I've had no reply, only from his Agent in Dublin. His Lordship is in London and the Agent will be coming to clear out the barn next week.'

'I'm still going to post it,' Annie said.

'He's not there, he's in London,' came the reply.

'He'll read it. And when he does . . .' Annie couldn't continue.

The teacher put her arms around Annie. 'I'm sorry Annie. If I had any money of my own, I'd pay the rent myself.'

The two of them began to prepare for the last day of the school.

Galway. Winter and Spring, 1846

On the west coast of Ireland, the winter months were hungry for Jane and her family. Jane and her father, tramped the road into Galway and for miles around the town in the search for work that would pay enough to feed them. By the time March blew in, the family had been short on food for weeks and were on the verge of starving. Jane's mother finally agreed to take the younger children into the workhouse for a few months to ensure they were fed.

Jane and her father stayed on in the cabin, although legally they were supposed to quit it and go to the Workhouse, too. They sorted out food for the two of them with the little work her father could find. They knew soon enough their own eviction notice would arrive. Jane's dreams of her cousin, Brendan's, eviction and murder stayed with her, she would wake in the middle of the night breathless, feeling the weight of Brendan's body and tasting his blood. When she did wake, she'd get no more sleep, and paced the small room, trying not to wake her father.

* * *

The following week, Jane and her father went to visit the

rest of the family in the workhouse. This was a large stone construction, built on the edge of the town. Its imposing exterior disguised the fact that it was filled with starving and sick from the town and county. When they arrived, Jane saw a crowd of people outside the workhouse door, pushing and shoving. Those nearest the door hammered on it.

'Daddy, what's happening?' To Jane it seemed as if a riot was about to break out. She heard shouting from women and men in the crowd. 'Warden! Warden, let us in!'

A voice from inside roared back. 'No-one is allowed in or out. The workhouse is in quarantine with dysentery and fever.'

At this news a great ragged cry went up. 'No!' Jane got caught up in the crowd as it surged towards the door. She was dragged along and tried to stay on her feet.

'Janey, Jane! Come to me,' her father shouted. He reached for her hand and hauled her out of the moving mass of desperate people. 'There's a back way into this building. Quick, come on.'

Police constables raced through to the front of the crowd. At the same time, Jane and her father hurried back out onto the road and along towards the edge of the workhouse wall that stretched around the site. As soon as they were out of view, Jane got a leg-up onto the wall and her father hauled himself up beside her, then they both jumped down on the other side. Jane's father fell heavily.

'Oof! Give me a minute, *a ghrá,* my love.'

'Daddy, are you hurt?' Jane helped him to stand.

'Come on, we must see your mother and the boys.' But he couldn't walk without leaning on her shoulder. They made it as far as the door. 'Go on and find your mother. Bring her out to me.'

* * *

Her father sat beside the back door while Jane went inside the workhouse. She moved through crowds of women and children sitting on the floor and avoided looking at uniformed wardens. Damp stone floors and indifferent grey walls offered a hard face turned towards these poor souls. Jane shivered at the sight of a child's bare legs and feet, crusted with dirt, bones gleaming through the skin; thin and stretched at knees and ankles. 'God help them all in here' she whispered to herself as she turned into a long dormitory. 'And my mother and brothers? Where are they? Who's that sitting with Joe and Seamus on that bed? My mother?'

The cacophony of sounds, children's voices, shouting and crying, bounced off the walls and the high ceiling. Jane's ears buzzed, her vision blurred, and the stink of dirty clothes, vomit and old soup turned her stomach. She swallowed hard and breathed lightly. Thankfully, she could see no wardens in this end of the room and she kissed her mother's worn face.

'Mam, we've come to see you. How are you?' Jane hid her shock at the change in her mother after just a week in this place.

'Janey, thank God you've come,' her mother's voice cracked and she leaned her face against Jane's cheek. Jane felt her mother's dry skin, saw it was blotched and yellow. Her mother's hair appeared to have turned almost completely grey, unwashed and straggling down her back. Jane's brothers sat together on the edge of the narrow bed.

'Have you come to bring us home, Janey?' Nine-year-old

Seamus asked.

Jane hugged both her brothers. 'My darlings.' She turned back to her mother. 'Daddy has come too. He's here, just outside the back door. Come and see him.'

'Can we bring the boys, Janey?'

'Yes, we'll go together. I'll help mam. Let's go.' They made their way along the corridors and down the stairs to where Jane's father waited in the yard. He hugged his wife and his sons. 'Sit here with me and tell me how you've been.'

'Look at me, Dara,' Jane's mother said. 'I'm like a beggar on the side of the road. Dear God, what are we come to?' She picked at the ragged worn cloth of her skirt and tears tumbled down her lined face.

Jane's father embraced his wife. 'Margaret, *a chroí*, my heart. Stay here, where you have some food. There'll be work in a few weeks and I'll have you out of here, I promise. I've written to your brother, Tomás, in Waterford. I'm just waiting to hear back from him. He'll help us, I'm sure.'

Jane's mother brushed her hair back from her face, then she noticed the blood on his shin bone below the end of his knee breeches. 'Dara, what happened you?'

'I fell getting over the wall to get in here' He smiled. 'I used to be good at climbing, Margaret. Do you remember?'

Jane and her brothers watched their parents' brief moment of intimacy, as their mother leaned in and kissed him. 'Only to come and see me. Yes, I remember, *acroí*, my heart.'

'Hold on for a few weeks, Margaret. I'll find work and come for you and the boys.' Jane saw tears gleamed in her father's eyes.

Jane embraced her brothers and her mother and watched them walk away, back to their lonely purgatory. She was left numb, not understanding how things had come to this pass.

* * *

'Help me stand, Janey, we've got to get out of here,' her father said. But he groaned in pain as he tried to get up off the floor, his face streamed with sweat. 'Dear God, I think I've broken something in my leg.'

He breathed hard, hauled himself up and held on to the wall with one hand as he got his balance and eased the weight onto his good leg, then leaned against the stone wall of the workhouse.

'Daddy, let me go and find someone to come and help.'

'No. We need to get out of here first. I don't want anyone asking questions about how we got in. It might make things worse for your poor mother and brothers.'

The damp oozed from the stone walls through their clothes and into their bodies and Jane shivered. 'Lean on me, Daddy, and we'll go out through the workhouse so we don't have to climb the wall. They'll think we belong here.'

'Let's try, my girl,' her father said. 'Don't tell your mother, she has enough to worry about.'

Jane's felt her father's weight on her shoulders as they went through the door and moved off along the dank corridor. Stairs led to the front of the building and her father sat on the steps and hauled himself up backwards one step at a time. His arms trembled and his face was red and sweating, but he didn't make a sound.

At the top he lay against the wall and groaned. 'Ah, I can feel the bones grating together. I can't go any further, get me some help, Janey.'

Jane left him there and ran towards the main door. She saw a nurse and called out to her.

'I need help. My father fell, and I think his leg is broken.'

The nurse turned and walked quickly back with Jane. She didn't question her about what they were doing in the workhouse, just nodded to Dara and gently felt his lower leg.

'I can feel a broken bone here,' the nurse said. 'You must come to the infirmary to have it set. Wait here until I'll fetch some porters, they'll help you.'

Jane sat with her father until two orderlies arrived with a stretcher and they helped him to lie on it. Jane held her father's hand as they brought him to the hospital ward on the other side of the workhouse building.

The infirmary ward was laid out much as the workhouse wards, with just the one long ward filled with narrow beds. The difference between the two was that in the workhouse, people were sitting on the side of their beds or moving around the ward. Jane saw upwards of fifty people all prone on their beds, most not moving.

The next thing she noticed was the unbreathable stench. These poor souls had dysentery and many were lying on soiled beds in their own excrement. The few staff on the ward were overwhelmed by the calls from those able to speak, while the sicker ones just lay there quietly and awaited their fate.

Jane gagged as she tasted a mouthful of foul air. 'He can't stay here,' she said to the nurse.

'This is the last bed in the place. There'll be a doctor through shortly and he'll arrange for a surgeon to set your father's leg. You can stay or go, but I can't do any more for you, I have others to attend to.' With those words, she left them.

Jane's father took her hand. 'Girl, you need to get out of

here. I'll wait to see the doctor and then get home somehow.'

'Daddy, I'm not leaving you.' Jane lifted his hand and kissed it. 'Now, lie down, and don't move your leg until the doctor gets here.'

Jane stroked her father's hair back from his forehead and he closed his eyes. She continued stroking his thick dark hair until his face relaxed and he slept, breathing deeply. Jane tried not to look around her but could not block out the sounds and smells of the sick and the dying.

* * *

The surgeon set the leg in a splint later that day. Dara hobbled out onto the road with Jane. He had a wooden crutch to lean on and they got a lift with a farmer heading out of town who kindly dropped them off at their cabin.

Once inside, her father collapsed on the bed. Jane could see he was exhausted and the pain in his leg had been exacerbated by the stress of movement.

'Thank God we're home, Janey,' he said. 'I'll rest now and tomorrow my leg'll start to heal. You're just the best girl a father could wish for.'

But whatever the best girl did was no use. Her father suffered agonies of pain, and over the next two weeks the skin on his leg turned red, then purple, then black. The blackness moved up his leg, inch by inch, until his whole body burned. And there was no doctor to call, so Jane called Father Hanrahan to come and see her father.

'Dara, we need to get you back to the infirmary,' the priest said. 'They can look after you there.'

Her father wouldn't budge. 'No, sure they're all worse off

than me in there. I'm staying here, Father. I'll get better, God willing.'

* * *

The Almighty Father was not willing. Jane's precious daddy died in his bed just ten days later. Father Hanrahan gave him the last rites and arranged a burial in the old graveyard. There was no money to pay for it and Jane was the only mourner on that bright spring day with the elm trees coming into bud and blackbirds building their nests.

The day after the funeral, Jane walked along the road to the workhouse in Galway. She was full of sorrow and dread at having to tell her mother and brothers. This time she managed to get inside the building, but she couldn't find her family.

'They're in the infirmary,' a warden pointed the way for Jane.

Puzzled as to why they were there, she prayed to God her mother had not got the fever, she followed the corridor through to the adjoining building and made her way onto the main ward her father had been on, and saw it was still crowded with beds. As well, there were mattresses on the floor, down the centre of the long ward. There were now twice the number of people on the ward.

'Where did all these people come from?' Jane gagged at the smells of urine, faeces and vomit and she covered her mouth with her hand. She looked around for a nurse to speak to but they were all were busy with the patients so she waited until one was free. An orderly wheeled up a trolley, left it by the door and hurried off. Jane could see the shape of a body and the outline of a face and skull under the sheet. She let her hand fall away from her mouth. She blessed herself and whispered a prayer, then saw a nurse nearby.

'*Dia dhuit*, God be with you. I'm looking for my mother and brothers. Margaret Keating is my mother and my brothers are Joe and Seamus. I'm told they are on this ward.'

The nurse, a worn out creature, looked at her. 'Are you Jane? Your mother was asking for you.'

'My father was sick at home,' Jane said. 'I had to look after him. Can I see my mam?'

The nurse put her hand out and laid it on Jane's arm. 'You're too late, girl. I'm really sorry for your troubles. They were brought here yesterday with the relapsing fever.'

'Too late? For what?' Jane asked. 'I need to see them and tell them about Daddy.'

Jane read the sorrowful face of the nurse and shook her head. 'No, you've got the wrong people.' She put her hands over her ears to ward off the words she saw coming out of the mouth of the nurse who caught Jane's hands in hers and continued to speak.

'Jane, listen to me. Your mother and brothers are in the mortuary, you can go there now and say goodbye to them. They've been very ill and their deaths were a blessed release.'

The words echoed inside Jane's head and made no sense at all. The nurse walked her to the door of the ward and showed her the corridor to the back door and the path to the mortuary.

* * *

Jane put one foot in front of the other and eventually got to the mortuary, just next to the cemetery. She walked past newly-dug graves and saw many freshly-filled ones, the cemetery was almost full. She was certain the nurse had made a mistake. But she had to come here and prove it. Her mother and brothers were tucked away in a quiet ward and she would find them soon, that was for sure. Her heart stuttered in her chest.

She pushed open the heavy door to the mortuary and cold air enveloped her. An orderly pushed a covered trolley along the hall and she stopped him.

'*Dia dhuit*,' she said. 'A nurse told me my mother and brothers are here, but I think I've been sent to the wrong place.'

'Who are they?' The orderly asked. 'I'll help you to find them.'

'Margaret Keating and my brothers, Seamus and Joe.'

'Ah yes, they are here. Come and I'll show you.' He left the trolley with its silent corpse beside the wall and motioned for her to follow him.

Jane still didn't believe. She followed the orderly to a nearby room, with side tables along the walls. Shrouded figures lay on the tables.

'These are the recently dead. They are waiting for the priest to come and bless them,' the orderly informed her. 'Your mother and brothers were brought in last night, God be merciful to them.' He crossed himself and left her there.

Jane slowly picked up the edge of the rough blanket covering the body of the adult and looked at the grey face of her poor mother. Her body was ready for burial with a bandage looped under her jaw and tied off on the top of her head. Her mother's eyes were closed and she looked to be sleeping. But her face had a grey pallor and her lips were tinged with dark blue. Jane leaned over to kiss her mother's face and felt the icy coldness of it against her lips. Only then did she accept the death she saw in front of her. She looked across at the two small bodies next to her mother. She touched them, lifted the covers and kissed her brothers' faces. She stood there in the room full of the dead and prayed for their souls. Jane's face was cold like theirs, but her heart beat and her breath hung in the air, unlike theirs. Then it was, that she finally understood. She was all alone in the world.

Waterford. End of March, 1846

It was early morning, and Annie began to build up the fire for the day. She stepped outside the cabin to fetch some kindling and stood for a moment to look further past the small dwellings. She saw empty fields all the way down to the river. Next month, the tenants would plant seed potatoes for the autumn crop, those that hadn't already been cooked and eaten. That left six months of hunger between now and their main food crop. She looked up to the heavens; the moon was still out, a silver arc in the sky. It stood at an angle and appeared to stare back at her.

Annie walked back into the cabin and placed small pieces of the dry kindling on top of the embers of yesterday's fire. She blew lightly, to coax a flame, then added larger pieces of wood and turf. The kindling caught light and flames grew and spread along the pieces of dry wood, which burned and blackened, then heated the turf until it glowed orange. The earthy smell of the dry turf mingled with the crisply burning kindling, like an incense burner, and perfumed the interior of the cabin. Annie blessed herself. The start of another day, thanks be to God. Through the tiny window, she saw turf smoke from other cabins in the village. With no chimneys, the smoke just eased its way out under the turf roofs of the cabins.

Finn and Katty slept on in their bed in the corner of the single room. Annie stood for a moment, looking down at them, both with dark curls framing the long, slim faces of the Power family. 'Just me and Da to protect them. Mam, pray for us.' The children were stirring, would wake soon for their breakfast. She smiled as her Da kissed her cheek.

'Da, we'll be needing another sack of oats before the week is out.'

'Don't worry, we'll get it. I won't be long.' She felt his hand on her shoulder as he left the cabin to milk their cow. Annie took after her mother, who had been the opposite in looks to the dark Irish Powers, with her copper curls and green eyes. In particular, Annie remembered her mother's smile and her singing voice. She would never forget the day, eight years ago, when her mam had died and left them with newborn Katty.

Annie turned to lift the bag of oats. She reached to the bottom for the last few grains. There was enough left to make a couple of small oat cakes for Finn and Katty, and maybe some soup for the dinner. Another hungry day ahead, she thought, and what of tomorrow and the day after? She hoped her father was right, and he would get another bag of oats for them.

Her brother and sister were still sleeping, and she left the cabin quietly, on her way to the spring to collect water. She called to her father, who was milking the cow at the side of the cabin. 'I won't be long.' As she walked along the path through the village of small, turf-roofed homes, she passed Brín's cabin. She hadn't seen him lately, but she didn't call at the door; she was just too shabby in her working boots and old clothes.

* * *

Blackbirds on the hedgerow, both males and females, were singing their call-and-answer songs in preparation for the new set of chicks in a few weeks. Their songs sounded like small bells and echoed over and back. The sun was almost above the horizon, and cast long shadows over the stone walls and on to the tracks of the lane. It was still chilly this early in the morning but the light of the sun warmed her soul, like a promise of better things. Please God, she prayed.

Annie walked back home carrying the full bucket and saw Brín's mother, Marie, coming out with her water bucket.

'*Dia dhuit,* Annie. We've not seen you for a while, how are things?'

Annie stopped and returned the greeting, noting that her neighbour looked ill and exhausted.

'Not good, I'm sorry to say, Marie. Sure, we're feeling the loss of our potatoes, like everyone here,' she replied. 'Tell me, how's Brín?'

'Ah, Annie, I forgot. I've been meaning to come and tell you Brín's news, but I've not left the house. I've been so unwell.' The older woman smoothed her hair and Annie saw how the weight had dropped off her recently. Her face was thin and grey with worry and she appeared to tremble as she spoke.

'Tell me, what news? Not bad news, surely?' Annie put the bucket down hard, and water sloshed over the rim.

'He's gone over to England to work. He said he couldn't stay here and starve. He went last week.' Her neighbour reached out and took Annie's hand and held it. 'He asked me to speak to you and tell you he sends his best regards. His cousin in England sent for him – there's work in a new factory in

Liverpool.' Marie paused. 'You know yourself what terrible straits we are in.'

Annie nodded her understanding, not speaking.

'Forgive me for telling you like this. He left a letter for you.' Marie went back into the cabin to fetch the letter, gave it to Annie, then went on her way to the well.

Tears streamed down Annie's face, her lashes stuck to her cheeks as she hurried on with the letter unopened in her hand. Brín had gone and not said goodbye. They were promised to each other. Surely, he would have come and told her. Why not?

The cheery song of the blackbirds still radiated across the barren fields. The sounds came towards her on the light breeze, mocking now, and pierced her head and heart like the tolling of the church bell at a funeral mass. How strange that in a few moments everything could change.

* * *

At home, there was still the breakfast to get for Katty and Finn. Annie dried her tears and set to making the breakfast oatcakes then put them on the hot griddle to bake. She poured out two cups of still-warm milk from the cow.

'Come on, darlings, your breakfast is ready.' Finn and Katty sat up to the table by the window and crunched on the oatcakes and drank the milk. Once fed, they washed their hands and face in a basin of water and dressed, ready for the day. Annie sat on the stool by the fire and started to plait Katty's long dark hair. Katty wriggled as Annie smoothed her tangled curls.

'Ow, Annie. Don't be pulling it.'

'If you would sit still for a minute, it'll be done in no time, missy.' Annie replied as she quickly tied off the long plait. 'There. It's done. Get your books out and we'll start work.'

Katty and Finn took out their school books, slates and pencils, then sat at the small table by the window.

'Annie, why can't we go to school in Waterford?' Finn asked. 'I could walk there.'

Annie looked at Finn. He was the image of his father, with his dark looks, and a wide mouth, not smiling now. Tears glistened in his eyes.

'I'll see about it soon, Finn. I promise. In the meantime you and Katty will learn maths and English with me so you won't forget anything. Come on, now, let's make a start.'

They began with arithmetic and although Katty was the younger by a few years, she was well able to keep up with Finn.

'Now, here's a problem for you to solve,' Annie began. 'I have a gallon of milk to take to market. How many pints of milk do I have?'

'I know,' Katty said. 'It's eight pints to a gallon.'

'Clever girl, Katty. We'll head into the market this afternoon and see if we can sell these eight pints of milk. Then we'll spend that money on a bag of oats. Now, your next task is to write a sign for the milk. You can use your slates.'

Finn and Katty worked on their signs and Annie took out her journal and began to record the news she had of Brín. She remembered the letter, and opened it.

'What's that, Annie?' Finn asked.

'Never you mind, brother, get on with your work.'

It was the first letter Brín had ever written her, and his

handwriting was hard to read. Where had he got the paper and the pen? He must have gone into the Post Office in town to write it, she decided, and began to read.

Annie, I'm sorry not to tell you to your face, but it's just too hard a thing to do. I have the chance of work with my cousin in Liverpool and I'm leaving today. You know my mam needs me to earn some money. If not, she'll starve. There's no room in my head or my heart for anything else, Annie. You know what I mean.

God bless you, Brín.

Annie's hand shook as she read the words on the page, but she acknowledged the truth of them. She screwed up the paper, put it in her pocket and blinked away tears.

Later, she got the chance to speak alone with her father and showed him the letter.

'Da, I just don't understand why he wouldn't come and talk to me and say goodbye.'

'Annie, *a stór*, my star, that's such bad news. I'd say he didn't want to add to your troubles, or his for that matter. But you're right, my girl, he really should have come and said goodbye to you.' Her father shook his head.

'I don't think he loved me enough to tell me,' she replied. 'Either that or he's a coward.' The doubts, seeded in her heart, now spoken aloud, bloomed in her mind. He's a coward.

Sitting by the hearth, they drank their milk, and Pat said. 'This last six months have been hard for everyone since the potato crop failed.' They sat in silence watching the flames.

'You know, Annie, since your mother died, you've been a great help to me, and a mother to little Katty and Finn. The time's not right to marry now, you know this. Sure, God help Brín, he must look after his poor mother. Let's get through this trouble, and pray God that better times will come.'

Annie stood up, kicked her old working boots into the corner of the room and paced the floor. She looked at her hands, they were bony and covered with the thinnest of worn, dry skin. She pulled at her hair, which had once been thick and full of curls and felt it dry and lank on her shoulders. It was a ragged mess, down to her waist.

'Better times, Da? I can't even go to mass on Sunday to pray. You should have known I won't be able to go to mass when you pawned my mother's cloak and my good boots. We've no proper food to eat, and no decent clothes to wear, even for Finn and Katty to go into town to school.' She stood by the fire, her head bent. 'You pawned my clothes, but kept the donkey and cart and the cow! It's no wonder Brín left.'

'Annie, I'm sorry. My coat and good breeches have gone too. I've pawned everything we can spare. I can't pawn the cow, she'll soon have to be sold, then we'll have no milk. And I've tried to sell the ass, but no-one wants the poor old *crathur*. Sure, God bless him, he's practically good for nothing.'

Annie was not to be consoled. 'And my mother's cloak and my boots? How will you get them back?'

Her father stood and put his hands on her shoulders. 'Listen to me, girl. I wrote to your aunt Bridie in New York, months ago, and asked her to help us if she could. I'm waiting on a reply. It'll be here any day now.' She heard his voice break. 'If she does send some money, I'll get your cloak and boots back, I promise you.'

Annie could see the torment in his eyes and relented. 'I'm sorry too, Da. I know you're doing your best for us. I'm not much help when I act like a spoilt child, now am I?' She went over to him and kissed his cheek. 'I love you, Da.'

Yet the tipping point moved nearer like a dark ravenous

wolf, but they dare not speak of it.

Galway. End of March, 1846

J ane stayed in the cabin for two days and two nights after her father died. She slept for hours, almost the sleep of death, and when she woke, she prayed, then slept again. The third morning, she collected water from the spring behind the cabin, threw the last of the turf sods onto the banked fire, and heated the water in the small black kettle. There were no tea leaves, but the water warmed her stomach, although her fingers trembled as she lifted the cup to her lips. She slept again, in the bed her father had died in, heard his voice in her dreams. On the fourth morning, she sat up, reached for the cup of water and sipped the last of it.

'You can't go on like this, Janey,' she said out loud. 'You'll soon be dead alongside mammy, daddy and the boys.' The water replenished her tears and she wiped them away from her sore eyes. She felt her skin stretched tight across the unfamiliar sharpness of her cheekbones.

She lay back on the bed and felt her father's spirit nearby, not in a dream, but a comforting reality.

'Well, daddy, what do you say I do now?'

His voice echoed instantly in her head. 'You know what to do Janey, *a mhuirnín*. My love.'

'I can't stay here on my own, that's for sure.' Jane sighed and looked up at the inside of the turf roof. It was dark and dry from the heat of the fire kept burning day and night. Her eye was caught by a patch of light colour in the darkened eaves, between the roof and the wall. She narrowed her eyes to focus and saw something caught between the rafter and the wall. She stood up on the bed to investigate and reached up and pulled out a piece of pale cloth, part of an old neckerchief belonging to her father. She instantly recognised the metallic clink, sat back down on the bed to unwrap the fabric and gawped as three silver shillings rolled out onto the mattress. Her father must have hidden them up there and somehow, he'd forgotten about them.

She nodded slowly, understanding. 'Thank you, daddy. Yes, I know what to do.'

Jane got up from the bed, wrapped the coins back in the fabric and put them in the pocket of her knee breeches. She slipped her feet into boots, picked up her father's old jacket then left the cabin, pulling the door shut behind her. It took her just one minute to leave home.

* * *

She walked along the lane away from the cabin, hearing her boots crunch on the hard ground. Although it was getting on for late morning, the spring sun was still low in the sky, its beams caught and glinted on the edges of the limestone wall that separated small fields from the roadway.

After a mile or so, she approached the churchyard and stood at the newly-filled grave of her father. She recalled Father Hanrahan's words at the funeral. "The kingdom of heaven is a far better place than our earthly home".

'No. That's not right. Daddy's place is here with me, Lord. And so is mammy's and my brothers.'

She turned and walked on to the small house beside the church where Father Hanrahan lived. She knocked on the door. Mrs Flynn, the priest's housekeeper, opened the door.

'Ah, it's Jane Keating, you poor child,' Mrs Flynn said. 'Come in, come in. I heard about your poor mother and brothers, and so soon after your father.' The housekeeper was a small-boned woman, in her fifties, neatly dressed in a dark skirt and blouse, with a black widow's cap on her head. 'You'll be wanting to see Father, then?'

Jane nodded.

'Come through, and I'll tell him you're here.' Jane followed Mrs Flynn along the hall into the back kitchen. She walked into the warm kitchen, filled with the rich smell of a broth cooking, and staggered. She put her hand out and held on to the doorway. The soft face of the housekeeper came up close to hers.

'Why, girl, sit yourself down at the table.' Mrs Flynn pulled a chair out for Jane, then dished up a bowl of stew from the pot on the range. 'I'd say you're hungry? Here, get that into you while I call Father.'

Jane sat and stared at the food in the bowl, there was meat in it, rabbit maybe. She breathed in the aroma as she leaned over the bowl and dipped her spoon into the barley-thickened gravy, small pieces of orange carrot glistened on the spoon, next to the pale meat. Jane ate her first hot food in days, and had her first taste of meat in weeks.

She went to stand up when the priest came in, dressed in his black cassock, a small wooden crucifix hung from a chain around his neck.

'Janey Keating, how have you been girl? No, don't stop eating. You must be hungry all on your own up there in that cabin. I was going to call up today and see how you are. But you're here now, you can tell me yourself.'

Jane ate a few more spoonfuls while the priest sat across from her at the table. The chair he sat in, had padded arms and a cushion for his back, and he made himself comfortable.

'Mrs Flynn, is the kettle hot? We'll have some tea, if you'd be so kind.' He had a deep rumbling voice and it somehow soothed the ache in Jane's head.

'There's tea on the pot, Father,' Mrs Flynn replied and brought over two cups and saucers to the table. She poured the black tea into the cups and left the kitchen, closing the door behind her.

The priest sat and sipped his tea while Jane finished the bowl of stew. 'Now then, Jane, you're fed. Have some tea and tell me how you've been these last few days. Sure that's a terrible thing to lose your whole family so suddenly, God rest them,' and he blessed himself.

'*Go raibh maith agat,*' she thanked him, but couldn't speak of her lost family. 'My mother's brother, Tomás Power, lives in Waterford, he has a farm there. Mammy and daddy wrote to him before all this happened. I need to go and find him, he'll help me, I'm sure.'

'And tell me this now,' the priest asked, 'how are you going to get there? Sure Waterford is more than a hundred miles from here.' Jane sat in silence and looked at her cup.

'I suppose you could always stay and go into the workhouse in Galway, but you might not like that, hm?'

Jane shook her head. 'No, not the workhouse. I'm going to Waterford, Father. Can you direct me?'

There was a small window, just beside the door leading into the garden of the house. The window had glass in and Jane looked through and noticed movement in the trees at the bottom of the garden. She saw blackbirds flying in and out of the bare branches, twigs in their beaks, they were nesting already. She heard her daddy's voice in her head. 'Yes, it's spring, *acushla,* and summer will surely follow.'

The priest stood up from the table. 'I'll just be a minute.'

He left the kitchen and she sat and waited, her mind made up. Wherever she went, it would be away from Galway.

The priest came back with a large book and set it down on the table.

'Right, let's clear a space.' He moved the bowl and cups over to the sink, came back and opened the book. Jane saw it was a book of maps.

He turned to the page showing a large map of Ireland, and put his finger on the spot on the west coast. 'Now, as I'm sure you know Jane, this is where we are. Galway, on the bay leading out to the Atlantic Ocean and all the way across to North America.'

Jane managed a small smile. 'Yes, Father, we learnt this in school.'

'Then you know where Waterford is, over here on the south-east coast.' He pointed to the estuary and the River Suir running out to the Irish Sea.

'I'm not sure how I would get there. I was hoping you can help me.'

He looked at her. 'Well, there'll be a post carriage going across the country, but they'll cost a fair bit. I don't suppose you have any money?'

'I have a few shillings,' she said, 'but I don't mind walking.

I'll get a lift when I get on the road. I just need to know which roads to take.'

'Right so, let's have a look here.' They both leaned their heads over the map, her straight black hair against the priest's thinning scalp. 'You'll need to head inland around the bay then south to Ennis. From there, keep going south to Limerick and then turn southeast across the country towards Tipperary town. By then you'll be within fifty miles of Waterford. It's a straight road through from there. Will I write it down for you?' he asked.

'No, I'll remember. South to Ennis, then Limerick. Southeast to Tipperary town and on to Waterford.' She held her forefinger in front of her and moved it down and across as she memorised the route, then nodded.

'Thank you, Father. I know where I'm going now,' and she smiled at him.

The priest looked at her. 'You're a brave soul, Jane Keating. I'll pray for a safe journey for you.' He pointed to her legs. 'I see you still have the knee breeches on.'

'I get all tangled up in skirts, Father. And I think I'll be safer as a boy when I'm on the road.'

'Well, you're still God's beloved child, whatever clothes you're wearing.'

'I just need one more thing, Father. My hair is too long. Do you have a scissors I can cut it with?'

'Mrs Flynn!' the priest called. 'Come in and find a scissors for young Jane.'

The housekeeper wasn't far. Jane guessed she was just on the other side of the door. The priest explained. 'She's off to find family in Waterford. She's going to be a boy on her journey, too. Do we have a scissors to give her hair a trim?'

The housekeeper pulled open a drawer in the dresser and held up a sharp pair of scissors. 'Now, hold still there.' She lifted a handful of Jane's hair to cut it, and laid the fine dark lengths on the table. Jane reached out to touch her silky hair and felt the strangeness of it being separated from her and the lightness on her scalp.

'Well, now you'll pass for a boy,' Mrs Flynn said, when she had finished and stood back to look at her work. 'And a very handsome one too, with your fine cheek-bones and those grey eyes!'

Jane put her hand up and felt her neck and the ends of her hair. 'Thank you, Mrs Flynn.' She looked from the housekeeper to the priest. 'I'll be on my way.'

The priest said, 'Mrs Flynn will pack up a bag of food for your journey and I'll give you my blessing.'

Jane knelt and bent her head while the priest laid his hand on her head. 'Dear Lord and Saviour, bless and comfort young Jane for the loss of her family. Keep her safe from peril. In the name of the Father, the Son and the Holy Ghost. Amen.'

'Give me one more minute,' Mrs Flynn said. 'We've got a fresh loaf here and there's some cheese. Oh yes, and we have a few apples in the larder.' The housekeeper wrapped the bread and cheese in a linen cloth and put the food into a jute bag. Then she filled a bottle with water, put a cork into it, and added it to the bag.

'Here girl, you can have this bag,' she said. 'It'll go nicely over your shoulder.'

'Will you be going back home before you leave?' the priest asked.

Jane hadn't thought, but no, there was nothing there for her. Her plan was now clear.

'No, I'll start now. Thank you both. I'll not forget your kindness.'

She turned and waved when she got to the end of the lane then started on her walk to Waterford.

The West of Ireland

Jane got her first lift with an old farmer in a cart loaded
with hay.

'*Dia dhuit*, God be with you,' he said, 'hop up here beside
me. Where are you heading to?'

'*Dia is Mhuire dhuit*,' Jane replied. 'I'm going to Ennis.'

'Well, you're in luck, young fella. I'll let you off in Gort.
That'll get you half way.' The farmer was dark haired and
wiry in build, with a white clay pipe stuck in the side of his
mouth. He looked at Jane from under his bushy eyebrows, as
she climbed up and sat beside him, then he clicked the reins
for the horse to move off, they were on their way.

'You're not from the town yourself?' he asked.

'Just to the north of Galway town,' Jane replied.

'Ah, that's why I didn't know you.' He paused to suck on his
pipe. 'And tell me this now, what are you doing travelling on
your own?'

Jane turned her head towards him and narrowed her eyes. 'I
have no family left here,' she replied, then looked away across
the fields as the horse and cart rattled along the miles towards
Gort. After the look she gave him, he didn't ask any more
questions.

The farmer's silence gave Jane time to think up her new

name, if she was to pass as a boy. Something similar to Jane. What about Jack? Jane to Jack Keating. That'll do, she decided. She turned and looked back over her shoulder. Galway had vanished in the hills.

'Will I ever come back here?' she whispered.

'What's that? What did you say, young fella?' the farmer asked.

'My name is Jack Keating, and thank you for the lift.'

'You're welcome, Jack. It's a hard time of year to be on the move though. That snow on the fields there is taking its time to clear,' the farmer said. 'But spring is on the way. Thank God.'

Jane looked across the low stone wall beside the roadway. The fields were a dull brown, there was no life in them yet. Old snow congregated beside the surrounding wall, pale grey and dirty-looking as it banked up, trying to stay in the shadow of the wall and exist for another day, before melting away into the earth.

* * *

The afternoon had turned into evening by the time Jane, now Jack, jumped down off the cart onto Market Square in Gort.

'There won't be much in the way of a lift for you to Ennis at this time on a Saturday,' the farmer said. 'Find a bed for the night, young fella. You'll be lucky to get a lift in the morning, too. Sunday morning, everyone will be at mass.' He waved and clicked the horse to move on. *'Slán.'*

Jack lifted her hand in a salute. *'Go raibh maith agat.'*

The main square was almost empty of people. It was dusk, with a cold rain falling. Jack stood outside a pale grey limestone building with a wide arched doorway and arches to the windows on both floors. She looked across to the other side of the square and saw a great new church with a bell tower. At that moment the bells began to ring out. The Angelus bells, of course. She remembered, and blessed herself, and said the Angelus prayer as she walked over to the church.

The door was open and a few people were leaving, so she slipped in and sat quietly at the back of the church and watched the priest blow out the candles on the altar. She saw a confessional nearby and when the priest knelt in genuflexion before the altar, she quickly opened the confessional door, slipped into the small dark space and pulled the door closed.

The priest's soft footsteps padded along the nave as he went to the door of the church, and closed it as he left. The metal key squealed in the lock, then there was silence. Jack was alone.

After a few minutes, she stepped out of the confessional and made her way to a wooden bench. She sat down and took out the bread and cheese Mrs Flynn had packed earlier that day. The crumbly cheese left a sharp, intense taste on her tongue and she drank the water and ate half the bread.

She saw the large crucifix above the altar and blessed herself. 'Thank you, Lord, for the help I've had today. Welcome mammy and daddy into your kingdom. Look after Joe and Seamus. Eternal rest grant unto them, and let perpetual light shine upon them. May they rest in peace. Amen.' The words echoed around the church walls but brought no comfort. She was alone in the world. Would she ever get used to it?

The bench was solid oak and, lying on it, Jack was thankful for the folded jute bag to use as a pillow. She dozed briefly throughout the cold night and dreamed of her lost family.

In her dream, her father spoke to her. 'Keep going, Janey.'

* * *

It was early, and the sound of the key in the lock woke Jack. She gathered up her bag and slipped into the confessional and peeped through a crack in the door. The priest came in and briefly knelt in front of the altar, then he went to the sacristy to put on his robes for early mass. Jack hoped he wouldn't notice the full chamber pot in the sacristy. Better not stay for mass then. She opened the door and crept out into the grey morning light.

Back at the market square, where Jack had alighted the previous evening, she continued on across the bridge over the river, heading south. The only people she saw were on their way to Sunday mass in the town. The rain from the previous day had cleared and the morning was fine, although puddles lay on the road. Jack saw the last of the snow had been washed away overnight. She made good progress, passed only a few people and covered the miles.

When she reached Ennis, she continued on past the town, and walked more miles until evening came. She watched from the cover of an elm tree beside the road as a farmer brought his horses into a barn, then left them in their warm shelter for the night. The animals didn't mind some company and Jack was grateful for the sounds of their breath in the barn. The smell of the horses and hay reminded her of back home, when she had helped her father at his work on local farms.

* * *

On the Monday morning, Jack continued walking towards Limerick for a few miles. It was still cold but the sky was the palest blue. And below the blue, lay a flat bank of pale cloud, coloured through with rose light from the rising sun in the east. The sound of a horse's hooves came up behind Jack and she turned and waved to the driver of a cart heading her way. There were two people on it, a boy and a girl, both around Jack's age.

They greeted Jack in Gaelic. *'Dia dhuit.'*

'Dia is Mhuire dhuit.' Jack returned the greeting, and continued to speak in Gaelic. 'I'm heading for Limerick. Are you going that way?'

'Not right into the city,' the boy said, 'but near enough.'

The girl moved up and made space for Jack, and on they went. The three of them perched on the seat of the cart pulled by an ancient nag of a horse.

The girl smiled at Jack. 'We're off to the creamery.'

Jack turned to see cans of milk standing in the bed of the cart. 'Ah, you have plenty of milk there.'

'We're blessed, we have some good cows.' The brother, yet to speak, twitched the reins and nodded. 'Where're you off to?' the girl asked Jack.

'I'm going to Waterford, I have family there. My name is Jack Keating and I'm from Galway.' The more times Jack said this, the more she began to believe it.

The girl nodded. 'There's been plenty of people on the road since the start of the year. Times are hard with the loss of the potato crop.'

'Are they lost here too?'

'Oh yes. We had a field of potatoes to dig, but we only got a few good ones. Most of them came up rotten. We're thankful, we have milk to sell and can buy bread. Others are not so fortunate.'

The girl's brother finally spoke. 'Some are breaking the law to get food. Just last week a gang of armed men broke into a big farm near us and took away all the food out of the house.'

The horse ambled along the rutted road and the three young people sat together, without glancing at the empty fields they passed.

After an hour they came to a halt at a crossroads. 'We turn off here,' the girl said. 'Limerick is just an hour's walk ahead.' She shook hands with Jack. 'God go with you on your journey.'

Her brother touched his cap and clicked the horse to turn off the main road.

Jack continued her journey on foot. It wasn't yet noon and she was rested after her lift on the cart. She walked on briskly.

Small cabins beside the road gave way to more prosperous looking farmsteads. Up ahead, Jack saw stone towers and a church spire. 'This must be Limerick. Just the river Shannon to cross and you're almost there, girl. That's good going.'

Walking along the road she looked across the river and saw a large, new, two-storey building with a slate roof and faced with narrow dark windows. The whole thing was built from grey sandstone blocks, much like the workhouse in Galway.

She walked over to the group of people standing outside the building. They looked like family groups, mothers and fathers with young children and grandparents.

Jack raised her hand in greeting. She looked like one of them, shabby and unwashed after two days on the road, and her clothes had been worn out before she started.

She greeted a couple with small children gathered around them.

'I'm travelling through on my way to Waterford from Galway,' she explained.

The man wasn't old but looked tired and angry. 'You may keep on walking then, for you'll get no comfort here.'

'I don't plan to stay. Is this the workhouse, then?' She nodded towards the building.

'It is, and it's full and won't take us in,' the man said. 'We've been out here since yesterday, begging for shelter. They say there's no room.'

'But, sure that's terrible. What brought you here?'

'We've been evicted from our land, and we've nowhere else to go,' he said.

The man's wife put her arm through his and said to him. 'They'll have to take us in, darlin'. They won't watch us starve on the road, now will they?'

Jack could see the woman was shivering beneath her thin shawl and light skirt. Their four young children sat on the road nearby, barefoot and mute.

The woman's husband said, 'I spoke to the Superintendent in there. He rebuked me for being impatient. And my wife and children, out here in the weather.' He sighed. To Jane it sounded almost like a sob. 'What we are in dread of is this. That while the gentlemen are doing their best, and the government is doing its best, ourselves and our little families will die of the hunger.'

Jack reached into her purse and pulled out one of her shillings. She gave it to the man. 'I'm sorry I can't give you more, but I'll say a prayer for you in your troubles.'

She walked on towards the bridge and looked up the river to see ancient stone turrets of King John's castle, built right down to the river bank. 'Limerick. I'd say I'm about halfway to Waterford. What do you say, daddy?'

Jack got no reply. Was she losing him, the further away she travelled from Galway?

* * *

The waters of the Shannon flowed strong and dark under the bridge. Jack stopped halfway across to watch the river on its journey to the Atlantic Ocean, then walked on across, and turned towards the quay, bustling with ships and fishing boats. She bought a small loaf from a bakery, found a place to sit and eat and looked down the river towards the castle. Her appetite faded when she saw more homeless people. Thankfully, they were lined up at a cart with a boiler of soup on the back. She finished her food.

Rested, she hitched the bag on her shoulder, and set off on the road south out of the town. The signpost read, 'Tipperary 25 miles'. She'd be there by nightfall with the help of a lift or two.

She walked fast for a couple of hours and felt the wind hum past her ears and the cold burrow into her bones and teeth. A further layer of sound joined the humming. Higher, fiercer wind rattled through the bare branches of stunted trees lining the road. Like a fiddle and *bodráhn* going at it together. Still, at least it wasn't raining.

She saw a small cottage beside the road with the door half-open, so she knocked. '*Dia dhuit*,' she called out.

She heard the response in Gaelic and stepped into the room. A young woman sat beside a small turf fire, a baby at her breast, with her shawl wrapped around it and herself.

Jack continued to speak in Gaelic. 'Can I trouble you for a

drink of water?'

'There's water in the bucket there by the door, a cup here on the table. Help yourself and come and sit by the fire with me.'

Jack smiled and helped herself to a drink. '*Go raibh maith agat,*' she thanked her. 'I'm Jack Keating, I'm travelling from Galway across to family in Waterford.'

'You must be tired walking the road, then,' the woman replied. She was only a few years older than Jack by the look of her. One of those small, dark-haired Irish women with ivory skin, but thin and anxious looking.

'I had a few lifts on the way. Your baby there. Is it a boy or a child?'

'This is Siobhan, she's just three months old.' The woman lifted the edge of the shawl for Jack to see.

'Ah, God bless her, she's lovely. Are you here on your own?'

'Michael, my husband, is working on the roads for the Relief Committee. Sure God help him, it's hard being out in this weather. He doesn't earn enough to feed us, but it's something at least.'

'Did you know there's a soup kitchen in Limerick? I saw it earlier today. They were feeding a lot of people.'

'I heard it had been stopped last week. They said people were taking advantage. Even those who have food were turning up.' The woman smiled. 'I might just get into town and join the queue, as long as they're not dishing out the Indian corn.'

'Indian corn? What's that?'

'We got hold of some last week, from the Government Relief Committee. And it's yellow. I tell you, we were both sick after eating it. Michael thinks they're trying to kill us all off.' She seemed to find her comment amusing.

Jack stood. 'Thank you for your hospitality. I must get on my way.'

'*Slán abhaile*, safe journey,' the woman said, as Jack left.

Jack walked a few steps then stopped at the edge of the road and took the kerchief out of her pocket. There was one shilling and sixpence left. She took out the sixpence and went back into the cottage, held up the coin, put it on the table and turned and left again.

A lift on a cart took care of ten or more miles of the journey and then she walked again. She was only a couple of hours now from Tipperary Town.

Gifts from New York

The first Monday in April, Annie's Da called into the Post Office in Waterford to check on the reply from his sister-in-law, Bridie. At long last, a parcel had arrived from America. He put it on the back of the cart and set off home along the road running parallel to the river. That spring morning, the fields appeared to show signs of new growth, some potato fields evidenced green tops, like small flags of hope.

Katty danced around the room when they saw the large box come all the way from New York. Finn, growing into a man now, helped his father to place it in the middle of the floor. Katty had recently lost her milk-teeth, and the gaps in her new teeth made her lisp, as her voice joined with Finn's. 'Daddy, open it quickly. Let's see what's in it.'

Their father took a knife to the layers of strong brown paper tied with thick twine. Katty's busy hands both helped and hindered the task and slowly the parcel revealed its contents. Below the brown paper there was a letter from Bridie, then another layer of wrapping paper.

'Well, I'll just read the letter before opening the rest of the parcel.' There was a humorous glint in their father's eyes. 'What do you say, my darlings?'

'Da!' By now even Annie was jumping up and down with anticipation. 'We need to see what Auntie Bridie sent!'

Their father put the letter to one side and unwrapped the last of the paper. Layer upon layer of colourful clothes were revealed. Warm flannel petticoats and dresses for the girls; a two pairs of knee breeches, one for Pat and one for Finn, together with a woollen waistcoat and jacket each. Scarves, shoes and boots were tucked inside the items of clothing. Precious gifts all the way from New York, sent with love from their mother's sister.

Annie held up a pale blue woollen dress, the exact colour of the spring sky outside the cabin. A white cotton collar lay like small clouds against the blue fabric. The skirt reached to her ankles, a perfect length.

'This is the loveliest dress I've ever seen.' She selected a pair of leather shoes that were just a little on the large side, two white aprons, a lace-trimmed cap and some cotton stockings. Annie felt a wide smile return to her face. The last item was a vivid red shawl and she wound it around her shoulders and tied it at her waist. The feel of the fine wool was like a mother's loving touch, full of warmth.

'Annie, you look like a grand lady,' Katty said. 'Is there anything for me?'

Annie quickly looked through the pile of clothing and found a smaller, yellow dress. Katty tried it on. It fitted well, was long, but Katty would soon grow into it. Finn and Da had sorted out their gifts and the whole family stared at each other in delight.

'We are well set up with fine clothes, and thank God for these blessed gifts,' their father said.

'Now children, sit down here by the fire with me, while I

read you Bridie's letter.' Pat sat Katty on his knee while Annie and Finn sat on stools.

1st February 1846
  'My dear Pat,'

  'I hope this letter and parcel arrives safely to you in Waterford. I picked out some clothes that I think will suit the children. Anything left over, you can sell them with my blessing. Give my love to Annie, Finn and Caitrín. I can only imagine how big they have grown in the ten years I have been here in New York. Sure, little Caitrín was not even born when I left.

  I think of you all every day in this time of great trouble for Ireland. The news we get over here is so frightening to all of Irish birth and, God knows, all with any charitable feeling. I have been down to the docks in New York to see for myself what I have only read in the newspapers. I can tell you there are hundreds, if not thousands, of our countrymen and women arriving each week with their children. Many of them are ill and destitute and they are just thrown onto the dockside. I dread to think what will become of them in this great city. I only hope and pray they have some family here they can call on for help.

  My dear brother-in-law, I know from your earlier letters that you will not leave Ireland, but if you ever decide to come, or need to send the children to safety, then there is a home here with me as long as you need it. Since my dear Eamon died, I'm all alone in my little apartment.

  You have all my love and prayers for your safekeeping. I've put twenty dollars to help with the rent or for whatever you may need. You should get five pounds for this.

  Your loving sister and aunt.
  Bridie

The little family sat by the turf fire and the heat drifted into the woollen shawl Annie had wrapped around herself. The pot hanging above the fire had started to bubble and the smell of the soup cooking for dinner, filled the air and warmed their hearts.

'Let's kneel and thank God for this gift from Bridie,' Pat said. 'She has her own troubles and works hard in New York. She's a great woman to think of us in our hour of need'. Pat knelt down and blessed himself as the children knelt with him.

'Thank you Lord, for this generous gift from Bridie. Keep our family safe in this time of great hunger. Let our Landlord and the British Government come to our aid until the blight passes. We ask this in the name of the Father, the Son and the Holy Ghost. Amen.'

* * *

The next day, Pat went into Waterford to the pawnbroker and retrieved Annie's cloak and boots and his own pawned clothes. She hugged her mother's cloak when her Da handed it to her.

'Da, promise me you won't pawn this again.'

'Annie, *a chroí*, my heart, you know I can't make that promise. We still have no potatoes and must buy oats and barley. This money from Bridie will last us a month or so, but there's no work for me. I just can't find any.' Pat rubbed his eyes in frustration. He stopped and took a breath. 'I have some good news though. The Society of Friends have opened up a soup kitchen in Waterford. It's a bit of a distance to travel, but if we do run out of food, we can get a bowl of soup for our dinner instead of going hungry.'

'What is the Siety of Friends, Da?' Katty asked.

'It's Society, Katty, it means a group of people,' their Da told her. 'They're good people, not Catholic like ourselves, but they believe in doing charitable works. I hear they've set up these soup kitchens in lots of towns across Ireland, may God bless them in their work.' Pat blessed himself. 'Now children, I have an idea. There's some spare clothes left from Bridie's parcel. Will you take them into the market in Waterford next week and see if you can sell them? Maybe we can buy another sack of oats with the money you make. But before you go anywhere, we need to sit down and write our thanks to Bridie and tell her we have the parcel and the money and a few bits left over to sell.'

'It'll give us a chance to show off our new clothes from America.' Annie kissed her father's cheek. She wished that Brín could see her in her finery, maybe then they could go back to how things were between them.

Katty did her little jig around the room while Annie helped their father with the letter, then planned their trip to market. The Power family had a day out to look forward to.

The Midlands

J ack approached Tipperary town just as the sun was
setting and the rain started to fall. The blisters on her
heels stung, and her stomach ached from eating the last
of the bread and the remains of Mrs Flynn's cheese. Somehow,
dry bread didn't satisfy her hunger like a cooked potato used
to. She walked past low stone buildings on the main street.
Ahead, she saw a line of people queuing to enter a doorway,
and she walked along to see where they were going. She hoped
it might be a soup kitchen and imagined sipping a hot cup of
broth.

The knee breeches and jacket were too big to fit comfortably
but at least the loose fabric disguised her breasts. Days of
walking had completed the transformation into Jack Keating
and she felt comfortable in her disguise.

A notice on the door read - Public Meeting to Report on
Potato Crops. Monday 30th March at 7 p.m. The constable on
the door, checking people entering, seemed to know everyone
by name. There'd be no soup in there. She debated with
herself to go in out of the rain or look further to find a soup
kitchen. A drop of rain fell from the gutter onto the top of
her head and soaked through her hair. She felt the icy water
on her scalp and brushed away the trickle on her forehead.

She'd go in if she could, just to get out of the weather.

She paused for a moment to think. She was a stranger to the town, would she be allowed in? A woman approached, heading for the meeting. She glanced at Jack, for a moment, then looked again, smiled and nodded. She was a brisk-moving, solid woman of fifty years or so, her greying hair neatly tied under a frilled black cap, the dull black of her widow's garments relieved by a moss and heather-coloured shawl. Her cloak and her smile helped Jack to take a chance on her.

'*Dia dhuit*, will you be kind enough to let me walk into the meeting with you?' Jack asked.

'*Dia is Muire dhuit.* Sure, you're welcome to come in with me.' The woman adjusted her cloak and peered closely at Jack. 'You're not from around here. What do you want with the meeting?'

'I'm from Galway. My name is Jack Keating and I'm on my way to Waterford. I thought to maybe find a bed for the night and something to eat, but then I saw this meeting. I'll get a sit down at least.'

'Ah so, come in and sit with me then, Jack.' She put her arm through Jack's. 'Take no notice of the constable on the door. He gets a bit full of himself in his uniform. I'm Nora Sheedy. If he asks we'll say you're my . . . grandson come to visit.'

Mrs Sheedy greeted the constable. 'Good evening, Kevin, you'll have your hands full with this crowd tonight.'

'Well, Nora, and who's this young person, then?' the constable asked.

Nora patted Jack's arm and introduced him. 'Kevin, this is Jack, my grandson from Galway, come to visit.'

They passed into the building and entered the meeting room

which was almost full with men and women; farmers, day labourers and tradespeople. Jack took a seat beside Nora. She could almost feel the pungent smell, from the damp, woollen clothing of those present, pressing into her face like a suffocating fog, making it hard to breathe. Anxious, low-voiced conversations hummed around, and uniformed constabulary stood at the edge of the stage.

Night had closed in and faint beams of moonlight glimmered across the shutters in the windows. Oil lamps on the stage illuminated the chairman who stood to open the meeting and the murmuring ceased. He spoke in English, and adjusted the waistcoat of his well-cut suit. His shirt collar gleamed in the lamplight.

.'Good evening everyone, and thank you for coming. Most of you will know me. I'm Andrew Clancy, Chairman of the town council. I have been asked by the Government in Dublin to collect information about the potato crops and any news of blight or murrain around the county. So we'll start then. Who will go first?'

Jack's 'grandmother' immediately stood to speak and got a muted cheer from the crowd.

'Good evening, neighbours. I'm Nora Sheedy.' She spoke in Gaelic. Then her face lost the smile and her mouth narrowed into a line as she switched to English.

'Mr Chairman, I'd like to report that last month I dug thirteen barrels of potatoes, and they were all sound when I dug them. I checked them the next morning and of the thirteen barrels, there were only two fit for my pigs to eat and, God help us, none, not a one, was fit for human consumption. They had all rotted with the blight.' She remained standing and looked around at her neighbours, who sat in silence.

'Mr Clancy,' Nora continued. 'I hope you've brought us here to tell us the government in Dublin is sending some help in our hour of need and not just gathering information.'

People nodded in agreement and then took turns to speak of their own crop failures.

The Chairman explained. 'I have not heard of any help forthcoming, Mrs Sheedy. I've been told there are potatoes in other parts of the country, so it might be just here that the blight has attacked. This may just be a local emergency.'

Nora stood again. 'Mr Clancy, sir, you know well that most people here, and their families, have run out of food. And what will we do, I ask you? In God's name, what will we do in our 'local emergency?' Nora took her seat again, her face grim.

The man in front of Nora, jumped up and his Gaelic words echoed around the room.

'Jesus, help us. Would they have us starve to death?'

Another male voice from the back of the room joined in. 'I'll not starve like a dog in the street.'

Mr Clancy called for order. 'You all know this meeting will be cut short if it is disorderly. I'll have no shouting out. Constables, the next person who disrupts the meeting will be arrested. And speak in English, all of you!'

The Chairman continued in a quieter voice. 'So, my friends, you ask what can we do? The council will be sending our report to Dublin Castle and when I have further news, I will make sure you hear it,' he paused. 'But so far, I'm sorry to say, the government appears deaf to our cries for bread.'

Jack stood and raised her hand to speak. Mr Clancy acknowledged her and she adjusted the pitch of her voice.

'Mr Chairman,' she said. 'Thank you, sir. You say there's

abundant food in the country. But in the last week, on my travels from Galway to here, I have not seen one part of the west or the midlands where food is abundant. Everywhere is afflicted with potato rot, sickness and eviction. I've seen whole families sitting on the side of the road as I passed. I haven't seen any help anywhere, apart from a Quaker soup kitchen in Limerick.' She sat down and took a deep breath.

The two men who had spoken earlier stood up again, one shook his fist, both shouted out. Others stood too, adding their voices and the meeting started to break into disarray. A constable moved towards Jack. The young stranger made an easier target than angry grown men. Jack ducked past Nora and had nearly made it to the door but tripped on the outstretched foot of a second officer and fell. Both officers caught her and half dragged her out of the room as if she were a wayward drunkard.

'You're under arrest, boy, for causing a disturbance in the meeting.'

'I only spoke the truth. Let me go,' Jack protested.

* * *

The constables marched her across the road to the police station, threw her in a cell and locked it.

'The magistrate will deal with you in the morning, trouble-maker.'

After the cell door slammed shut, Jack stood in the dark and felt her way to a narrow cot with a rough, stinking blanket. The cold stone walls of the cell reminded Jack of the workhouse, and her mother's face flashed across her vision. She breathed in the smells of mouldy air and old urine, pressed her hand against the hunger cramps in her stomach, then fell into a deep, troubled sleep on the hard bunk. In her dream, she'd been discovered . . . She stood on the stage in the moonlit meeting hall, naked and exposed to the silent stares of faceless strangers.

* * *

The next morning, Jack's hands were manacled and she was escorted to the court-room. It was in the same building, with the same stone walls and small windows that kept out the light. Jack waited for the judge to speak.

'You are fortunate not to be transported for your crime, young man,' the Judge said. 'However, I have been approached by your grandmother, Mrs Sheedy. She has begged the court's clemency. She tells me your mother and father died recently and you have come to live with her in a sad state of distress.'

Jack looked around the courtroom and spotted her. The Widow Sheedy's black and grey curls, stocky build and Galway cloak were unmistakable. She nodded to Jack, her face unsmiling and resolute.

The Judged continued. 'Mrs Sheedy has assured the court that your actions last night were as a result of your bereavement. She will stand as guarantor for your future good conduct.'

The Judge straightened his wig and paused. 'Well, young man. What do you say to that?'

'Thank you, Your Honour. I'm sorry if I caused trouble at the meeting, but I only spoke the truth.'

The Judge sighed and looked at Mrs Sheedy then back to Jack. 'If you come before the court again, for 'speaking the truth', you won't get away so lightly. Now get off home with your grandmother, and don't let me see you again.'

The constable unlocked the manacles on her wrists and Jack left the courtroom with Mrs Sheedy. Neither spoke till they were outside on the road and Mrs Sheedy hugged Jack.

* * *

'I couldn't leave you in that jail, Jack. They would have transported you as soon as look at you. Then where would you be?' The widow paused and her eyes twinkled. 'What with you being a girl.'

Jack laughed and tears came to her eyes. 'How did you guess, Mrs Sheedy?'

'Call me Nora. Sure, aren't I a mother and a grandmother? I've raised both girls and boys. I can tell the difference, even if those idiot guards and the Judge can't.' Mrs Sheedy smiled at Jack, then pointed to a pony and trap, waiting at the side of the road.

'Let's get you out of here. Hop up next to me.' They both climbed onto the driver's seat. Nora took the reins and clicked for the pony to trot on. They left the town and headed east.

After an hour, they stopped to rest the pony. Nora took out a bag of bread and butter and shared it with Jack. 'I'm only sorry I don't have any potatoes for you, girl. But, sure you know that. There isn't one left in the county that you could eat.'

Jack shook her head. 'There's none anywhere in the entire country I'd say, Nora. What'll we do with no potatoes?'

'God help us, that's all I can say. My children are all long gone to America. They did the right thing. I'm only sorry I didn't go with them.' Nora turned and touched Jack on the shoulder. 'If you get the chance, then take it and go, get out of this place. Boy or girl, you'll be better off anywhere else.'

'I've got to find my uncle in Waterford. He'll help me,' Jack paused. 'Tell me, Nora, how did you know my mother and father had died recently?'

'God love you, child. I've seen the sad look about you,' the widow replied. 'Sure, you wouldn't be travelling alone if you had a mammy and daddy to look after you, now would you? And what is your real name anyhow?'

'Jane Keating.'

Nora brought Jack as far as the crossroads outside Cahir. It was late afternoon and the sky was filled with clouds.

'I have to turn back now, Jack. We've come a good twelve miles or more, but you're still in Tipperary, so mind yourself, in case any of them constables are out and about,' Nora advised. 'Keep on walking and head east,' she pointed along the road. 'This road will bring you to Clonmel and Carrick, then Waterford. A day or so walking, I'd say. But find a barn to get some rest later and you'll get a lift in the morning, there'll be plenty out on the roads.'

'Nora, thank you.' Jack threw her arms around the woman and hugged her then turned and jumped down on to the road and waited while Nora swung the trap around. Nora raised the whip to salute Jack.

'*Slán abhaile!* God bless you!' Mrs Sheedy jiggled the reins, clicked for the pony and headed back to Tipperary town.

* * *

Jack walked until it got dark. She spent the hours on the

road thinking about her mother and father and her brothers. She tried to think of happier times, but all she could see in her mind's eye were the dead, grey faces of her mother and brothers in the mortuary. All she could remember was her father's agony as the infection in his leg spread up through his body. She passed dark fields and thought of Brendan lying in his grave beside the hedgerow back in Galway and said a prayer for his little family in the workhouse. At least they were safe and would survive this disaster.

When Jack had passed through the town of Clonmel, she relaxed to think she was now next door to county Waterford. Not too much further to get to her uncle Tomás.

She found a barn for a few hours' sleep on soft hay and her only companions were a family of pigs that the farmer had brought in for the night. For the first time in weeks Jack's sleep was undisturbed and she woke refreshed the next morning for the last day of her journey.

Waterford Market

The market was up at the top of the town right beside the ancient walls of the city, and was situated on a large open square, surrounded by stone-built shops and houses. Stalls and carts displayed foodstuffs and clothes, and people from the town and countryside sold their produce and bought food. On one stall, dark green, spring cabbages were displayed next to purple beets, and narrow, green-stemmed scallions. Open sacks of oats and barley stood beside a large weighing scale on another stall.

Annie stopped at a cart piled high with pats of butter, cheese and eggs for sale. Next to it, another cart had half a dozen dead hens hung up by their feet, their russet feathers ruffling in the breeze. Annie's mouth watered as she tried to remember when she had last eaten chicken. It seemed like in another life. It was clear, too, with all this food on offer, that not everyone was going hungry.

Annie, Finn and Katty, spread out their spare New York clothes on the back of their cart. Katty and Finn saw some of their old school-friends were in town and joined them to play and chat, while Annie, in her American dress and shawl, soon attracted a crowd of interested buyers. Most of them were just looking, not buying. One, a short woman wrapped in a warm cloak, greeted Annie.

'Annie, well, how're you, girl?'

Annie looked up to see an old friend of her mother and her heart sank. 'Maura, I'm well, and you?' she asked of the biggest gossip in Waterford.

'Managing, is all I can say, darlin'. You're all dressed up in your finery, I see. And what have you got here?'

'We had a parcel from my aunt Bridie in New York. There's some bits left over and I'm here to sell them.'

'Let me have a look and see what I can buy then. I'm short on stockings and I like the look of that skirt. It'll go well on my girl at home.' Maura rummaged through the items on the cart. It was only when the woman touched the clothes that Annie had to swallow her sudden anger. To have to sell these lovely gifts from her aunt and watch them being pawed over by that gossip's fat fingers, who, at the same time as she examined each piece of clothing, asked Annie if she'd heard the latest news from Dublin.

'What news?'

'There's a rumour, and it's only a rumour, mind you,' Maura said, and licked her lips, as if tasting the words. 'That your Lord Ashling is going to evict his tenants if they haven't paid their rent this year. I thought, as you're one of his tenants, you'd have heard.'

Maura stopped, and squinted at Annie, like a hawk on a mouse, then she picked up a pair of stockings as if to examine them.

'No, no,' Annie replied. 'I've not heard anything. Anyway, I'm sure his Lordship wouldn't do such a thing.' Annie tried to smile, but her face had stiffened, as if it had frozen over, and she pressed her lips together.

'Well, it's just a rotten rumour,' Maura said. 'Take no notice. Here, I'll pay you for these and be on my way. How much do I owe you?'

The woman paid for the skirt and stockings and said. 'Give my best to your poor father, now won't you, girl?

Annie nodded, breathed out and turned back to the stall. Thank God, Finn and Katty weren't here. Her breathing steadied as she tidied up the rest of the clothes.

The day passed quickly and with most of the American clothes sold, Annie decided to start packing up. She called her brother and sister over to help.

Jack arrives in Waterford

Early the next morning, it looked set to be a fine day when Jack set out again. She got a lift as far as Carrick-on-Suir, then walked the road for a few hours. The walk was no bother, the day was mild, and she looked forward to arriving in Waterford. She tried not to think of her family every single minute of the walk.

She finished the last crumbs of the food Nora had given her, then stopped by a spring to get a drink of water and wash her face and hands. The countryside around was a mix of wooded hillsides and small fields along the side of the road. Jack saw there were crops showing through in some of the fields, turnips and spring cabbages but no potatoes here either. Some fields had livestock; sheep and cattle. The place definitely looked a little more prosperous than where she had come from.

She reached a bridge and crossed the River Suir; now she was in Waterford and walked along the quay. She saw an ancient town, with great warehouses and hotels along the quay facing a dozen or more ships tied up alongside. Jack quickened her pace. She'd find out where her uncle Tomás lived and be there before the end of today. Her mother's brother would be her family now.

Jack followed a road up away from the quay, and past a fine cathedral on the main street that was otherwise full of small shops. There'd be a market-place somewhere near, so she continued on until she found it at the top of the town. Evening was drawing on and the traders had started to pack up their stalls.

* * *

She looked around to find a friendly face and saw a young woman of about the same age as herself, a little older maybe. She was tall with dark, copper hair curling all the way down her back and she wore a soft, pale blue dress that showed off her narrow frame and slim waist. The tiny white collar on the neck of the dress framed her face while a bright red shawl covered her arms and shoulders. At that moment, she smiled at a younger girl with her, and continued to pack up her stall.

Jack watched as the young woman folded some clothes and carefully laid them into a box, and then began to count her money. She had a long face with straight dark brows that outlined green eyes and pale skin stretched over fine bones in her cheeks. Freckles sprinkled over her nose and her wide mouth was now closed as she glanced over at Jack, as if conscious of being watched.

Meeting

Annie counted her money, and noticed a stranger near the cart. A skinny boy, about thirteen years old, a bit older than Finn, and definitely a beggar; ragged, starving and dirty. He didn't look like he had money to spend, that was for sure. She wrapped the coins in her purse and tied it to her waist. Yes, plenty of money for a sack of oats and some vegetables. She'd let her Da haggle for the food.

She began to pack up the last few clothes that hadn't sold. She felt the boy was still there, could smell the unwashed odour off him. She looked over at him, what did he want? He certainly wasn't getting her money.

'*Dia dhuit,*' the boy said in Irish then switched to English. 'I've just got here and I need some find some family of mine. I wonder if you'd know of them?'

For his young age, Annie thought, he seemed very confident despite his dirty appearance. His accent was not local, maybe west of Ireland. Somewhere over that way.

'*Dia is Muire duit,*' Annie replied to his Irish greeting. 'Well, I'm from around here, so yes, I know a few people. What's their name?'

'I'm looking for the Power family of Waterford, they're relations of my mother. My name is Jack Keating and I've travelled from Galway to find them.' To Annie, the boy suddenly looked like a tired child.

At the mention of her family name, Annie smiled.

'You're speaking to a Power of Waterford,' she said, 'but there are lots of families by that name in this part of the country. I'm Annie. Come and sit here and tell me which Power family.' She sat on the edge of the cart and patted the space beside her. Maybe he's genuine, she thought, we'll soon find out.

Jack explained who she was looking for. 'My uncle's name is Tomás Power, he lives just outside Waterford. He's my mother's brother. They have a small farm and his wife, Elizabeth, runs a public house on the Waterford road. Would you know it? It's called Harte's?'

As the boy recounted the information about his family, Annie felt her face freeze at the mention of the public house on the outskirts of the town. She did indeed know of them. She sent Katty off to find Finn, and when they were alone, she slowly broke the awful news.

'I don't know them, but I've heard of them,' she said. 'I'm really sorry to tell you this, but Tomás and Elizabeth Power both died last month, from the sweating sickness.'

Jack closed her eyes, bent her head and cried. 'No, please say no.'

Annie put her arm around Jack's shoulders and felt the frail bones in the young person's back and arms. What would the poor thing do now, after this news?

Finn and Katty arrived back and Annie introduced Jack and explained about Jack's uncle and aunt.

'That's really sad. I'm sorry for your trouble,' Finn said.

'Thank you.' Jack wiped her face with her hand and stood up. 'I'll be on my way.'

'Let's get something to eat before we go.' Annie looked at Jack. 'Will you join us for a bite to eat?' The boy was clearly half starved.

'I will, and thank you.' The offer of food seemed to cheer Jack up a little.

Annie bought a loaf of bread and some cheese, and they sat on the back of the cart to eat. They shared it gladly with the hungry stranger.

'There don't seem to be so many affected by the potato blight here. Is that so?' Jack asked, while they ate.

'It looks like it here on the market,' Annie replied. 'Farming families have more to fall back on, it seems. But come out to where we are and you'll see plenty of hungry families. Then there's the really poor people of the town. Well, the workhouse is full.'

'Yes, I see. Just like back at home.' Jack nodded and finished the bread then stood to leave. 'I'll go now. Thank you for sharing your meal with me. *Go raibh maith agat.*'

'Where will you go?' Annie asked.

'I'm not sure yet, but I'll find somewhere,' Jack replied, and nodded to Finn and Katty. 'Goodbye.'

'Sure, come home with us, why don't you?' Finn said. 'Da would like to meet you. He can tell you about your uncle. Maybe there's more family around who can help you.'

Jack looked at Finn. 'Do you think there might be more family for me in Waterford?'

'Come with us, and we'll soon find out. If anyone knows, it'll be our Da!' Finn replied.

Annie looked at Finn and pressed her lips together. Jesus, Mary and Joseph, we don't need another mouth at the table. Jack looked so hopeful now, that she nodded in agreement.

'Right so, Finn and Katty,' she said. 'Take Jack with you and make sure the donkey is well-watered before the journey home. I'll finish up here and then we'll be off.'

* * *

While she finished packing up, Annie chatted to the farmer's wife on a neighbouring stall.

'That bread was the best I've tasted for a long while. Thank you,' Annie said.

'You're welcome girl,' the woman replied. 'I see you've sold most of the clothes you brought. That was a good day's work.'

'The money will keep us going for a while,' Annie replied. 'But tell me, have you not been affected by the blight at all?'

The farmer's wife was a fine-looking, sturdy woman, well-turned out for her day at the market. Her hair was pinned up under a snow-white, frilled cap and her cloak and skirt were clearly new.

'We're fortunate to have a decent size farm,' the woman replied. 'Our main crop is wheat, but we have dairy cows and I make the butter and cheese I sell here, along with the bread, of course. You can see for yourself how the price of wheat has gone up these last few months.' The woman paused. 'You're not from the town yourself?'

'No, we're tenants on Lord Ashling's estate. Do you know it?' she asked.

'Ah, sure of course I do,' the woman replied. 'I will say I've heard stories of evictions around the county, but I think they are only rumours. Lord Ashling wouldn't do that to any of his tenants, now would he?'

Annie saw Finn, Katty and Jack coming back with the donkey. Thank God, they didn't hear that. Rumours everywhere. They hitched up the cart and were soon ready to go.

Jack and Annie sat on the cart while Finn and Katty ran alongside the cart to give the old donkey a race.

'Come on, Annie, or we'll be home before you,' shouted Katty as her bare feet flew over the road back to Ashling.

'I'm not going to whip this poor *crathur* just for your amusement,' Annie replied. 'Now run on ahead home and tell Da our good news.'

As the donkey trotted along, Annie felt the weight of the coins in her pocket. The money from her aunt Bridie and this money would keep them going. Her father could pay the quarter's rent, and feed the family for a while. Da might even get some work. She refused even think about the rumours. As long as the rent was paid, they'd be safe.

Ashling, Waterford

K atty and Finn had arrived home well before them and Da was waiting outside the cabin to take a look at their visitor.

'Come and say hello to Da,' Annie said. The two jumped down from the cart. Jack shook hands with Annie's father.

'Welcome, Jack. Come in and have a seat by the fire.'

It was getting on for evening and the turf fire warmed the small room. Finn and Katty went off to unhitch the donkey and get him a drink of water.

'Da, you listen to Jack's story,' Annie said, 'and I'll get the supper on. We did well at the market. Did Finn and Katty tell you?'

'They did so. You're great, the three of you,' Annie's father replied. 'Jack, come over to the fire and sit beside me.'

Annie had brought home some vegetables from the market. While she prepared the food she listened to Jack's account of his family and his journey from Galway. She washed the spring cabbage and beets then chopped them, peeled and sliced the scallions and added both to yesterday's soup in the pot. She added a few handfuls of barley to thicken it, then a pinch of salt and more water. She hung the pot on the hook over the fire and left it to cook.

'I bought a half-ounce of tea, for a special treat for us.' Annie said. She filled a kettle of water and put it to heat on the fire beside the pot. When the water had boiled, she made the tea. The three of them sat around the fire and sipped the dark brew.

'My girl, you've done a good day's work today,' her father said. 'We've a fine dinner to look forward to and tea.'

He looked at Jack who was gradually warming up by the fire. 'And we have a visitor. Sure, we're blessed this day.' He took his pipe out of his pocket and put it in the corner of his mouth, unlit.

On hearing about Jack's family in Waterford, he nodded. 'I knew a Tomás Power, I think he was from a farming family in Passage, though we're not related. There's a lot of Power families around Waterford and the county.'

Da looked closely at Jack as if trying to decide how old he was. 'Tomás married Elizabeth Harte. The Harte's owned the public house on the Dunmore road and Tomás and Elizabeth took it over. They had no children unfortunately. So, you're Jack Keating, and your mother was a Power from Waterford. Tomás's older sister, Margaret, would have been your mother then?'

'Yes, Margaret was my mother,' Jack replied.

'Ah sure, it's terribly sad for you to lose your whole family like that.' Da looked closely at Jack. 'And you've been on the road, travelling, for how long now?'

'Three days.'

'And which way did you come?'

'Down through Ennis, Limerick then Tipperary and now here. I walked most of it but I got lifts some of the way,' Jack said.

'Did you meet with any danger on your travels?'

Annie was puzzled by the questions her Da asked. Was he not convinced by Jack's story?

Jack looked at Annie's father, sighed, then stood up and turned to face them. 'I'm truly sorry. I haven't told you the full story.'

Annie looked at her father; when he narrowed his eyes like that, she knew he was not happy.

'Well, young man, now you've come into our home and drank our tea, you may tell us the rest of it,' her Da said. His voice had an edge to it that Annie knew was rarely used. She squeezed onto the chair beside her father and looked at their visitor. Jack's face was grey and strained.

'To start with I'm not a boy, I'm a girl. My name is Jane Keating and I'm fifteen.'

Annie looked at Jack and then looked again; she had seen how slight Jack was when she first met her, and now that Jack had taken her coat off, Annie saw her waist and her chest was definitely female. She looked at her father and he nodded as if he had spotted something was amiss.

'The part about my family is all true,' Jack continued. 'My mother and brothers died in the workhouse in Galway. Daddy fell and broke his leg and he died of an infection two weeks ago. It's all true. The thing that's not true is, I'm not a boy. I dressed as a boy to make it easier for me to travel alone.'

'Well, I would never have guessed,' Annie said. 'Your name is Jane? Well!' She laughed. 'What a story. What will we call you – Jack or Jane?'

'Call me Jack. I'll be Jane again when I get things sorted out.' Jack replied. 'For now, I'm better off as a boy. I feel safer this way. I'm very sorry for deceiving you.'

'I thought there was something not right about you, Jack,' Annie's father said and put a taper to the fire. 'But I can see you've had your troubles. If it's all right with Annie, you're welcome to stay here until you decide what to do.'

'And that's not all,' Jack said. 'On my way here, I was at a meeting in Tipperary town. People were reporting on their potato crops and some of them got really angry. I stood up and told them what it was like in Galway and the towns I had passed through. I got arrested for my troubles. I was fortunate a good woman, Mrs Sheedy, spoke up for me, or I'd have been put in prison.'

'Well now, it seems to me you've had far too much of an exciting time on your travels here.' Annie's Da lit his pipe and nodded. 'Sure, that's a grand story for your children one day, please God,' and he smiled.

'Thank you, *go raibh maith agat*,' said Jack. Annie saw a small smile. 'I'm just so tired.' Jack's voice broke. 'It's good to be off the road, sitting by this fire and in good company.'

Annie's father took his pipe out and tapped it. 'We'd better tell Finn and Katty that you're staying and that you're not a boy! Call them in, and let's get some supper, that soup smells nearly ready. I don't know about you girls,' he laughed, 'but I'm starving.'

The soup needed another half an hour so Finn played them a few airs on his tin whistle while Katty showed off her dance steps.

Jack had found a home for a while.

The Nation newspaper

A few days later, Annie's father had managed to get some work on the roads. Jack went with him and between them they earned enough money to buy a good supper. Pat had also bought, second-hand, a copy of a newspaper from one of the workers in the road gang. When they got home, Jack helped Annie to prepare the supper while the Da sat in his chair by the fire and took the newspaper out of his jacket pocket.

'Well now, Annie, you too, Finn. Come and look at what I got hold of today,' their father said.

'It's a newspaper,' Finn said, and they all laughed.

'Yes, son. Very amusing. But this is what they call a nationalist newspaper. The people who write it want Ireland to manage its own affairs and not be ruled from London.' He pointed to the banner on the front page. 'The Nation. It's the Irish nation, they're talking about. They're reporting on evictions and say people should fight against them.'

'Will they get into trouble for that, Da? Sure England won't like that,' Annie said.

'I expect if they sell a lot of newspapers then they surely will get into trouble with the government.'

Annie looked over her Da's shoulder and read along with

him. The pages rustled as he turned to read on.

'What's that, Da?' Annie asked and pointed to the next page. 'That's a poem, let me read it. It's about the potato blight!'

'Speranza, that sounds like a woman's name,' her father added.

'Yes, it does.' Annie looked from the paper to her father. 'They print poems, Da. Will I send one of my poems do you think? They might print it.'

'I see no harm in trying, *acushla*,' her Da replied. 'The address is here on the front page. Number four, D'Olier Street, in Dublin.'

* * *

After they had eaten supper, Annie sat down at the small table and made space for her paper and pen. Evening was drawing in so she pulled the shutter away from the window to let in the last of the daylight. She shivered as cold air crept in.

'Don't be long, Annie, or we'll freeze,' Finn said.

'You're right. There's a bit of candle left, I'll use that instead.' She stood and pulled the wooden screen back across the window to keep out the draft, lit the stub of a candle and began to write.

Dear Miss Speranza, *Dia dhuit*,

I have just read your poem, The Stricken Land, in The Nation newspaper. I write to tell you that I think it is a wonderful poem, especially the part about the mothers who cannot feed their children.

"Would to God we were dead –
Our children swoon before us, and we cannot give them bread."

Miss Speranza, I see this happening in my village of Ashling,

126

near Waterford. The blight has destroyed everyone's potato crop here and all go hungry. My father had to pawn our good clothes to get money to buy food for me and my brother and sister. Lately, we've heard rumours we're all to be evicted from our homes and everyone is afraid of what will become of us.

I have written some poems myself and will add one to this letter that you may find time to read.

May God's blessings be upon you.

Annie Power

Annie took out a fresh sheet of her precious paper and copied out one of her poems, then read it out to her family and Jack.

Have Mercy

Lord of Ashling, you are a kind landlord to your people.

Yet they suffer for the want of a few potatoes.

Please help us in our hour of need.

Children go hungry and their mothers grieve to see them so.

Fathers look for work and cannot earn enough to buy food for the table.

May God and His Lordship have mercy on us,

We will be grateful for his kindness for ever.

'Ah, Annie, that's a lovely poem,' Katty said. The two girls hugged. 'Thank you, *astór*,' Annie replied. Jack read it and nodded. 'It is all true, Annie.'

Annie folded the two sheets together and used some old candle wax to seal them. She addressed the outer layer to Speranza at The Nation in Dublin.

The Persephone

The next morning, Annie walked the road into Waterford to post her letter. Jack had gone with Annie's father on the donkey and cart to help finish the job they had in Dunmore. Finn was to take care of Katty and the two of them planned to collect seaweed on the beach.

Annie wrapped her cloak tight and pulled the hood down around her eyes, for the sky was overcast and there was a light drizzle in the air. She shivered with cold and even though she had eaten her supper the previous evening her stomach wasn't full. Lately it seemed to ache permanently with hunger; her body felt hollow and light, like a bird about to fly away, with nothing to hold her to the earth.

She had walked a couple of miles when a farmer passed her in his cart and stopped.

'Annie Power, *Dia dhuit*,' he greeted her. 'Where are you off to, girl?'

'*Dia is Mhuire dhuit*, Mr Shaughnessy,' she replied. 'I'm going in to Waterford. Are you going that way?'

'I'm off to Wexford, so jump up and I'll give you a lift to the quay in town. It'll save your legs one way at least, girl.'

She climbed up to sit beside him, grateful for the offer of a lift. She felt strangely weary after only walking part of the way.

'Tell me, how're you getting on these days?' the old farmer asked her. 'I haven't seen your father for a while. Is he well?'

'He's well, thank you. He's been out every day looking for work on the road gangs and he got three days in Dunmore this week, thank God.'

The cart rattled along the road towards the town.

'I don't understand these roadworks,' Mr Shaughnessy grumbled. 'Sure they just seem to be building roads and walls that go nowhere. They should just give away the money and save everyone a load of heartache. Better yet, just give out food until this trouble passes.'

'Mmm, I think you're right.' Annie sat and watched the miles pass by on the winding road to town. They got to the quay and Mr Shaughnessy stopped halfway along to let her off.

'Here you are now, girl. Give my regards to your father, won't you?'

'I will to be sure. *Slán*, and have a safe journey to Wexford.'

* * *

The farmer drove his cart off towards the bridge. Annie turned into the entrance to the Post Office on the quay, stepped up to the counter and waited to be served. She took out her letter and placed it with her Da's penny in front of the clerk.

'For Dublin, please,' she said.

The clerk, a skinny older chap with steel spectacles balanced on his beaky nose, lifted the letter and turned it over in his hands, as if it were a nettle and might sting.

'Hmm, The Nation newspaper and what is your business with that rag, might I ask, Miss?'

'Sure, it's my business, is what, and none of yours, sir.' Annie stood while he huffed and stamped the letter then put it in the large post-bag beside him. Her poem was on its way. With luck it would be published in "that rag".

Annie left the Post Office and stood beside the entrance while she looked out over the river. There was no market that day and consequently, most of the local fishing boats were tied up beside the wide quay. Some larger ships were anchored further along the quay. Annie watched as barrels of wheat and oats, tubs of butter, and other produce, all stacked up on the quayside, were loaded by stevedores. Where's it all going and who's selling it, while we scrabble for food? She sighed and shook her head. It all made no sense.

Further up the river, she saw a larger, three-masted ship, anchored just in front of the bridge. The name of the ship, The Persephone, gleamed in freshly applied gold paint along its side. She could make out some seamen busying themselves on deck, as they prepared to leave.

She strolled over towards the ship and joined two other onlookers who nodded to her and continued talking.

The older of the two men, who clearly knew his way around a ship, pointed out some of the ship's rigging to his younger companion.

* * *

The three of them stood and watched the work on board the ship. After a few minutes, a long, black carriage pull up next to the Persephone's gangplank. The tide was high and sunlight reflected off the water onto the glossy side of the carriage which appeared to move as if alive with silvery fish.

Suddenly, a cohort of seamen rushed down the gangplank from the ship to the carriage, and they held pistols in the air, ready to fire. A uniformed officer jumped down from the seat next to the carriage driver and unlocked the side door. Annie and her companions watched as the occupants stepped down onto the quayside. They were prisoners, each one chained to the other by a heavy iron chain which went through a leg-iron on the ankle of each man, woman and child.

The seamen lined them up on the quay, there were ten prisoners in all, dirty and silent. They were quickly hauled along by their chains onto the ship's deck where they stood for inspection by the Captain and were then led down into the depths of the ship. As soon as he had handed them over, the officer jumped back up beside the driver and the carriage drove off.

All was quiet again save for the cries of the seagulls as they swooped around the ship's rigging.

'Well!' exclaimed Annie. 'What was all that?'

'Those poor souls are to be transported, Miss,' the mariner said.

'Transported? Where to?'

'Why to New South Wales, of course, for their crimes,' he replied. 'They'll never see this town again, that's for sure.'

Annie's voice cracked. 'But some of them are just girls and boys. How can they be criminals?'

'Oh, 'tis easy enough, when you're starving and see a loaf of bread you could eat. That's enough to get you deported, don't you see?' the older man said. 'Stealing's a crime even if you're starving. It's a hanging offence, actually. So they're getting away easy.'

The mariner sucked on his empty clay pipe. 'I expect they'll be better off where they're going. At least they'll be fed.'

His companion huffed, but had nothing to add to that truth.

Annie stood for a while and watched the seamen on the ship's deck continue their work preparing the Persephone for sea. Her heart went out to the boys and girls on the ship. Was this the last time they'd see their homeland?

She turned and said goodbye to the two men and started to walk back along the quay. She had no idea how long it would take to get to New South Wales or what would become of the young people she saw. She looked up at the sky over the ship. They would surely live under a different sky to this one. Annie whispered a prayer for their safe-keeping and continued to walk the road home.

End of April, 1846

It was getting on for the end of April. Annie had called in to the Post Office every week to check if she had received a reply from Speranza at The Nation. This week, there was a letter for her. She broke the seal straight away and began to read.

The Nation Newspaper
D'Olier Street
Dublin
23rd April 1846

My dear Annie,

Thank you for your letter, and thank you for your kind compliments about my poem. It is a wonderful thing to have one's work published.

I have some good news for you. I showed your poem to Mr Gavan Duffy, the Leaderwriter of The Nation, and he tells me he will be pleased to publish it in the next edition. I urged him to pay you for your beautiful work and he has agreed. I will let you know about payment when the poem has been published.

The newspaper is also interested to publish work about the potato blight that afflicts our country. Send your news to Mr Duffy, at the above address.

Do continue to write poetry. I think you have a gift for this art form and send you my best regards.

Yours sincerely

Speranza (Jane Elgee)

Annie hurried home to show the letter to her Da, and he hugged her.

'You'll be a famous writer one day, my girl,' he said, then added. 'Let's hope His Lordship doesn't take offence at your poem.'

'No. If he reads it he'll help us, I'm certain of that. I'll show this to Jack. Where is she?'

'She went to the beach with Finn and Katty. They've gone to look for seaweed.'

Annie found the three of them hunting for seaweed among the rocks at the water's edge. They had a decent bag of the black seaweed and would dry it by the fire before eating it.

They stopped work and sat on the larger stones while Annie told them her news from Dublin.

'You must write more poems, Annie, you'll soon be famous.' Jack paused then looked at Finn and Katty. 'Will you two bring the seaweed up the cabin and start it drying? We'll follow you up soon. I want to talk to your sister.'

They agreed and set off for home.

* * *

Annie was curious. What did Jack want?

'I need to tell you something, my friend,' Jack said. 'I'll be moving on soon.'

'Ah, sure don't say that,' Annie replied. 'You must stay. We love you.' Annie looked at Jack's unsmiling face.

'Annie, I can't stay here and live on your generosity for much longer, much as it pleases me,' Jack said. 'I've been reading The Nation, too, and Mr Gavan Duffy writes about an uprising to be free from the British government. He calls on all men to fight to make Ireland a free country.'

'But Jack, you're not a man. Girls can't go and fight.' Annie smiled at the thought.

'It's not just that, Annie. I've heard the rumours and so have you. The Landlord is making plans to clear the estate here and eviction is on the way. I've seen it in Galway and it's coming here. Eviction is coming and I can't stay and watch another one. I can't bear to think about my cousin Brendan's eviction. That was the start of all our troubles, my mother and brothers, and my father. I have to get out of here before it happens again.' Tears flooded from Jack's eyes and trickled down her face.

Annie shook her head. 'No, they're just rumours, they're not true. You mustn't believe them.' She reached out and caught Jack's hand. 'Don't cry.'

'It's coming, Annie, even if you won't think about it,' Jack wiped her eyes and leaned down to pick some shells from between the rocks. She threw them out to the river, where they splashed and sank, to be recycled back to the strand by the tide and the waves, crushed into ever smaller pieces.

Jack's words settled into Annie's brain and she stood and straightened her skirt.

'What'll we do if we're thrown onto the road, then? We'll not survive till the autumn crop is ready. Sure, what am I saying? If they clear the estate, there'll be no autumn crop, and no-one to dig it.'

Annie looked along the narrow laneway from the road to the strand and saw Katty skipping back towards them.

Annie spoke quickly. 'Jack, if you go, then I'll go with you. I'll go to His Lordship in Dublin and beg him for a stay on the evictions. What do you say?'

Before she could reply, Katty arrived breathless and smiling. 'Annie and Jack, come on, supper's ready.'

Annie and Jack caught Katty, a hand in each of theirs, and swung her along the lane as they walked home, counting. '*A haon, a dó, a trí*, one, two three, and up she goes!'

* * *

After supper, Jack walked outside with Annie's father to explain her plans. Annie stood at the door and listened.

'I'll be sorry to see you go, Jack,' her father said. 'You've lifted our spirits these last few weeks. I know Annie will be sad to say goodbye.'

Annie came over to join them. 'Da, I'm going too.'

'What in God's name are you saying girl?' her father looked at her and shook his head. 'Don't talk foolish nonsense.'

'I'll go and see His Lordship in Dublin and ask him to put a stay on the evictions he has planned for this whole village.' She put her hand on her father's arm and lowered her voice in case the children heard. 'Da, how will we live if we're thrown onto the road?'

'Annie, you're making this up. Stop this wild talk, we won't be evicted. And you're not leaving us, we need you here. That's my last word, daughter. My last word,' Annie's father shrugged off her hand and walked off along the lane.

Annie turned to Jack. 'What'll I do?"

'Your father's right, he needs you here. Katty and Finn need you. You have to stay. But, will you do something for me, Annie?'

'To be sure.'

'I want you to write to the editor of The Nation and tell them I'm coming to Dublin. Ask them if there's any work for me at the paper. Tell them I'm a boy and I'll do anything.'

Annie shook off her disappointment. She'd think about it later. She stretched her hand out to her friend.

'Come inside, we'll write the letter now.' They wrote the letter and posted it off to Dublin the next morning.

Early May 1846

For the next few days, her father spoke only briefly to Annie. She knew he was still angry that she would leave them, even for a short time, so she busied herself with work, cooking and cleaning, and teaching the children their letters and numbers. Jack joined them and somehow the lessons became even more fun.

Jack also began to make preparations to leave. Her knee breeches still had some life left in them, but she replaced her worn-out jacket with an old jacket belonging to Pat. This got a smile out of Pat when he saw a female wearing his clothes and the atmosphere thawed a little.

Annie had made a few oat-cakes on the morning Jack was to leave. She knew that Jack planned to hitch a ride to Dublin. There were plenty of carts going that way with room for another on board. If not, then Jack was well used to walking.

'It's only a hundred miles, and the weather's a bit more settled, so I won't get too wet.'

Annie offered to take her friend as far as the bridge in Waterford. Jack accepted and said heartfelt goodbyes to Annie's father, brother and sister, then she jumped up onto the cart beside Annie and they left.

An hour later they stopped at the bridge that crossed the

river from Waterford into Wexford and Jack turned to Annie.

'I'll get a lift from here. Thank you for all your kindness, dear Annie. We'll meet again, please God.'

'I just want to go with you,' Annie said. 'I'll write to you at the newspaper offices. God bless you, my darling.' The two friends hugged and Jack jumped down from the cart then Annie guided the donkey to turn.

'Come on, tk, tk, let's go home.' Annie looked at Jack standing by the side of the road; a skinny boy with a jute bag over her shoulder. Jack raised her hand and Annie tried to smile, then looked away, as she began to retrace her journey back to Ashling. It was a hard road going back, for she'd lost another friend. Please God, they would meet again, unlike poor Eileen, whom she'd meet in heaven one day. She knew she'd never see Brín again. Although she had loved him, he wouldn't come back from England. Her father spoke the truth when he said these times were not right for marrying.

'I could've just kept going with Jack. I have the few pence for the toll across the bridge, then we'd have been free. Free of all this,' Annie said as she blinked away tears. 'Da and me, we're just slaves to the landlord, and if we can't pay the rent, we're no use.' Annie made a promise to herself. 'Finn and Katty will grow up free, they won't be slaves.'

The old donkey pulled the small cart up the hill out of the town and took her back to her small cabin on the Landlord's estate.

* * *

When Annie got back to the cabins, she saw Brín's mother, Marie, walking along the laneway with a full bucket of water.

'How's Brín?' she asked.

'He sent me some money last week, thank God. But I'm in two minds whether to pay the rent, what with these rumours of eviction. Anyway, tell me Annie, did Jack get away to Dublin?'

'Yes, he did and thank you,' Annie said as she slowed the cart to a stop and jumped down to walk with her neighbour. 'I wanted to go with him and find His Lordship in Dublin, but Da won't have it.'

'To talk to His Lordship about the evictions? Jesus, Mary and Joseph, what'll become of us?'

Annie let the reins hang loose and the donkey followed the two women as they walked back to the cabins. Her neighbour continued.

'As if that's not enough, did you hear there's sweating sickness in the village? Seamus McCormick and his family are all sick with it.'

'What's that? No, I've not seen anyone lately and Da's been away working most days. Is it dangerous?'

'I don't know, but some of them are really poorly with it. The little ones seem to be worse off. Please God, it'll pass quickly.'

They reached Marie's cabin and Annie continued her walk back home. She unhitched the cart and gave the donkey a drink of water, then opened the gate to their small field and let the animal in. She patted him on his back. 'Thank you, my friend.'

Da was at home with Finn and Katty.

'Jack's going to write and let us know when she arrives,' she said.

'Sure that's good news,' her father replied. 'Come and sit

down, daughter. You must've been sorry to say goodbye.'

'I'll be fine, Da.' Annie said, and warmed her hands by the fire. 'I was talking to Marie and she said the McCormicks are all sick with the sweating sickness. Did you hear that?'

'No I hadn't heard, but we seem to be cursed lately, my girl,' her Da said. He leaned towards the fire and lit a taper to put to his pipe. There was a tiny shred of tobacco in it and he breathed in the smoke. 'I must get more work to keep us going, but there's just a day here and there lately, not enough to keep us for more than a day or so.'

'What about the money from Aunt Bridie?'

'Sure, I paid the quarter's rent with most of that.'

Annie bit her lip and decided not to tell her father about Marie not paying her rent.

'I saw some fishing boats on the river on the way back,' Annie said. 'They'll be going out from Dunmore, now the weather has settled a bit. What do you say I go and buy some mackerel and see what I can sell up in the hills around Crannagh?'

'That's a great idea,' her Da replied. 'But I don't have any spare money for you to buy the fish.'

'They might let me have some on credit. I'll pay when I've sold it. What do you say, Finn and Katty? Will we go first thing in the morning?'

It was agreed, and it settled her mind a bit to have something else to think about other than the constant worry of eviction.

Buying and selling mackerel

They were up early to do their morning tasks. Annie rekindled the fire and cooked up some oatmeal porridge, Finn fetched water from the spring, while Da and Katty milked the cow.

The two younger ones each had a bowl of porridge. Annie and her Da made do with a cup of hot water mixed with a drop of milk, for they had run out of tea a while back. It was time to go on the road.

Annie said, 'Katty, get your ribbons and we'll do your hair, *acushla.*'

When Katty's plaits were done, Annie climbed the ladder to the roof store in the cabin and took down the creel. The woven basket felt soft and worn between her fingers and the shoulder straps frayed where it had been carried by her mother before her. By the time Finn had led the donkey and cart to the door, both Annie and Katty were ready.

'We'll get something to eat on our travels, I'm sure,' she said to her siblings, as she waited for them to climb onto the small cart. She looked at Finn who hadn't moved, his feet planted on the road. She recognised that stubborn look on his face.

'I want to drive the cart,' he said. 'You said I could the last time, don't you remember?'

'Finnie! Go on then.' She let him take the driving seat and sat next to him, while Katty sat behind them in the cart, and off they went.

The road to Dunmore was a trek for the poor old donkey, so at the foot of some of the higher hills, they all got off the cart and walked up to the top. Sometimes Katty and Annie raced each other to the top of a hill, while Finn led the donkey, then they all jumped back on the cart and let it glide down the other side. The river to their left was wide and silver-bright that morning and there were a few fishing boats out trawling their nets. The early summer sun gleamed in the sky and hedgerows bloomed with hawthorn. Annie inhaled the sweet scent of the sparkling white blossom and, after a while, they arrived at Dunmore, a large fishing village at the estuary of the river. Out beyond the edge of land, Annie saw the pewter coloured ocean, and farther out, the horizon, where pale sky and sea merged.

* * *

Finn hitched the cart to the harbour wall while Annie put her basket on her back. 'Let's see what they have for us,' she said, as the three of them walked along the quayside.

There were around ten or so boats moored on the water beside the quay. Most were small fishing boats, each with their wooden oars laid along the length of the boat. Above, on the quay, nets were draped and spread out for repair and to clean off the seaweed. Seagulls and kittiwakes flew above the boats and nets, lured by the smell of the just-caught fish, their harsh calls reverberated around the quays. There must have been fifty or more birds diving and skittering around, over and back to their nesting places on the cliffs nearby.

Annie, and her mother before her, had both been regular buyers of fish in the past. Lately though, there'd been no money to buy fish to sell on, and no-one to sell them to.

One of fishermen called her over. 'Annie, *Dia dhuit!* I've not seen you for a while. Are you buying? I've a good catch of mackerel here, come and take a look.'

'*Dia dhuit,* Fergal. It's good to see you, how are you?' she asked as she walked over to his boat.

'Sure, it's quiet enough lately. How's your Daddy?' Fergal was a man in his forties, short and rangy with a mottled beard and a black seaman's cap topping off his bony face. In fact, to Annie, he was beginning to look like the mackerel he had in the box at his feet.

'Da's well, thank you. He's out every day looking for work. He gets a day, here or there,' she replied. 'Let's see your catch then. Katty and Finn, come over and we'll tell Fergal what we think of his catch.'

She smiled as Katty peered into the fish boxes laid out on the quay. Finn, like Annie, was an old hand at selling fish, but he was more interested in Fergal's boat.

'They love a bit of fish, Fergal,' Annie said, 'but cooked first.' They both smiled at her joke.

'There's four dozen in that box there, Annie. Just two shillings for the lot.' Fergal took the creel and proceeded to fill it with gleaming, scaly, just-caught fish.

'Wait, Fergal!' Annie said, and reached to take back the basket. 'We haven't agreed a price. And,' she paused, 'I've no money to pay you straight away. I'll take half the box and pay you when we come back later. What do you say?'

'I trust you, Annie. Here's two dozen,' he said, and counted out the fish into the creel. 'See what you can sell and then pay me a shilling on your way back. Sure, there's no-one else buying around here.' He shrugged and looked up along the quay, Annie was the only customer.

'Thank you, Fergal, you're great.' She picked up the basket of fish. 'We'll call back this way later.'

They shook hands on it. Fergal's hands were thick-skinned, dirty and scarred from the fishing. Hers, slim and long-fingered, but hardened from digging potatoes with her father.

* * *

The three Powers headed away from the harbour, up into the hills, and jolted along narrow lanes overgrown by grass. Now, the donkey moved nimbly over the bumps, and they bounced along at speed until they reached the first house on their round.

The woman of the house took four fish and haggled over the price until both she and Annie were satisfied, then they moved on to the next smallholding along the lane. This was deserted, the cottage door swung on its hinges. Inside, the fire was just ashes in the grate. There was no sign of habitation, other than a nest of birds in the rafters.

'Where are they?' Finn asked, as Annie climbed back up on to the cart.

'Gone. Let's try further on. Eamon Byrne lives just up the lane. He was at the school a few years ago. He'll tell us.' They saw more empty cottages, and one or two of them had their roofs pulled down, leaving just bare stone walls.

At the Byrne's small cottage, two black and white collies sat beside at the door, as if on guard. Finn stopped the cart, but there was no-one around.

Annie jumped down. 'Stay here with Katty. I won't be long.'

She knocked on the door and called out the Irish greeting. *'Dhia dhuit.'* A low sound reached her ears, so she walked in.

'Oh, thank God, come in girl,' a voice whispered from the corner.

'Why, Mrs Byrne, what is it, are you sick?' Annie asked.

'Come in, come in and I'll tell you all about it,' the woman replied.

Mrs Byrne lay on the bed, her face was white and she shivered with a fever. She was wrapped in a blanket but the fire was cold in the grate and the air in the cabin felt damp.

'But where's Eamon?' Annie asked. Mrs Byrne's son, a bachelor, lived with his mother on the few acres they farmed.

'Oh, we've been so unfortunate, the dear Lord help us,' Mrs Byrne said. 'Eamon had an accident on the road works last week and he's in the Infirmary in Waterford. Now I'm sick and have no-one to look after me.'

'Sure, that's terrible news! Well, we're here now and I'll get Finnie to light the fire and get you a drink, Mrs Byrne.'

'You're a great girl, so you are. I've not seen a blessed soul for a week.' The woman began to cry softly. Big tears ran down her tired, cold face.

'I'm out selling fish, or I wouldn't have found you. Who can I call on to come and help?'

'I don't want to be any trouble, but the Bradys will come and give me a hand. They live up by the Crannagh, do you know it?'

'Yes, I know it. We'll light your fire and get a drink of water for you and then we'll go and find the Bradys.'

'God bless you, girl,' the woman said and blessed herself

with her rosary beads. She began to pray while Finn set and lit the fire.

At the Crannagh, they relayed their news to the Bradys who promised to go straight over, and then went on their way again. The country around Dunmore had lots of small farms and they called at several of them. Some bought fish, but many more farmhouses were deserted. Annie couldn't understand why.

The mackerel were hard to sell, although she got rid of a dozen and a half. People who were at home just didn't have any money or anything to barter with. Annie had hoped to get some oats or eggs in exchange for her fish but came away empty-handed. She could see those homesteads that had been abandoned were open to the elements. Even the ones that still had families living in them looked sorry and dirty.

On their return journey, they called in to Mrs Byrne and she was sitting up having a feed of the mackerel Annie had sold her. The Bradys had promised to call in each day.

Back in Dunmore, Annie settled up with Fergal. She bought another half dozen mackerel and they went home with a fish supper and money to spare.

* * *

'I'll do that again, Da,' she said, when they got home. 'But the whole country around seems to have changed.'

'In what way, Annie?'

'Sure, God help them, some of them have nothing, even their clothes are dirty and torn. I saw some half-naked children in a few of the cabins up around Crannagh.'

Annie's father poked at the turf on the fire and orange sparks flew up in a swirl.

'I'm sorry I brought Finn and Katty along to see that,' Annie finished.

Her Da stayed silent and chewed on the end of his pipe.

'Well, I've a bit of good news, Annie,' he said. 'I planted some seed potatoes today for an early crop. Please God they'll come through sound in a few months.'

Annie bit her lip and took a deep breath before she spoke.

'Things are changing, Da. Can't you see it?' she asked him. 'Even some of the small-holdings were abandoned. The families have gone off to America or British North America,' she paused. 'They've left the land!'

Her father seemed to have closed his mind or just couldn't understand what was happening. He repeated the only remedy he had.

'Better times will come, girl. I'm sure of it. We just need to sit tight and pray.' He didn't look at her, just sat there and stared into the heart of the fire.

* * *

That evening the family sat around the table and had a big feed of mackerel. Annie had cleaned the fish and placed them on the turf fire, skin down, where they cooked in a few minutes. She piled them on a wooden platter in the middle of the table. Before they started to eat, Da said the Grace, then they tucked in, eating with their fingers.

'Ow, Annie, these are too hot to hold!' Finn complained.

'Sure, blow on them why don't you?' she asked and leaned across to blow some cooling air across the plate of fish.

Katty giggled. 'Annie, you're funny! Blow on one for me.'

Annie picked up a mackerel, blew on it, then carefully pulled away the narrow spine and feathery bones of the fish. She handed the fillet to Katty.

'Here darling, it's cool enough to eat,' Annie said and she glanced over to see her father smile as he watched his children eat a hearty meal.

'Do you remember when your mother was alive?' he asked. 'She'd cook the mackerel just as you have, Annie, and they'd be there on the table beside a pot of potatoes.'

'She was the best mother,' Annie replied. 'She's watching over us in heaven, I'm sure.'

Silence stretched across the table like a pall until Katty broke the spell with a cough.

'Ah, there's a bone stuck in my teeth!' She pulled at a shiny, narrow bone and held it up. 'Look!'

They laughed, and ate until all the fish were gone. That night, after they had prayed the rosary, the children went to bed with full stomachs.

Annie cleaned off the table and threw the skin and bones of the fish on to the midden at the back of the cabin. She came back in, swept the floor then added a little more turf to bank down the fire.

'There now, we'll be warm tonight.'

She placed her journal and pen on the table, and there was a stub of candle left for her to write by.

'Annie, come and sit with me before you start your writing.' Her Da's voice was low so as not to disturb the sleeping children.

She pulled a stool over beside him and they sat close together.

'I've been thinking about what you said earlier,' he said.

'About what, Da?'

'When you said all our neighbours are leaving. The ones who are better off than we are and won't stay and see this through.' Her father scratched his hair and rubbed his chin. 'I thought the Butlers were the only ones going from around here. But I'm wrong, aren't I?'

Annie nodded. 'What do you think we should do?'

She leaned in and put her head on his shoulder, then she put her hand on his arm and he looked at her. She saw his eyes were filled with tears.

'I don't know anymore.' Her Da's voice broke and he picked up her hand and kissed it. 'We don't have the money to go anywhere. If the rumours are true then evictions are on the way. And if that happens we'll end up in the workhouse, God forbid. That'll be the end of us. But that won't happen, I've paid the rent. They won't throw us out.' He didn't seem too sure, for all his talk, Annie thought. And they both knew the next quarter's rent would come due soon.

'Da,' Annie's face almost touched his as she spoke. 'Let me go to Dublin to find His Lordship. He won't turn us out when he knows how desperate we are. I'll remind him we've paid the rent. Jack's there, she'll help me'

'Sure, you're a great girl, Annie. But our Landlord won't take any notice of a young one on her own.' He cleared his throat and continued. 'I've been thinking about that, too. I'll go. I've been to Dublin before and I'll be able to find him. He knows me and his agent knows me. They know I'm a good tenant. They'll listen.'

Her father moved away from her, let go of her hand and stood up. 'Yes, I'll go. You must stay here and look after Finn and Katty.'

Annie didn't argue, no matter how much she wanted to. Her father had decided. He would leave in two days time for Dublin and she must stay behind.

She sat at the table and recorded all this in her journal. She didn't know then, but everything was about to change.

Fever

The day after their feed of mackerel, their neighbour, Marie called to the cabin.

'Pat, can you help me?' she asked. 'I've not seen Theresa O'Malley for a few days. Their door is shut and I knocked but I can't see any sign of her or the boys.'

'Have you seen her, Annie?' her father asked, but Annie shook her head. 'That's strange. I know Davey's away working but the family are not gone anywhere. I'll come with you to take a look. Annie, pass me my jacket, girl. I won't be but a few minutes.'

'I'll come with you,' Annie said. 'Finn, keep an eye on the fire, it'll need a bit more turf in a minute.'

Annie and her Da left with Marie and walked back along the lane to the far end of the village. Theresa's cabin was silent, so her Da knocked and then banged on the door.

'Theresa, Theresa, are you in there?' he called. 'It's Pat Power, I've come to see how you are.' He banged on the door again.

There was still no answer, so he pushed the door open. Annie stood beside him and looked into the silent room. The wooden shutters were pulled across the tiny cabin window and the room was in shadow. The rank air caught in the back of Annie's throat.

'*Dia dhuit*, Theresa! It's Pat here,' her Da repeated. 'Can I come in?' He motioned to Annie and Marie to wait outside. From the doorway, Annie saw Theresa lying on the bed with a young child in her arms and another child asleep beside her. She heard Theresa whisper.

'Ah, 'tis you Pat, come in. The little ones are very sick, look at them. I think they might need a doctor.' Theresa cradled her sleeping three-year-old son, Rory, in her arms. The poor woman's face was haggard, her skin was bleached of colour and her eyes stared at Annie's father.

Annie held her breath as Pat felt the boy's face, and then looked at the other child lying beside his mother on the bed. 'Let me help you with Rory,' he said to Theresa.

Her father gently took Rory from Theresa's arms and laid him down next to the child on the bed then settled the two children and covered them with a blanket.

'Now, come outside with me and we'll talk. There's a good woman,' Annie's father said.

Theresa stood up and looked at the boys. 'Be careful they don't get cold, Pat.'

Pat put his arm around her and they walked out of the cabin into the air. Theresa was bare-foot and dressed only in a shift, and she trembled as she leaned against Annie's father. Pat shook his head at Annie and Marie as he helped Theresa to sit on the low wall beside the cabin, then he closed his eyes and blessed himself.

'Theresa,' he said. 'God bless you. Your two boys have gone to God. You can see that, surely?' Annie looked at her father then over at Marie, as they both understood what he had said.

Theresa put her hands up to her head and sobbed. 'I thought

if I prayed hard enough, the good Lord would work a miracle and give me back my children, but I've been punished for my sins.'

Annie's Da spoke again. 'Rory and John can't stay in the bed like that, Theresa. I'll call the priest to come over and say the last rites for them.'

'What'll I do, Pat? What'll I tell their father? she asked. The poor woman, sick and half-starved, looked to Annie's father for an answer.

'Let's look after the children first, Theresa,' he said. 'Let's do this thing first.'

* * *

Annie went with her Da to the priest's house to tell him what had happened. She was in a state of disbelief as they walked the road to the chapel. 'What happened, Da? Sure, they can't be dead. They were playing with Katty yesterday.' Her father had no answer. He just shook his head.

The priest got his bag of holy oils and set out back to the village with them.

Pat sent Annie home to Finn and Katty. He stayed with Marie and Theresa while the priest administered the Last Rites to the two boys.

'Da, will I go over and sit with Theresa for a while?' Annie asked her father when he came back to the cabin.

'No, Marie's still there,' her Da said. 'I'll head off in a while to help dig a grave for the boys and see they're decently buried. I'd say we could both do with a cup of tea, daughter. Is the kettle hot?'

Pat sat in his chair and lit his clay pipe while Annie made

tea for them. She breathed in the smell of the tobacco and sipped her drink.

'Why did they die, daddy?' Katty asked.

'They got sick, darling,' he explained. 'I think it was that fever. But we can say a prayer for their souls. I pity their poor father when he comes home.'

'Will we get sick too, Da?' Finn asked.

'No, you won't,' Annie replied. 'Now, come and kneel down and we'll pray for John and Rory. In the name of the Father, the Son and the Holy Ghost. Eternal rest grant unto them, O Lord. . . '

When the prayer was finished, Annie sent Finn and Katty out to get the cart ready for their father. He'd use it to take the children's bodies to the graveyard and stay to help with the burial.

* * *

When her father got back later, he spoke to Annie. 'You know it's a strange sickness. Those children's poor faces were all swollen and the cabin just stank of mouse droppings. God only knows what that is. I didn't see any mice around, and the place looked clean enough.'

Annie remarked on the smell he brought in with him. 'That mousey smell is on your clothes, Da,' she said. 'Here, give me your jacket and I'll shake it off outside. There's hot water on the fire, use it to wash that smell off your face and hands.'

'Thank you, daughter. I'm weary to tell the truth.' Her father slumped into his chair. 'Burying children is not a task I'd ever imagined doing.'

Annie sat next to her Da and kissed his cheek. 'You're a

saint that's what I say. Now give me your jacket.'

She went outside and shook the jacket till the smell had almost gone. Then went back in and said her night prayers.

* * *

The next morning, Pat was still tired and stayed in bed while Annie and the children did their jobs. Annie brought him a cup of tea but he shook his head. 'I don't want anything to drink.' She felt his face, it was hot, and his forehead and cheeks were flushed.

'What's wrong, Da?'

'I don't feel well,' he said. 'I've a fierce pain in my head. I just hope I haven't got the fever that killed them two poor children.'

'No, that's not possible. You're just tired from yesterday. Here, sit up and have a drink of tea. I'll get your pipe for you.'

He waved away the tea and the offer of his pipe. 'Take Finn and Katty out of here, Annie. I don't want them to see me sick, they'll only worry.' Then he lay back on the bed; his face was wet with sweat.

Annie called Finn and Katty. 'Come on you two, we're going to visit Marie. Say goodbye to Daddy and we'll go now.'

'Daddy, what's wrong, are you sick?' Finn asked.

'I'm just tired that's all. I'll have a rest here for a while, son,' Da said. 'Go off with Annie, and tell Marie I was asking for her. I'll get kisses from you both later.' Their father lay back on the bed and closed his eyes.

Pat Power

During the following weeks, Annie spent all her time nursing her father. She helped him to wash and tried to get him to eat some porridge or soup. Finn and Katty had their slates and books at Marie's and they studied hard and prayed for their father to get well. Marie fed them and they slept in her son's empty bed.

The fever abated a little, but it had left Pat weak and he stayed in bed. Thankfully, Annie remained unaffected by the fever and she spent her days sitting with her father. One day he would be on the mend, and the next day, his face would be flushed with heat. On good days, he often spoke about the two younger children.

'They'll be scholars, Annie. Clever, like their sister. We must see to it that they go back to school when this is over. Promise me this, daughter.'

'I promise you, Da. Katty and Finn will make you proud, we all will. Sure, don't they just love their books? And they both have a lovely writing hand. Don't you worry about us now, Da. Just get yourself well.' Brave words, but her heart stuttered with fear when she looked at his gaunt face.

* * *

157

It was early morning on the final day.

'Daughter, this fever has got the better of me,' her father said. His voice was low and hoarse from the burning temperature.

'No, Da, don't say that!' Annie took his hand in hers and kissed it. 'You're getting better. You must get better.'

'I've seen death before, my girl. It's here, now. I want you to go and fetch Father Corcoran. Ask him to give me the Last Rites. Don't be crying. Go off and tell him to come now.' He squeezed her hand. 'Go on.' Her father lay back on the bed, exhausted and breathless.

Annie's felt as if her heart was breaking as she raced over to Marie's. 'Da's asking for the priest! He says he's dying.'

Then she saw Finn and Katty were there, and they looked at her, stunned. Katty burst into tears. 'Daddy!'

Marie blessed herself, stood up and took off her apron. 'Well then, you children had better go over to your father. I'll go and call Father Corcoran.'

The three of them raced back to the cabin. Katty threw herself on the bed beside her father. 'Daddy, don't die!' she cried.

'*Acushla*, Katty.' Da spoke in a whisper. 'Hold my hand there. You too, Finnie.' He took a deep breath before he could speak again. 'It's my time to go and join your mother. Sure hasn't she been waiting patiently for me all these years?'

Katty cried and cried until she had cried herself to sleep. Annie and Finn sat with their father until the priest came. He said the last prayers and anointed Pat with the oil of extreme unction, then left them to keep vigil with their father into the night.

Pat didn't speak after the Last Rites. He gradually lapsed into a deep sleep and after a while his breaths became less frequent. Annie dipped a cloth into cool water and brushed his tangled, greying hair back from his forehead. The fever began to diminish in his body as his heartbeat slowed, yet he muttered and moved his arms around. Annie put her hand over his and held it there, and he quietened. Finn held his father's other hand. Katty dozed on Annie's knee with her head on her sister's shoulder, her dark curls against Annie's chin.

Neighbours came and went, prayed and offered their sympathy. The night passed slowly. Annie lay Katty down on their bed in the corner of the cabin. Then she and Finn and together with Marie and a few of their neighbours, knelt and prayed the rosary. They kept vigil until dawn broke and Pat Power drew his last faltering breath, and then silence. It was over.

* * *

Annie sat with her father's body while Marie carried Katty over to her cabin and put her onto the bed the Power children had shared for the last few weeks. Finn went with them and lay down beside his sister.

Marie returned to the cabin and closed the door. 'I'll help you lay out your father.' She put a bucket of water to heat on the fire, then helped Annie to strip her father's body and the two women washed it with great care. Annie combed her Da's hair and the two women dressed him in his shirt and breeches then wrapped him in a blanket from the bed. Finally, they placed two pennies on his closed eyes and it was done. Pat Power was ready for his burial.

Together, they tidied the room, emptied the bucket of water

and cleared away the undershirt Pat had died in and the cloths they had used to wash his body. When all that was done, they sat beside him and drank a cup of tea together.

Annie thought back to her mother's death. She had died in childbirth when Annie had been only a child herself. The women of the village had looked after her. Annie looked at Marie and nodded.

'You were there, too, for my mother. I remember.'

The older woman nodded. This time, Pat had prepared Annie for his death, and her good neighbour, Marie, had been by her side to help her through it.

'*Go raibh maith agut*, thank you,' Annie whispered.

'You've done well by your father. He'd be proud of you.'

At noon, Marie offered to go to the priest's house to arrange the burial for the next day. There was a family plot in the graveyard where their mother, Caitrin Power, lay. Finn and Katty went with Marie.

After they left, Annie sat at the table and wrote a letter to Bridie in New York and one to Jack, care of The Nation newspaper in Dublin. She took out her journal and recorded the death of her father, then she looked around her. The fire had gone out, the shutters were still closed.

Just she, Annie Power, sitting beside her father's body in the dim light of her empty home.

* * *

Finn and Katty didn't move back to the cabin after their Da died. They stayed on with Marie. She helped Annie arrange the burial for her father. Pat and his wife, Caitlin Power, were finally reunited in death.

The day after the burial, Annie cleaned and tidied the cabin. She washed her Da's remaining clothes; his old breeches, his jacket and his spare shirt, and hung them to dry on the hedge beside the cabin. Then she cleaned his boots. The following day, she tied the boots and the clothes into a bundle, went into Waterford, and sold her father's possessions to the pawn shop. She put his clay pipe in her bag with her journals, her pen and ink and her rosary beads.

* * *

Annie left the cabin, and called over to Marie's with her water bucket. She motioned for Marie to come out, leaving the two children, Katty and Finn inside. Her neighbour picked up her bucket and they walked together to the spring for water.

Annie stopped before they got to the spring, she pressed her lips tightly together to stop them trembling, then she took a deep breath and spoke.

'You've been a true friend to my family. I can't repay your kindness, Marie. But I need you to do one more thing for me.' She held on tightly to the iron handle of the bucket, fingernails digging into her palm.

'Tell me what it is girl, and if I can do it, I will.'

Annie saw how strained and worn Marie looked after the recent deaths of her neighbours. There seemed to be no end to this hardship.

They continued walking towards the spring. The crystal water bubbled as it passed over the smooth white stones lining the base of the spring. Green sprigs of grass overhung the water and a blackbird flew up and away at their approach, its sweet call echoed in the air as evening drew in. Annie cupped a handful of the clear water and drank it. She could almost taste the ancient stones it had flowed across.

'You've heard the rumours, that we're all to be evicted. Before he died, Da was going to Dublin to ask Lord Ashling not to evict us. We paid the rent up to Easter. But we need a stay on the rest of the year's rent. At least until this is over.'

She waited as her neighbour stooped to lay the bucket in the spring and fill it with icy water.

'I've heard those rumours too, Annie. Brín's sent me a few shillings from England, but it's not enough to pay the rent. I can't see us being left here much longer. He's not a sentimental man, our landlord. Will he give all of us a stay, do you think?' Annie watched Marie dry her hands on her apron and adjust her shawl.

'I don't know. But it's what Da wanted to do.' She bent down and put her own bucket in the water to fill it. 'I've decided, I'm going to Dublin, in Da's place. Jack is there and he'll help me find Lord Ashling.' She paused as she saw Marie's face. 'Finn is old enough to look after Katty, but I don't want them on their own. Will you keep them with you for another week or so, until I get back?'

Marie shook her head. 'Sure, I have barely enough money to live on, Annie. I can't keep feeding them, girl.'

'I have three shillings here. That'll keep them, won't it?' asked Annie. 'I'll leave you the donkey and cart. Finn and Katty will milk the cow. You'll get a few shillings for the two animals if anything happens to me. But sure, the poor *crathurs* are on their last legs. You might have trouble selling them.' She smiled grimly and paused. 'I have the money for the ferry to Dublin. Please say you'll look after them.' Annie took the money from her skirt pocket and held it out.

Marie reached over and took the coins from Annie's out-stretched hand. 'Don't stay away too long, Annie. They need you, not me.'

'*Go raibh maith agut*. Thank you. I'm sure His Lordship will listen when he knows our situation here. We've always paid our rent. I'll go and tell Finn and Katty now. Then I'll leave first thing in the morning.'

The two women turned and walked back to Marie's cabin.

* * *

Annie called Finn and Katty to come outside. The sun was dropping lower in the sky and the clear sky foretold a cold night ahead of them.

'Finn, will you carry the bucket home for me? Katty, take my hand. Let's get home. I have some important news to tell the two of you.'

Annie looked at them, her precious brother and sister. Could she say the words?

They arrived back at the cabin and Annie opened the shutters on the window and rekindled the fire with some twigs and broken turf.

She sat with them at the table and the fire in the grate started to crackle as it took hold.

'Now, you know we have no potatoes', she said. 'They were all destroyed by the blight. Then Auntie Bridie sent us some money. Da paid the rent and bought food. Most of that money's been spent. And you know Da was going to ask our landlord, Lord Ashling, for a stay on the next quarter's rent.'

'Why do we need to ask for a stay on the rent?' asked Finn. He looked at her. 'Sure, can't we just pay it when we get more money?'

'No,' she replied. 'Lord Ashling owns all this land and this cabin and he can throw us out of here if we don't pay the rent. In fact, he can evict us, even if we do pay the rent.' Finn's face darkened as he understood.

'Listen to me.' She held out both hands for them to hold. 'I'm going to Lord Ashling's house in Dublin and I'll ask him to give us a few months until this potato blight is over. Me and Finn can work over the summer and earn money. Then, in autumn, when the next crop comes in, we'll be fine.'

'How will you get to Dublin, Annie?' Finn asked.

'There's a ferry that goes twice a week from Passage. I've enough for my fare.'

'I'll come too,' Katty said. 'When His Lordship sees how good we are, he'll help us.' She held on tight to Annie's hand. Katty was eight years old and still didn't understand what was happening to them.

'That's the hard part, *acroí*, my heart,' Annie said. 'You must both stay here with Marie. I only have enough money to get myself to Dublin. But Jack's there, and I know she'll help me.'

'I'll look after Katty,' Finn said. 'Don't worry about us. And I'll keep an eye on the cabin.' Finn looked away from his sisters and blinked back tears.

'Thank you, Finn. I've given Marie money for your food and she'll make sure you're both fed. I'll be away no longer than a week or two, my darlings.' Annie looked at Finn's hungry face as she spoke. His eyes were old and weary for his young years, yet he braced his shoulders back.

Katty finally understood. 'No, Annie, you can't leave me.'

She clung to her sister.

'Darling, I won't be gone for long.' Annie's head whirled with the promises she was making. 'Let's go back over now and I'll say goodbye. Your clothes and books are still there.'

'You're not going today, Annie!' Katty said and shook her head, her dark curls tumbled around her little face.

Annie bent and hugged her sister. 'I'll be going first thing tomorrow. There's an early ferry from Passage. The sooner I go, the quicker I'll come back with good news. Come on with me and we'll go back to Marie's. She knows already.'

'No, no! I won't go. I'm staying here. That's what Da wanted. You said!' Katty let go of Annie's hand. 'You can't go and leave us. Da said you'd look after us. He did, he did!' She ran over to the bed in the corner and threw herself onto it and cried and cried, her small body racked with sobs.

'Dear God! Katty, don't upset yourself so.' Annie followed her over to the bed and lay down beside her. Now, her own tears fell, and the two sisters wept for their dead father and their lost life together.

'Finn, come over here to me,' she said after a few minutes. She sat up and pulled Katty and Finn to her and wiped her face dry.

'Now, listen to me, both of you. This is hard, but if I don't go and speak to His Lordship then we won't be left stay here. There's a workhouse in Waterford and it's full of poor people who have been evicted. Lots of them are getting sick and dying. We can't go there. Da wanted us to stay here, that was his dying wish, all he wanted for us. So I have to try. You two must be brave and strong and pray for me. Will you do that?'

Katty nodded and reached up to untie the ribbon her father had given her for Christmas. She silently handed it to Annie who took it and hugged her.

The three siblings sat quietly together as they accepted this truth. One of them would have to leave the others, to try to save them all.

* * *

Later, they arrived back at their neighbour's cabin.

'You've told them?' Marie asked. Annie nodded, unable to speak.

'They'll be fine with me, don't you worry. And I have Finn here, he's almost a man, now. You'll help, won't you, Finn?'

Finn nodded, then put his arm around Katty and bent down to her. 'Katty, say *slán abhaile,* safe journey, to Annie, and then I have a new story to tell you before bed. About princesses who were turned into swans. Would you believe that?'

Katty held on to Annie's hand and looked out under her eyelashes at Finn. 'No,' she said. 'I don't want a story. I want to go with Annie.'

Finn persisted. 'It's a story about fairies, with magic in it.'

Katty loosened her grip and looked at Annie.

Annie hugged them both, her arms strong around them. 'I'll be home before you know it,' she said and turned to leave.

Finn caught hold of Annie's hand. 'Don't be gone too long, sister.' She nodded to him. Then she turned and left.

* * *

Night was drawing in when Annie got back to the cabin and stood the bucket of water on the burning turf sods in the grate and left it to heat.

She took out the blue dress, stockings and underwear sent by her Aunt Bridie from New York. She had only worn the clothes twice, once for the market and once at Christmas and now she spread them on the bed. She poured some of the warmed water from the bucket into a wooden tub that she used for washing, and saved a drop in a bowl for the morning. She stripped off her old skirt and blouse, her vest and drawers. She bent over the tub and put her hair into the water to soap away the dust and tears of the last week. She rinsed it off with the last of the clean water in the bucket and rubbed it dry with a cloth. Then she knelt by the tub and used the last sliver of soap to wash her face and hands, her neck and chest and arms. She stepped into the tub and crouched down to wash the rest of her body and dried off quickly.

She put the clean underwear on then sat on the stool by the fire and ruffled her hair to let it dry off in the heat; she felt the curls springing out from her head with the heat from the fire. She poured some of the water from the tub onto the fire to damp it down then took the tub outside, emptied it and left it outside the door. Please God, she'd use it again.

It was dark by now and she lay down on the bed and tried to sleep. This was her last night at home, and she prayed for her father and Finn and Katty, then she prayed for herself. She had been terrified when her father told her he was dying. With Marie's help she had been strong for her father. Annie was determined that Finn and Katty would not have to suffer another death in the family for many years to come. But she felt so alone, she missed her father, her friend, Eileen, and Brín. And she missed Jack. But they'd meet again in Dublin.

* * *

Annie got up before dawn and used the privy at the back of the cabin, came back in and rinsed her face and hands, then put on her dress and buttoned up the front. She pulled on woollen stockings and laced up her boots.

Her last task was to finish packing her bag. Her journals, rosary beads, pen and ink were already in the bag, together with her father's clay pipe. She added her old skirt and blouse and her new shawl.

She wrapped her mother's cloak around her tightly and pulled the hood up, then picked up the bag and set off to walk the few miles to Passage East village. She'd bought a ticket in Waterford, the day before, and had now spent the last of her money. If she had to, she'd walk the road back home.

Finn Power

At the same time as Annie was walking to the ferry, Finn set out for the hills above the cabins. He wore a hood over his face and shoulders in case he was seen by the game-keepers. When he reached his spot he settled down to wait for the sun to brighten the hedgerows. As soon as it was light enough, he took off the hood and searched out the snares he had set under the hedges the day before. The first snare was empty and he left it in place. He took a breath and checked the second snare. Yes, he'd caught a rabbit. The animal had struggled against the snare but now lay exhausted. Finn released the rabbit's leg from the wire snare and used both hands to wring its neck. Dinner.

He reset the snare and left both wires in place for one more day, then he'd move them. He stayed crouched for a few moments and listened to the sound of the wind in the trees overhead and the grass rustling. He stood and checked along the lane, no movement. It was early and he didn't expect to see the game-keepers out at this hour, but they'd be on patrol soon. He checked back on the snares to be sure they were well-hidden, then he put his hood back on to cover his face and began to jog along the lane. He had the rabbit in one hand and a small knife in the other.

He covered the ground to the tenant farmer's fields in just ten minutes. The farmer was usually up and about early, too, so Finn needed to act fast. He stayed close to the low stone wall around the first field. He needed to go round this field of oats and get to the edge of the next field over. The only sound was the song of the blackbirds. He crept towards the field he wanted; the one full of turnips. When he got there, he reached in and pulled a couple of turnips out of the ground. He heard dogs barking, grabbed two more and bent low to run back around the field to the laneway. He laughed, for if he was caught now with the rabbit and the turnips he'd be lucky to escape with a jail sentence, but more likely, transportation.

Finn kept running in case the farmer let the dogs loose. He slowed as he reached the road to the cabins and looked out across the river. The Dublin ferry was heading downriver towards the Irish Sea. He thought he could see Annie in her blue dress and waved, then ran on and didn't stop until he got back to his own cabin. He put the hood under the bed, then went on over to Marie's. Both she and Katty were up and dressed.

'I've got dinner,' he said and held up the plump rabbit by the legs, and shook the turnips.

Marie smiled. 'Ah! That's where you've been. Here, give them to me. I'll skin the rabbit for the pot. Just make sure you don't get caught, young man.'

'They won't catch me. They're too old and slow,' Finn said. The farmer could spare a few turnips from his field to help out a neighbour, he was a good Catholic after all. Finn saw him at mass every week. And wild animals belonged to no-one, in Finn's book. The law could go to hell. From now on, Finn would catch as many rabbits as they needed.

Leaving home

That morning, Annie was the only passenger on the ferry when it left Passage. When she stepped on board, she looked back at the small village crouched under steep, dark hills. The village itself was built on a flat outcrop of land that spread into the river, with a small harbour for fishing boats. The Waterford road wound up and away, back into the hills. It was still early, and there was no-one around to see her leave. She turned to look in her direction of travel down the river. The day was fine, but the ferry struggled to make headway against the incoming tide.

Annie's stomach churned as the ship sailed out into deeper water. She sat out on deck and waited as the ferry docked at Dunmore East to pick up more passengers. Fishermen were preparing their boats to leave for the day's fishing out in the estuary. She saw a figure waving on one of the boats and recognised Fergal; she waved back. She remembered the mackerel she had bought from him and the wonderful meal they had eaten together as a family. It seemed so long ago now, but was really only a few weeks. The ferry then moved out into the estuary and turned up into the Irish Sea towards Dublin. Being out in deep water made the boat roll even more and Annie held on to the wooden laths of her seat.

Several small children raced around the deck, laughing and calling to each other. They paid no mind to the movement of the ferry, and their laughter brought tears to her eyes. She'd see Finn and Katty again soon.

A woman came and sat next to her on the wooden bench and watched as Annie wiped her eyes.

'We're in hard times, girl. That's for sure,' the woman said. Annie nodded.

'Are you travelling alone then?' the woman asked. She was young, a few years older than Annie, long-faced with grey eyes and wore a fine woollen cloak with a frilled hood.

'Yes, I am,' Annie replied.

'Well, you'll not be alone for this part of your journey. We'll keep each other company. I'm Nora Flynn, and those three rapscallions are mine,' she said with some satisfaction.

'I'm Annie Power. *Dia dhuit,*' Annie said.

'James and Cillian, come and get something to eat. Here, bring Sile with you.' The woman called to her children and took out some bread and cheese. She divided it between the two small boys and the even smaller girl.

'Now, sit there,' she said to her children, 'and when you've eaten it you can go and look for the captain of the boat.'

Annie smiled at the thought of the captain's face when these three turned up.

The smell of the fresh-baked bread and the crumbly yellow cheese made Annie's mouth suddenly water. She looked away as Nora took out more and began to eat.

She heard Nora speak. 'Would you have a bit of something to eat with me, Annie? Sure, I've more than enough for myself here.'

The fresh bread almost melted on Annie's tongue. The

sharp, rich taste of the cheese complimented the yeastiness of the bread and gradually settled her stomach. She smiled at Nora.

'Thank you. I was hungry.'

As they chatted, Annie's guilt about leaving Katty and Finn eased somewhat. She was doing the right thing, she explained to her new friend.

'The only things we have left are the half acre and the cabin. If we lose those, then God knows what will become of us.'

'Well girl,' Nora replied. 'I'm off to Liverpool to join my husband. He has work there.'

'My neighbour's son went there, earlier this year,' Annie said. She didn't say that he was her sweetheart. That was all in the past now.

'Well, the factories are full with us Irish working all hours. My husband, God bless him, says he got the last job in the place and we'll stay there until this blight passes.'

'Then you'll come home?' Annie asked.

'Ah yes. The rent is paid up for the next quarter and I've put a lock on the cabin door. It'll be there for us, please God, when this trouble is over.' Nora said and wiped the crumbs from her mouth with a soft cloth.

'My father said we'll never leave Ireland.'

'And what'll your father do if this blight doesn't end soon, tell me that now?'

Annie turned away from the sea and faced Nora. 'He died last week. And I truly don't know what we'll do. I'm going to see the landlord in Dublin to get a stay on the rent till this is over.' Then she turned away again to stare out to sea.

Nora chewed on her bread, nibbled a bit of cheese and said no more.

The two women sat together and watched the grey waves break along the ship's bow as the children raced each other up and down the deck. They, at least, were off on a great adventure.

* * *

The ferry docked at six o'clock that evening at Dublin's North Wall on the River Liffey and passengers disembarked. Annie said goodbye to Nora and her children and wished them well for their onward journey. She walked along the quays beside the Liffey and headed further into the city. The day had some brightness left, and thankfully no rain, but evening was closing in. She passed the Customs House, built by the British Government. It looked like a great, white stone monument, and it shone in the setting sun. It appeared to be newly built, but it was at odds with the people she saw. Wretched, homeless paupers by the looks of them, just sitting on the pavements. Many were only half-clad, and seemed to have lost all hope.

A child approached her, a bone-thin boy, his face was bruised, his breeches were in rags about his legs, and he was barefoot. 'Missus, do you have a few pence to spare? I need to buy something to eat.'

'My God! Where are your mother and father?' Annie saw that he was around the same age as Katty, but his little face and hands were filthy, his eyes were staring at her.

'Just give me some money or something to eat, please Missus.' He held his hand out to her.

Annie found a penny and a farthing in the bottom of her purse and handed it over. 'Here, it's all I have.' She handed it over and walked on quickly.

Why are all these people here? She asked herself. Surely they can't all be homeless? She looked around her. But the ones and twos she saw as she started her walk along the quays, turned into dozens as she got nearer the centre of Dublin. Many of them appeared to be in family groups. She hurried on. She'd find Jack first, at The Nation. She could hear Da's voice as he planned his own journey to Dublin. *'Get to Carlisle Bridge, cross it and find D'Olier Street and the newspaper offices. His Lordship's house is not far from there.'*

The bridge itself was a crumbling, stone-arched edifice, and she paused halfway across to look back along the Quay at the massive dome of the Custom House overseeing the work of import and export. She stood and counted the masts and sails of the ships docked there, loading grain and livestock for the markets in England. A busy port indicated money. So why are there so many people here with no homes to go to? No food to eat? It seems to be everywhere. She'd seen something similar in Waterford and couldn't make sense of it at all.

Annie walked carefully beside the traffic moving across the bridge. Large horses pulled great carts full of goods. They rumbled into the city before the day's businesses closed. The smells and noises of animals and people filled her nose and ears. The air from the river was stinking and pungent, not a bit like the crystal river that ran past her home. She turned away from the water; tall buildings rose up to four or even five stories and stretched the length of the road. They seemed to cut out the sky and air. Great whales of buildings beside which her own small cabin back in Ashling would be the size of a mackerel.

'Dear God, help me to arrive safely,' she murmured as she

pushed her way through the masses of people rushing up and down the pavement. She held up her skirt with one hand and skipped lightly past horse-pulled carriages on the roadway filled with even more people, on their way to only God knew where, and dodged piles of horse manure and steaming yellow puddles.

* * *

She reached D'Olier Street and searched for the office of The Nation newspaper. A brass sign over the doorway of a building announced the name she was looking for. The building itself was built of pale stone on the ground floor with tall, narrow glazed windows. The three stories above were built out of dark red bricks and seemed to press downwards to the street.

Annie approached the doorway and pushed it open. The oak door felt heavy against her hand and she let it close behind her as she stepped into the large hall.

'Good evening, Miss.' A hoarse voice sounded from a room off the hallway. Inside the small room, a young man sat at a desk piled high with papers. He had just turned out the oil lamp on the desk and the light faded. He had a small dark head with straight hair swept back from his narrow face and a pointed chin and nose.

A laugh escaped her. '*Dhia dhuit!*' She greeted him in Gaelic. She was so relieved to have arrived.

'Sorry Miss, I don't speak Irish. And we're closing, you'll need to come back tomorrow, so you will.' The little clerk stood and began to put his coat on.

'No, I need to speak to Speranza. I've come all the way from

176

Waterford to see her,' Annie explained.

'Well, as you can see, she's not here. They've all gone home for the day. Now, I'm locking up, so you need to go.'

He closed the door to his cubby-hole, took her by the elbow, and ushered her back out onto the street. Then he locked the door behind him.

'Wait, do you know Jack Keating?' she asked.

'He's away with the boss on business. Good night then. Come back tomorrow,' and he walked off in the direction of the river, whistling.

'Well, so this is Dublin!' Annie put her bag on the ground by the doorway and sat on it. 'I'll sleep on the streets of Dublin like the other poor souls I've seen. If they can do it . . .'

She pulled her shawl around her cloak and settled in for a cold night. Thoughts of her dear father kept her company. 'I don't know, Da,' she said. 'It doesn't feel like Ireland here. That young man is Irish, but he doesn't speak Gaelic!'

The Nation Newspaper

Night came on quickly, and she stayed perched on her bag in the doorway. The street quietened after a while, with just the odd horse-drawn carriage clopping through. Later, Annie watched street cleaners sweeping up the horse droppings, shovelling the manure onto the back of a cart. The stink off the river permeated the air, even though D'Olier Street was a little distance from the Liffey.

The moon was full, its glow outlined by thousands of stars in the sky. There were too many to count, most were tiny gleams of light, others were flickering red and blue jewels sprinkled on the ebony night sky. She sighted the North Star and her heart ached for her father. He often pointed out the star to her and said that if she ever became lost, it would help her find her way home. But she couldn't remember what he said to do, to find her way home, and now she'd never be able to ask him, never see his face again or hear his voice. She wanted to see Finn and Katty. Dear Lord, keep them safe, she prayed.

As the night drew on, she heard a church bell toll midnight. Even though it was May, the temperature had dropped and it began to freeze. Tiny ice crystals glistened on the pavement and she huddled down into her cloak and pulled the hood in around her face. She had never slept anywhere other than in the small cabin in Ashling, had always shared a warm bed with Katty and Finn, until the last few weeks, their soft bodies beside her and the sound of their quiet sleeping breaths. The night passed slowly and she listened out for the church bells as they tolled the night hours, then she prayed the Angelus at six o'clock in the morning.

* * *

An hour or so after daybreak, Annie heard the sound of scurrying footsteps along the pavement. The little rat-faced boy she had met the night before hurried towards the doorway. He glanced at Annie curled up in the corner and put his hand in his pocket to take out some keys. As he stepped over her, she lifted her foot an inch and he tripped, fell against the door and dropped the keys.

'Shit!' he said. Then he saw Annie move and said, 'I thought you were asleep.'

She looked at him. Yes, he still had that unfortunate face.

His sharp yellow teeth gleamed as he spoke. 'Wait here till I open the office, then you can come in.' He sniffed, then walked into the hallway and closed the door behind him.

Annie stood up and smiled to herself at the trip, while she straightened her dress. She pushed back her hair, it felt frizzed and tangled after the cold night air and she pressed it down with icy fingers. She smelt the stench from the river on her hands. It must be all over her.

Annie waited on the street to be allowed in. She was still there, when a horse-drawn carriage pulled up. The horse snorted noisily and tossed his head and the driver jumped down to open the carriage door. A tall, dark-haired young woman stepped down onto the pavement. She was of Annie's height and wore a dark green dress frilled at the neckline over which she wore a jacket trimmed with light brown fur. Her black hair was pulled back into an elaborate arrangement with pearl ornaments dotted through it.

This must be her. Annie stepped forward. '*Dhia dhuit*. Are you Speranza, the famous poet?'

The woman stopped and turned to look at Annie in her wrinkled clothes. 'And who are you to be asking?'

'My name is Annie Power. I've come from Waterford.' Annie couldn't seem to find the right words but continued. 'My friend, Jack Keating, is here. Do you know him?'

'Jack? Yes, I know him. He works here.' The woman still didn't identify herself, and turned away towards the door, dismissing Annie.

'Wait. Please,' Annie said. 'I wrote to you, I sent you a poem and you got it published. Don't you remember me?' Annie reached out as if to touch her, but stayed her hand.

Speranza stopped and turned back, her hand on the door. She looked back at Annie and let the door go.

'Well! You're my little Waterford poet, aren't you? Forgive me, of course I remember you, Annie Power.' Speranza took Annie by the hand and said, 'And you've come all the way to Dublin? Come into the office and we'll talk there. But your hands are freezing!'

Annie smelt the scent of roses and heard Speranza's clothes rustle as she moved, silk and lace swirling around her body. Annie knew that she must look and smell dirty after sleeping in the doorway all night, and she badly needed the privy.

Speranza led the way into a small, wood-panelled office off the hallway. There was just one narrow window overlooking the street. Annie glanced out across to the river where boats and barges were running under the bridge. She was here at last!

'Did you hear what I said, Annie?'

'I, I'm sorry. I'm just so . . .' Annie put her hand to her tangled hair and brushed it back from her face.

Speranza looked closely at Annie. 'When did you arrive in Dublin?'

'Last night. I got here just as the young man was closing the office.'

'Oh my word! What did you do then?'

'I slept outside, in the doorway. Well, I sat there all night waiting for you to get here,' Annie said and tried to smile. Her skin felt tight on her face and she shivered.

Speranza stepped back out into the hall and shouted. 'Michael! Get yourself in here, now!'

They both sat down and waited for Michael's footsteps to creep along the hall. He pointed his face around the door. 'Yes, Miss Speranza?'

'Annie tells me you threw her out of here and left her on the doorstep all night. What in God's name were you thinking?'

'She just turned up,' he replied. 'You weren't expecting her, that I know of.' His black eyes glittered as he looked from one woman to the other.

'Please don't be angry with Michael,' Annie said. 'He's right, you didn't know I was coming.'

'You're an idiot, Michael.' Speranza said. 'Get out of here and make us a tray of tea. Then I don't want to see your face again today.' Speranza waved her hand at him. 'Go!'

Michael closed the door quietly and tip-tapped off down the hall to the kitchen.

'There's something wrong with that boy, and it's not just his face.' Speranza said, then drew a deep breath. 'Now, what were we talking about? Annie, you look exhausted. There's a privy at the end of the hall and a washroom next door to it. There'll be hot water for you to have a little wash. That's if Michael has done his job. Then come back and we'll talk over a cup of tea.'

Annie used the privy and washed her face and hands. Yes, there was warm water and a clean towel. She swept her hair back with damp hands to get rid of the smell of the river, at least a bit of it, and tied it with Katty's ribbon into some sort of order. She rinsed her hands off again, dried them, and walked slowly back along the hallway. Dark lengths of timber ran to halfway up the walls, the same on the floor, the only light came in from the glass above the door into the building. She prayed Speranza would help her.

The tea was poured and the two women sat together while Annie recounted her story; the death of her father and her fears for herself and her brother and sister.

'The only plan I have is to find our landlord, Lord Ashling, and beg for time. We've run out of food. I've sold everything apart from the poor old donkey and cart. And no-one will buy the cow. There's just no money anywhere.' Annie stopped and sipped her tea. It had milk in it and tasted soft and looked pale in the small china cup, but she drank it down.

She noticed Speranza was writing down her words as she spoke.

'You don't mind, do you, Annie?' Speranza asked as Annie glanced at the notebook. 'I need to know everything I can about this wretched blight. From what I hear, it's having a terrible effect on the poorer parts of Ireland, and there are so many people, all flooding into Dublin!'

Annie shook her head. 'No, I don't mind. People who have money are leaving and they are not the poorest people. Those are just left behind and no-one cares.' She paused. 'Well, some do care. There's a soup-kitchen in the town, in Waterford,' she explained. 'We'll manage till the potato crop comes back in the autumn. That's if I can get some seed potatoes to plant, but the main thing is to keep a roof over our heads.'

'Annie, I am so sorry to hear your story. As you know, I've written poems about this problem, but you are the first whose story I have sat and listened to.'

Annie looked at Speranza, a wealthy young Anglo-Irish woman with a career as a poet, taking time to listen to a poor Catholic girl from down the country. They had nothing in common, apart from their poetry. Then she remembered.

'I wrote another poem for you,' she said. She picked up her bag and took out her journal. She opened it to the right page and handed it to Speranza. 'Here.'

Speranza read the poem. 'Is this true?' she asked.

'Yes, they were my neighbours' children. They died of the fever that killed my father. And their poor mother was demented by it. She ended up in the asylum.'

Speranza leaned over and took Annie's hand in hers. 'You must be very afraid for your brother and sister, and yourself.'

'I'm desperate,' Annie whispered. 'Please help me!'

Speranza pressed her lips together, then nodded. 'You can stay with me for a few days,' she said. 'I have rooms in town, for when I'm here at the paper. I think Jack and Charles will be back this afternoon. But first, let's get you something to eat.

'Thank you,' Annie replied. 'I need to talk to Jack, and I need to write a letter to my neighbour, and Katty and Finn.'

'Excellent. Letters first, then something to eat and we'll come back here.'

* * *

Later that afternoon, Jack and one of the owner-editors, Charles Gavan Duffy, arrived back at the newspaper offices. They had been to a Repeal meeting in Kildare, led by Daniel O'Connell, an Irish MP. O'Connell wanted the British government to repeal the Acts of Union and allow Ireland to have its own parliament in Dublin.

Gavan Duffy planned to write a report about what O'Connell and his supporters, the 'Old Irelanders' were calling for. Jack had accompanied him, as his assistant.

Gavan Duffy was speaking as Speranza and Annie came into the editing room.

'I'm telling you, Jack,' Gavan Duffy said. 'O'Connell will never agree to fight.'

Annie saw Jack and rushed over to embrace him. 'Jack, thank God!' She stood back and looked at her friend.

Jack was now dressed in fine new clothes. He wore dark woollen trousers instead of knee breeches, and a high-collared jacket over a white shirt and matching cravat.

'Annie, *acushla*, you came! It's so good to see you.'

Gavan Duffy looked at Speranza and raised his eyebrows and they left Annie and Jack to talk.

'How are you? And tell me, how are Finn and Katty?'

'They're well, Jack. Marie is taking care of them.' She paused, and waited for Jack to speak about her father.

'So, Pat agreed you could come to Dublin, then?' Jack seemed puzzled.

'You didn't get my letter?' Annie said and her eyes filled with tears.

'No. What happened, Annie?'

'Da got this terrible fever and it just burned him up. He tried so hard to get well. He suffered so much, then he died, last week.' She brushed at her eyes with her fingers. 'We're lost without him.'

'Oh no, Annie. Don't say that!' Jack's face contorted in pain, and she sat down heavily, as if her legs had given way. She leaned her head right down onto the table. 'Lord, how many more must we lose?'

After a few moments, Jack composed herself. She stood and reached out to Annie.

'Darling Annie, and poor Finn and Katty, to lose your father.'

'I had to leave them, Jack, to come here and see our landlord. We need that extension on the rent. If we don't get it, God knows what will become of us.'

'Let's get out into the air,' Jack said. 'I can't breathe in here.' She brushed her fingers over her eyes and then opened the door. She whispered a couple of words to Gavan Duffy and Speranza.

* * *

Once outside the building they walked towards the Liffey and strolled along the quay.

To an observer, they looked like a handsome young couple. Annie, with Katty's yellow ribbon through her hair. Jack was taller and better dressed than when he had left Waterford. Although a couple of years younger than Annie, and narrower around the shoulders, Jack could easily pass for Annie's brother or her intended.

They walked on past the bridge. Annie asked. 'Does anyone here know your secret?'

'No, no-one knows. Here, I'm young Jack Keating from Galway,' Jack replied. She shrugged. 'It'll come to an end soon, when I'll either be discovered or just move on. In the meantime, I'm learning how to typeset for the newspaper.' She turned towards Annie and smiled, her grey eyes glinted with humour. 'What do you say, Annie? Do I still look like a boy?'

Annie smiled back. 'If I didn't know differently, then I'd say you're a boy. But I do know differently.' She reached out and put her hand on Jack's arm. 'Who was the man you were with earlier? Could you tell him?'

Jack tried to laugh. 'Hah. No. They'd let me go. I'm no use as a girl, just trouble they don't need. Sure, we've travelled to these meetings together, me and Mr Gavan Duffy. It wouldn't be right if I was a girl. He just thinks I'm a very modest boy who won't get undressed in front of him. He's not shy though!'

'Jesus, Mary and Joseph!' Annie smiled at the thought. 'So what will you do, Jack?'

'Well, you know when I came here, I thought I could join Young Ireland in the revolution. But the Young Irelanders I've met just don't see how desperate people are. The only ones I can see with any sense are the main man, Charles Gavan Duffy, and John Mitchell, the leader writer,' Jack explained. 'Mr Gavan Duffy set up this newspaper, he's a barrister too. He gave me this job when he found out I was an orphan. He said he'd lost his parents at a young age. too. He's been really good to me.'

'Then, why can't you join them, the Young Irelanders?' Annie asked.

'It's not that I can't join them. But I can see there's just no chance of a rebellion now, that's for sure', Jack said, as they turned and began to walk back to the newspaper offices.

'Most of them are away with the fairies,' he explained. 'They seem to think starving people will have the strength to rise up against the British Government, who have an army they can bring down on our heads, any time they want to. God help these Young Irelanders to get a bit of sense, with their talk of revolution.' Jack paused to catch his breath.

'Then there's the Old Irelanders, the crowd who follow O'Connell. He just wants an Irish Parliament with Catholics in it, set up in Dublin. He's a pacifist. The two groups are scrapping amongst themselves with no thought for the likes of you or me and where our next meal will come from.'

Annie was silent for a few minutes. 'So what'll you do now? Will you stay here?'

'I was thinking of going back to Waterford with you, if you'll have me.'

Annie stopped walking and embraced her friend. 'Sure, why wouldn't I, Jack? I love you like a brother, or a sister.' She paused and smiled, then she turned away to look out over the river, at the brown water racing along below their feet.

'I've been so lonely since Da died,' she said. 'We could take care of each other, and Finn and Katty.'

Jack held her hand and Annie knew that, yes, she could go on with Jack's help. But first she had to get help from her landlord. They turned back towards D'Olier Street.

Before they arrived back at the newspaper office, Annie put her hand on Jack's arm to stop him walking further. They stood in by the side of a building to avoid being jostled by passers-by. Horses trotted along the road just a few feet away from them, some with riders and others in teams pulling carts and carriages. It had started to rain and she pulled her hood up around her head.

'Jack, if you really are coming back with me, then I think we should tell Speranza.'

'About me?'

'Yes, I don't want to deceive her.'

'But sure, she'll think I'm rotten.'

'No, she won't,' Annie said. 'She's going to help me, Jack, and you'll need to say it sooner or later. Won't you?'

'If they sack me, then I'll make my way to Waterford and wait for you there.'

'They won't sack you. They're good people. Come on, let's go and tell Speranza.'

Speranza was in her office, waiting for them to come back. 'I'm inviting you both to supper at my hotel,' she said. 'We'll have the food sent up to my rooms. Annie, you'll stay with me while we arrange for you to meet your landlord. I can help with that. And Jack, you'll join us, won't you?'

Jack smiled at her. 'Thank you, Miss Speranza, I'd like that. But I've got something to tell you first.'

'Well, will it keep until we get to my hotel? There's a cab waiting outside.'

Annie looked at Jack and they both nodded.

'Now I'm intrigued.' Speranza said. 'Come on, let's go.'

* * *

At the hotel, Speranza ordered supper for the three of them. 'You both need a good feed, from what I can see of you.'

Annie hadn't tasted meat for months and all three relished the chicken and ham pie served up to them. When they had finished eating, Jack began to relate her story.

'When I left Galway, I travelled in disguise for protection. It just wasn't safe on the roads. Annie knows about my disguise, no-one else here does. But it's time I told you, Miss Speranza.'

Speranza smiled. 'Why, Jack, what are you talking about? I can't see a disguise, unless you're a wealthy landowner, who travelled in rags.'

Jack shook her head. 'I'm not a boy, I'm a girl. My name is the same as yours. Jane, not Jack. My name is Jane Keating, and I'm fifteen years old.'

Annie saw Jack's eyes fill with tears. 'My family are from Galway and they all died last winter,' she continued. 'So I came to Waterford to find my uncle and aunt, but they had died of the fever. Annie and her father took pity on me. She's been like a sister to me.'

Annie reached over and held Jack's hand, while Speranza stood up from the table and came up close to Jack. She bent and peered at Jack's face and looked at her body.

'Well! I thought I was observant, yet here you are, a girl,' Speranza said. 'What fun you must have had, Jane!'

Jack smiled. 'It's not really fun, Miss Speranza. I had my monthly last week and that was hard to hide.'

'Jack!' Annie said.

Speranza clapped her hands and the three of them laughed together.

'Miss Speranza,' Jack continued, 'I've decided to go back to Waterford with Annie after she has met with her Landlord.

Will you keep my secret until I leave?'

'I won't tell a soul, Jack,' Speranza promised.

They moved over to the settee in the room and chatted about Annie's visit to the Landlord's house.

Later, Jack left to go back to The Nation and his late shift in the print room. Speranza went with him to review some poems for publication.

Annie stayed in the room and rested. She was tired after her night spent on the pavement. She lay on the feather bed, and let her aching body sink into the soft mattress. Her head was full of thoughts of the day, and the previous night she'd spent on the pavement. She wanted to kiss Speranza for offering her friendship and a place to stay. If not, Annie might have had another night in a doorway somewhere. But no, Jack would have helped her, she was sure of that. She turned over in the bed and smelt lavender from the pillow and breathed deeply. She let the scent of the lavender soothe her tired mind. Tomorrow she would see the landlord, he was sure to understand why they couldn't pay their rent at this time. Those stories of eviction Jack had witnessed in the west of Ireland, please God, let it not happen in Ashling.

Her thoughts turned to Katty and Finn. She'd bring back good news soon and they'd both go to the National school in the autumn. Her little family just needed to get through the next few months. Somehow, with no money and no food, whatever else happened, they had to keep a roof over their heads, they just had to.

She dozed while she waited for Speranza to come back from The Nation. Then Annie went back to bed and slept through the night.

Speranza

The next morning, Annie woke refreshed. She stretched in the soft bed and heard a knock on the door. A maid called, 'Miss, there's a bath ready for you.'

Annie took her first bath; she sank under the water and washed every bit of her body and her hair. She thought how lovely it would be to see Katty in a bath like this. They'd easily both fit in the huge, cast iron tub.

She dried herself off with a large bath towel, then, with her hair towel-dried, she combed and braided it tightly and let it hang down her back, heavy and damp. She put her borrowed nightgown back on and tapped on the door to Speranza's bedroom.

'Annie, come in and have some breakfast with me. You look well-rested.' Speranza was already up and dressed. Today, she wore a pale cream, silk dress with a light woven shawl around her shoulders. Her diamond bracelet shimmered in the morning light.

The two women sat at the table by the window and sipped tea. Outside, it was still raining and clouds hung low over Dublin. Their breakfast tray was filled with a silver teapot and milk jug, china cups and saucers. Alongside these sat a plate of fresh crusty bread with pats of yellow butter.

'Thank you, Miss Speranza. I'll have some tea with you, but I'm still full from the beautiful dinner and supper we had yesterday.' She smiled at her host, and prayed that Finn and Katty would have their breakfast at Marie's.

'We'll make a plan today, Annie, then we'll sort out some clothes for you. If you're staying for a few days then you need to be presentable.'

Annie put her cup down and looked at her hostess. 'Miss Speranza, why are you so good to me?'

'I admire your poems, *Miss* Annie. Do call me Speranza; we're both poets, both Irish women. In truth, I admire your bravery coming here to Dublin to try and save your home. I'd like to help you if I can.' Speranza held up her cup. 'Enough now, let's finish our tea. Then I'll lend you a dress to wear, and we'll go shopping. I have a dressmaker nearby.

'Thank you, but I have my new blue dress. My aunt sent it from America.'

'Ah yes, of course, the one you wore yesterday,' Speranza said. 'It's lovely. We'll go when you're ready.'

* * *

Later, they left the hotel and Speranza hailed a cab. When it came to a stop at the kerb, Speranza gave the address to the driver, they stepped up into the small compartment, and the horse trotted on. Speranza pointed out the buildings of Trinity College as they made their way to her dressmaker near Saint Stephen's Green. It only took a few minutes and she paid the driver when they pulled up outside a four-storey town-house.

The ground floor of the building was in use as a narrow, glass-fronted shop. A tall window at the side of the front door was filled with rolls of colourful, printed fabrics, and two dressmakers' mannequins displaying beautiful gowns. They entered the shop and a dark-skinned, elegant woman greeted them.

'*Mademoiselle* Speranza. Welcome.'

'*Bonjour,* Celeste,' Speranza replied. 'Please meet my friend, Annie. She's visiting from Waterford and she needs a new dress and coat. I told her you might have something ready for her to wear today. Can you help us?'

'*Mais oui.* Please come in and sit down.' Celeste led the way into a room that was both a shop and a workroom. The large window, with the mannequins and rolls of fabric, faced the street to the front, and floor length, double windows opened onto a garden at the back. Outside, the rain had turned to a fine mist, and the trees and shrubs appeared shrouded in lace.

More of the mannequins were placed around the walls and displayed dresses to perfection. Celeste herself, wore a dark red fitted dress with a low neckline. The tops of her breasts gleamed against the white edging of the dress.

Annie stared at this woman who spoke with a strange accent. Celeste's eyes were almond-shaped; they appeared black with long, dark lashes and slim, arched eyebrows. She had high cheekbones, and the colour of her skin, like pale tea, fascinated Annie. Black curls peeped out from under an elaborate arrangement of pale, rose silk wrapped around Celeste's head. A brilliant yellow jewel sparkled in the silk.

'Come here, my little friend, and let me measure you.'

Annie stood obediently to be measured, unable to speak. She felt Celeste's hands gently pulling the tape around her waist and across her shoulders. '*Mais*, but you are so thin, mademoiselle. Have you been ill?'

After a moment, Annie finally replied. 'No, not ill.'

'Ah, it is the potato disease, *non*? I will make you feel better with some new clothes. What do you say, Mademoiselle Speranza?'

Speranza nodded. 'Yes, Celeste. I think Annie could do with another good dress. This one she is wearing was sent by her lovely aunt, all the way from New York.'

'It is a beautiful dress, Annie. Tell me, what do you think of my creations here?'

'Did you make all these?'

'Of course. I have spent many years developing my skills, here in Dublin and in my hometown, Paris, also. But come and look, there are one or two dresses that you could try on right now.'

Celeste put out her hand. Annie held it and walked with the dressmaker to look more closely at the creations.

Annie tried on two dresses; one was too big, the other was an almost perfect fit, with just small adjustments needed around the shoulders and waist. It was made of the same fine, deep red fabric as Celeste's dress. Annie loved it.

It was agreed. Celeste would make the alterations and send the new dress and a matching jacket to the hotel for the following day.

* * *

After they left the dressmaker's, Annie and Speranza decided to walk back towards the hotel instead of taking another cab. The mist had burned off and it was now a warm day. As they walked, they passed an open-air market on St Stephen's Green. Annie saw more of the homeless families she had seen on her first night in Dublin.

'What is happening here, Speranza?'

'They're coming in from all over the country,' Speranza explained. 'God help them, there's nothing here for them. Those families you see are waiting for the soup kitchen to start up in the market. Look! Here it comes now.'

Annie saw a horse and cart pull up nearby with two women on board. She recognised a soup boiler on the back of the cart. The older woman called out a greeting in Gaelic. *'Dhia dhuit.'*

The woman wore a plain back dress, and was about forty or so, but she moved quickly and jumped down from the cart and dropped the horse's reins, for it to crop the grass.

The younger woman stepped to the back of the cart and removed the lid from the urn. Steam and the smell of food wafted over the market as the ragged crowd responded to the greeting and came closer to the cart.

The woman in black continued to speak in Irish and called the children to come forward first. Each child held a small dish or mug that was then filled with the hot soup and each was given a small crust of bread to dip in it. There must have been thirty or forty children and soon they were all served. Annie could hardly look at their small bodies, dirty and ragged. She saw a brother and sister the same age as Finn and Katty, and she wanted to cry. These were the sons and daughters of Ireland, too.

Annie and Speranza stood to one side, to witness the soup kitchen in action. It was quiet, with just the shuffling feet of the half-naked children and their whispered words of thanks, *'Go raibh maith agat'*. Then it was the turn of the adults. By now the urn was half empty and the two women adjusted the portion sizes to make sure everyone got some soup and a piece of bread.

The women must have fed almost a hundred people, some of whom sat on the grass to drink their soup. When they had finished, a few of them recited the rosary in thanks.

The women started to pack up the cart to leave. Annie and Speranza went over to speak to them. They told Annie and Speranza, that they were Quakers, and had been doing this work for the last two weeks as people began pouring into Dublin from the country.

'The Lord knows what is happening in the rest of Ireland,' the older woman said.

'Do you get help from the government?' Annie asked her.

'No,' the older woman replied. 'The Society of Friends has given us some money for this work. But in the main, it is our own money.'

The younger woman, clearly the daughter of the older woman, spoke. 'I fear that if we get many more people than the numbers we fed today, then we shan't be able to feed all of them. We may just cause offence to those who get nothing.'

The two women got back up onto the cart and drove off. Annie and Speranza looked at each other. Annie shook her head.

'Yet the market is still open and selling food. I don't understand, God help us.'

'Come on, Annie. Let's go back to the hotel.' Speranza linked her arm through Annie's and they walked on.

They made plans to see the Landlord. Speranza would call at Lord Ashling's Dublin townhouse that afternoon. She'd make an appointment for both of them. On her return, she brought bad news. Lord Ashling was in London with his agent on business. They would not be back until the end of the next week. Speranza had arranged for herself and Annie to call to the house on the following Friday morning. Annie agreed to wait until then. She had no choice.

Annie meets Thomas Meagher

At the newspaper offices the next day, Jack was at work in the print room down the hall, assisting with the type-setting for the next edition. Speranza read through one of Annie's poems.

'This is a lovely poem, Annie. You are gifted. I know you're disappointed you can't settle your business with Lord Ashling right away, but I have a suggestion for you. A job that will keep your mind busy until then.'

'What sort of job, Speranza?'

'I want to publish some stories and poems to shine a light on these terrible food shortages that are happening now. You can help me. I need to find out what is driving these poor people to Dublin.'

'Well, just go outside and ask some of them, why don't you? They'll tell you, as I did. It's all there. You just can't see it!' Annie took a deep breath. She couldn't be harsh to Speranza who had only tried to help. 'I'm sorry, Speranza. I don't mean to be sharp with you. It's just . . .'

'You're right, Annie, I can't see it here. I can only hear what they tell me. I've heard some terrible stories, but I don't know if they're true. Many say they are exaggerated. They say these people are lazy and don't want to work. I don't believe it, and neither do you.' Speranza stood and moved around the room as if searching for the right words.

'That's why I need your help,' she continued. 'Here's my suggestion. I want you to come to the west coast, to Sligo, and help me bring back a first-hand account of what we see there. The Nation will print the facts, and make the British Government take notice and act.' Annie saw a flush spread across Speranza's face and felt her fingers caught in a hard grip. 'Say you'll do it. Come with me!'

'You know that I can't do it,' Annie replied. 'Katty and Finn are the only ones I can think of. I have to get back to them as soon as possible. Speranza, you must understand.' Annie took her hand away from Speranza and caught the yellow ribbon holding her hair at the nape of her neck. She pulled the ribbon out and held it up to Speranza.

'This is all I have now of Katty and Finn!'

'Darling Annie. Calm yourself. I'm not keeping you away from them.' Speranza reached over to touch the ribbon wrapped in Katty's fingers. 'You can't go back to them empty-handed, so you must wait until next week and speak to the Landlord.

'In the meantime, you can do something to help your fellow countrymen and women and their children. Don't you see?' Speranza continued. She was clearly fired up with her idea of publishing the latest news of the potato blight. 'Spend the next few days with me on my research while you wait to see Lord Ashling. You'll earn some money doing it as well. I'll pay you to be my interpreter. What do you say?'

Annie leaned forward, rested her forehead on her hand and closed her eyes.

'I just want to go home. But you're right. I have a week,

then I'm going home. I'll help you.'

'Thank you, Annie. I promise I'll see you get away home as soon as you've had your meeting.' Speranza meant well, but her easy promise would be hard to fulfil, as events overtook them both.

* * *

Later that afternoon, Annie and Speranza went out for a stroll towards College Green. The day had brightened, buds were now in bloom on the trees around the park and blackbirds were busy building new nests in the branches. Small children ran to and fro and chased hoops under the gaze of their nursemaids.

In the same park, other families with children, slumped together in the corners, hungry and dirty. Annie's heart ached to see them. Who was looking after them?

The two women linked arms as they walked. Annie smelled the rose-scented perfume that Speranza favoured that day, and breathed a little easier.

'I spoke to my friend, Tom Meagher, yesterday,' Speranza said. 'You know his father is the Lord Mayor of Waterford?'

Annie smiled and nodded. ' Yes. They are both well-known in Waterford.'

'Tom is one of the Young Irelanders. And he is also lovely to look at.' Speranza added with a smile. 'Well, it appears Tom is going to Cork tomorrow and on his way he's going to stop off to visit his family in Waterford. He's offered to go out to Ashling and check on Katty and Finn. He can tell them you are here, that you're well, and send them your love. He's due in the office later this morning and we can talk to him. What do you say, Annie?'

'Yes, thank you so much.' Annie breathed a sigh of relief to think she could send news to her brother and sister and hear back from them. 'You are all so kind to me and my family.'

Speranza took Annie's hand in hers and they linked arms. 'Let's keep walking, my dear, and I'll tell you the rest of my plan.' Annie saw Speranza's eyes light up in anticipation.

They would travel to Sligo and spend a few days visiting some of the more remote towns and villages to gather facts about the potato blight on the West coast. Annie would be able to translate conversations into English, and help Speranza write up the news articles and poems. Speranza would draw sketches to illustrate scenes for the newspaper.

'I read there is a new process of making pictures without having to draw them. It's called Daguerrotype. I've seen portraits that just amaze one. For now though, my poor drawings will have to suffice,' Speranza said. She glanced at Annie to watch her reaction. 'You know, I think between us we could even earn enough to pay for tickets to North America for you, Katty and Finn.'

Annie stopped and turned to Speranza. 'I'll gladly earn some money, but it will pay the rent, Speranza. It's what my Da wanted for us.' She shook her head, but remembered back to the leaving wake for her friend Eileen, when Annie had longed to go with her to America. She dismissed the idea, but it seemed to stick in her mind. And her neighbour, Marie, had not paid her rent because of the rumours of eviction.

* * *

The meeting with Tom Meagher went well. He was young,

201

in his early twenties, Annie guessed. A strongly built man with thick, light-brown hair framing a slim, clean-shaven face. His nose was on the long side, but dark eyebrows set off clever brown eyes. He wore a tailored jacket that outlined his broad, sloping shoulders and narrow waist. Annie tried not to stare at the gleaming, starched shirt collar up around his jawline and the dark grey cravat tucked into his cream waistcoat, above long, narrow-legged trousers, instead of the knee breeches common in the rest of the country. Gleaming leather boots finished the outfit. She had never seen a man like this. Speranza was right; he was lovely to look at.

Tom flirted with Speranza, as was clearly their habit. Annie realised instantly, that he wouldn't flirt with her, a country girl, but she remained dumbstruck, so it was just as well.

It was agreed. Tom was leaving for Cork the next day. He'd call in to see Katty and Finn and tell them Annie was safely in Dublin, and that she planned to be back by the end of the next week. Annie and Speranza would have time for their research in Sligo and would travel back to Dublin for her meeting with the landlord. After the meeting, she would go straight home.

Tom took Annie's hand in his and kissed it. 'I'll bring you back word of your brother and sister, Annie. It will be my pleasure.' She blushed and looked at Speranza, who laughed. Annie thought, he must flirt with every woman he met.

'He's a bold man,' Speranza said to Annie. 'Stop it, Tom, she's only seventeen!'

'Annie, I'm amazed by your bravery,' Tom said. 'Don't worry about Katty and Finn, I'll tell them you'll be home soon.'

Tom turned to leave. 'Kiss me, Speranza, darling.'

'Get away with you!' Speranza replied, but she smiled at him and blew him a kiss. Annie and Speranza left the newspaper offices to make preparations for their own journey.

Sligo

F riday morning arrived. Annie and Speranza stepped out from the hotel lobby with their bags and took a cab to the General Post Office. The Royal Mail Coach was almost full but the women had managed to get tickets, the day before, for the last seats inside. It was six o'clock and the horses and carriage set off along the road to Sligo on the north-west coast of Ireland. Two of the men in the carriage lit up their pipes as soon as the journey started, and the cloying smell of tobacco enveloped both Annie and Speranza, making them cough.

When the coach stopped in a town later that morning, they both got up on the top of the carriage and wrapped themselves in musty travelling blankets. Here, at least, they could admire the mountains and fields and breathe in fresh air. The carriage stopped again at an inn in Mullingar for the passengers to have lunch. It was turning colder, so Annie and Speranza took their seats inside for the remainder of the journey. Thankfully, the two men who were smokers, settled down to snooze for the afternoon.

The women dozed, were shaken awake, and dozed again, through the afternoon and evening. It was dark, almost ten o'clock, when the carriage pulled up outside the Post Office in Sligo. The passengers, all stiff and weary, stepped down onto the roadway and stretched their aching limbs.

Annie and Speranza made their way to a nearby hotel recommended by the carriage driver. They would have to share a bed, but at least the bedroom would be theirs alone. Too tired to eat, they fell into bed and slept.

* * *

The next morning they had an early breakfast and set out to investigate. They had been advised by the owner of the hotel to walk out of town along the coast road to see the effects of the potato blight. 'Those poor souls don't have any other way of living, apart from their little plots of land and their potatoes,' the landlady had told them.

The two women were content to walk the three miles along the coast road towards the Atlantic Ocean. It was past the middle of May, the sun was up and fields on all sides were multi-coloured with stony outcrops on the hilly land. Dry-stone walls added a grey and white dappled effect to the green landscape. Most of the land thereabouts was turned over to cattle, but as they got nearer the coast the ground became more boggy and uneven.

Small cabins appeared dotted across the horizon, but there were no signs of habitation. Annie saw the dwellings were smaller than her cabin back at home, and built closer to the ground, giving just enough room for a small window and a low door. The cabin roofs were covered in turf sods from which grew long green grass, making the cabins appear as if they were just growing up out of the bog and had managed to grow so far, and no further. They still saw no people and the landscape was eerily silent.

They got nearer to one cabin set back off the road. 'Let's see if there is anyone at home,' Annie suggested.

'*Dia dhuit,*' she called the greeting at the doorway. The door stood ajar but no light could be seen even through the window. Annie peeped in and called again. She heard a whisper of movement, a light patter on the floor. And what was that smell? She tried to place it, then the odour reached the back of her throat and she gagged. She put a hand up to Speranza, then covered her mouth.

'Take care, Speranza!' she whispered. 'There's something dead in there, and I hear rats.' Both women moved through the doorway into the dimness of the cabin.

The room was very like Annie's home in Ashling, with the same few bits of furniture; a small table and a stool. Annie stepped inside, closely followed by Speranza. The fire in a cabin was usually never let go out. This one was unlit, with pale ashes in the grate.

Speranza let out a scream. 'My God. The rats are . . . . '

Annie grabbed a broom by the door and swung it at the dozen or so rats swarming over the bed in the corner, and the body on it. She breathed lightly. 'Jesus, Mary and Joseph. Get out, get out!' she shouted and swept the rats out of the cabin with the broom, almost tripping over Speranza in her haste. She was sweating by the time she had got rid of the last of them.

They stood and looked at the dead woman on the bed. The rats had feasted on her face. Her eyes were missing and her tongue was torn out. Her skin was blackened; the shift she wore was torn and soiled. The dense smell and the sight of her body forced them to turn away. Annie grabbed Speranza's hand and they both stumbled to the door and outside into the air.

Speranza bent over and retched. She vomited up her breakfast and coughed and cried. Annie leaned against the wall of the cabin and breathed shakily. She blessed herself, then closed her eyes and prayed for the poor soul on the bed. 'Eternal rest grant unto her, O Lord.'

'God help her, she must have some family. Where are they?' asked Speranza when she had recovered a little.

Annie pushed away from the wall and tried to shut the door. It was warped and didn't close fully, so she left it. The two women linked arms and walked on to the next cabin further along the road. They needed to find out about the dead woman. Neither could speak after the horror they had just left behind them. The sun still shone in the spring sky and the wind still blew through the hawthorn hedges.

The cabin door was open and the woman of the house came out to meet them as they approached.

'*Dia dhuit*', Annie said.

'*Dia is Mhuire dhuit*', responded the woman. She was barely five feet tall, not old, but her face was sunken with dark circles under her eyes, and thin to the point of emaciation.

'Who are you looking for?' The woman asked, in Irish. Most of her teeth were missing and she lisped when she spoke.

'We've come from Dublin. We've heard tales about the blight in this part of the country. We came to see for ourselves,' Annie explained.

'Oh, they're true alright,' the woman said. 'Sure, won't you come in and have a drink of water?'

They bent down to get under the low doorway and squeezed into her tiny living space. There was a wooden bench beside the fire, no other furniture.

'Have a seat there, while John fetches some water.'

The woman spoke to her young son, a frail boy of about ten years, who was crouched in the corner of the room.

'John, get up, there's a good boy and fetch some water for our visitors.'

The boy stood and picked up the empty bucket beside the door and set off to fetch water.

'Do you know there is a dead woman in the cabin back along the road there?' Annie asked when the boy had left.

'Ah, she died then, the poor soul. That'll be Peg O'Hara. She was the last of her family.' The woman shook her head. 'T'is a pity there's no-one to bury her. She would've wanted a decent burial.'

'There are rats eating her corpse,' Annie continued speaking in Irish. 'Where is everyone? We've only seen empty cabins in the last hour we've been walking.'

'They're all gone; either to the workhouse, or dead,' the woman said. 'Myself and John are the last family on this little patch of land. You can go into any of the cabins around and find more dead, if you wish to look.' The tiny woman, no bigger than a child, seemed to shrink into her rags.

'The landlord has been evicting as fast as he can,' she said. 'But he can't evict corpses. He'll be coming to level these cabins in the next week or two. Then he can level this roof over my dead body. I'm sending John into Sligo to the workhouse, but I'll not go.'

Annie looked at the pot over the fire. 'At least you have some food for your dinner in the pot.'

'Take a look,' the woman replied, and turned her head away and closed her eyes.

Annie stood and lifted the lid on the pot; reeking steam billowed out. She recognised the skinned body of a rat floating in a soup of blackened potatoes and dropped the lid back to cover the sight. Annie swallowed hard and beckoned Speranza to look in the pot. When she had seen the contents Speranza turned and bolted out of the cabin into the air.

'God help you,' Annie said to the woman.

The starving woman reached out her scrawny hand and whispered. 'Don't say anything to John.'

'Are you able to get him to the workhouse?' Annie asked and the woman nodded.

Speranza came back in, she looked pale and shaken. She had her purse in one hand and with the other she gave the woman a silver coin. 'Here, for you and your son, and may God bless you.'

John had still not come back with the water so they took their leave and walked back along the road intending to continue their journey. But first they had to pass the cabin with the dead woman inside.

As they reached the cabin, Annie noticed the door was further open than when she left.

'The rats are back,' she said, and looked inside to see the black vermin feasting on the body. 'I'll fix you,' she muttered. She picked up a spade next to the cabin door and turned.

'Wait here,' she said to Speranza. She re-traced her steps to the neighbour's cabin, knocked and went inside.

'Missus, the rats are back in Peg's cabin. I need to take a piece of your fire, if you can spare it.'

'Take what you want, Miss. You are a good soul to think of her,' the woman said.

Annie held the shovel of burning turf out in front of her and returned to the rat-infested cabin. Speranza collected a few twigs together and put them on the shovel. Annie unloaded the shovel onto the foot of the bed, on the straw-filled mattress. The rats ignored Annie, until the mattress caught fire, then they jumped off the bed and raced to the door. Annie and Speranza reached it first and pulled the door closed behind them.

Outside, Annie stretched up to the turf roof with the shovel and hacked at the turf until pieces of it fell in on the cabin. She was sweating again and looked through the small window. The bed was burning well now and the dry sods of turf from the roof acted as fuel to the fire. She couldn't see the woman's body for smoke and flames. She lifted the shovel and knocked back a couple of rats trying to scramble out through the window.

'Go to hell!' she shouted.

Annie and Speranza stood back and watched the cabin burn. The heat from the flames forced them to step further away. They listened as the rats squealed to get out and the fire crackled. They watched the hungry fire burn the little cabin to the ground. The smell of burning turf and wood overpowered the stink from the dead body.

As they began to leave, Speranza's legs gave way and Annie caught her before she could fall.

'Oh my God, Annie. Let's get away from here.'

* * *

In the following two days, Annie and Speranza travelled around Sligo and the surrounding countryside. They hired a pony and trap and went up past Ben Bulben, that great flat-topped mountain. They talked to priests, teachers and tenants. Everywhere they went, they heard and saw much the same story as on their first day.

When it was time to leave, they had gathered plenty of information for the newspaper to publish, and caught the same Royal Mail coach back to Dublin.

Annie now understood what her father had meant before he died, when he said he was familiar with death. Now she knew too, and her heart almost failed her.

The Landlord's Agent

Back in Dublin, it was the day of her meeting with the Landlord. Annie and Speranza stood before the Dublin townhouse of His Lordship, the owner of her patch of land, her cabin and most of the land for miles around that part of the county of Waterford.

Georgian windows on either side, framed the porticoed entrance to the three-storied building. She pulled the door-knob and heard the clangs echo inside the house. The door was opened by a tall man, dressed in black from head to toe. He was six feet or more and he looked down at the two women on his doorstep.

'Misses,' he asked, 'what is your business here?'

Annie stepped forward, but before she could speak, Speranza tapped her arm, and began to explain. 'We have an appointment to speak to Lord Ashling. Kindly tell him that Annie Power and Mademoiselle Speranza are here.'

'His Lordship is still away in London, Mademoiselle,' the man replied, and he went to close the door.

Speranza put her hand on the door to stop him. 'I was informed he would be back yesterday. I came here to enquire just last week and spoke to the housekeeper.'

The man, the butler, gave in to Speranza's insistence and

invited them in while he enquired if these two determined females had booked an appointment to speak to His Lordship and what he was to do with them.

They were shown into a large drawing room with the tall windows Annie had seen from outside, and sat on spindly, satin covered chairs, hemmed in by narrow wooden arms. The settee was covered in peach silk to match the chairs; elaborate woven rugs of creams and shades of azure, spread out over the hardwood floor.

Annie turned her head this way and that way, to look at the furnishings and fittings. A vast crystal chandelier hung from the ceiling and was reflected in the huge mirror above the marble fireplace. The musty smell of the room told her that windows were rarely opened and fires were rarely lit.

He must be very wealthy, she thought. Where did all the money come from, to pay for all this luxury? Her head felt light, as if she could just lift off the seat and touch the ceiling. She tried to steady her breathing and hoped there would be someone she could speak to. She couldn't go home empty-handed, that was for sure.

The women heard footsteps along the hallway and a large, brown-clad man walked into the room. They both stood at the same time. Speranza caught Annie's eye and shook her head; she had met Lord Ashling at a society event and this person was not he.

'Mademoiselle Speranza. It is an honour to meet you. I have heard of your fame as a poet. Indeed I have read your poems in the Nation newspaper. I'm Mr. Jones, His Lordship's agent. Tell me how I can be of assistance.' The agent's oily voice came from deep in his fat throat and he licked his lips as his eyes slid over Speranza's face and neck and across her chest.

Annie watched as Speranza ignored his greedy gaze. 'Mr Jones, thank you so much for seeing us. As I explained to the butler, we have an appointment to speak to Lord Ashling.'

Jones bowed to Speranza. 'I'm sorry to disappoint you, Mademoiselle. His Lordship was detained in London on Parliamentary business. I will do my best to help, if I can.'

'Please let me introduce my good friend, Miss Annie Power,' she said. 'Her family are tenants on His Lordship's estate in Waterford.'

Mr Jones's face darkened and his eyes narrowed. He turned in Annie's direction. 'Well, this is most unusual, I must say. What is your business here, Miss?' He frowned at Annie.

'Mr Jones, thank you for seeing me. You must know of our situation at Ashling,' Annie said. 'Our potato crop is lost to the blight and we're struggling to afford food, let alone the rent. I've come to Dublin in the hope that His Lordship will allow us to pay the rent we owe when our next crop comes in.'

Jones stood there and shook his head. 'No, no, no. I'll not allow this.'

'You don't understand, Mr Jones. Let me tell you, please.' Annie took a step towards him. 'There are twenty families on the estate. We had thirty children at the school in February. We must look after the children and their parents. Surely, you must see that.' She tried to smile at him, but he ignored her and addressed himself to Speranza.

'Enough!' Jones said. 'Mademoiselle Speranza, I am surprised you are involved in this. It's none of your concern.'

Speranza put her hand on Annie's arm and spoke to the agent. 'Mr Jones, I urge you to have compassion. Surely Lord Ashling will want to look after his struggling tenants? Other landlords have let off their tenants from the rent. I hear the Duke of Devonshire has agreed a reduction in the rent on his estate.'

Annie clasped her hands together. 'Mr Jones, I'm begging you. Please ask His Lordship to have mercy on my family and my neighbours. I have a younger brother and sister and we've gone hungry for months. My poor father died of fever, just two weeks ago.'

He looked from Annie to Speranza. 'This is a trick you two are playing on His Lordship. I know that many of you tenants, Miss Power,' he spat her name out, 'have the money to pay your rent, but you are putting on the poor-mouth to play on His Lordship's sympathy. You're a lazy and deceitful lot. Eviction will be well deserved when it comes.' Jones leaned forward as he spoke and the smell of his meaty breath wafted into Annie's face.

'You've had a wasted journey. His Lordship is not in any position to forego rents to one of his tenants, let alone the whole estate. Huh! I don't think so!' He turned away and walked to the door.

Annie followed him and she caught his arm. 'Mr Jones, don't go! It would only be for a few months. As soon as the next potato crop comes in. Then any money I earn will pay the rent. My brother can work, too.' Her voice broke as she tried to get him to hear what she was saying.

He turned towards Annie. 'Your father and your neighbours know they're all on conacre tenancies. They can be asked to leave at any time. They know this and it is the law, Miss Power.'

'But I told you, my father died just two weeks ago. You're not listening to me!' Annie's voice became shrill.

Jones shook his arm free. 'If other landlords fall for this trickery then that's their business. I get paid by Lord Ashling to manage the estate in Waterford and his properties here in Dublin. I follow His Lordship's wishes and they are clear.'

'Then what will become of Annie and her family?' Speranza demanded.

'As I have just said,' Jones repeated, showing his long, yellow teeth. 'His Lordship is legally entitled to evict for non-payment of rents. And I can tell you now, that I have been instructed to instigate eviction notices against all tenants on His Lordship's estate in Waterford.'

Annie heard these words as in a dream, then reached out and grabbed the lapels of his tweed jacket. 'You can't do this to us! We'll die!' Her breath was ragged.

'Don't you dare lay hands on me,' Jones said. He used both fat hands to push Annie away. Speranza caught her before she fell.

The butler appeared at the doorway. 'Mr Jones, sir, can I be of help?'

Jones turned away and Annie shouted. 'Please listen! My father died two weeks ago. We have nowhere to go!' She caught Jones's arm again to force him to listen.

'You're just lazy, the lot of you.' Jones said. 'And if your father is dead, then you have no claim on the land or the cabin. Good riddance! The sooner you're out the better.'

Annie pulled at his arm to stop him from leaving, realised what she had done, then let him go. He was caught off balance and stumbled against the door, it gave way, and he fell to the floor. He sat there, his face crimson, and looked up at the two horrified women.

'Get out! Both of you, get out of here!'

* * *

Speranza put her arm around Annie and pushed her out of the room, along the hallway and out of the front door onto the street. The door slammed shut behind them.

Speranza linked Annie's arm through hers.

'My God, what have I done?' asked Annie.

Speranza blew out a breath. 'Come, Annie, let's get away from here. We'll talk back at the hotel.' They walked quickly away.

The streets of Dublin had quietened as the evening drew on and street hawkers packed away their goods. There was still the occasional sound of a boat horn on the river and the rumble of carriages across the bridges. The two women arrived back at their hotel and Speranza ordered a tray of tea to be brought to their room.

Annie wiped away her tears. 'I'm sorry, Speranza. I shouldn't have shouted at him, or laid hands on him.'

'Hush, Annie,' Speranza replied. 'We'll think of something, my friend. We'll get Jack and Tom to help us. Hush now!'

Annie's head throbbed. 'Dear Lord, what am I to do? Katty and Finn. I promised I'd bring back good news. I can't go home and tell them we're to be evicted.'

'Let's have our tea and think up a plan. Darling girl, don't upset yourself so.' Speranza said, as she went to answer a knock on the door.

A hotel maid stood there with a note from the manager. Speranza took it from her, closed the door and walked back to the settee.

'No, it can't be,' she murmured. She sat beside Annie and read the note again.

217

She turned to Annie and put her arm around her. 'More trouble has found us, my friend. Mr Jones has laid a charge of assault against you. There are constables below in the lobby, come here to arrest you.'

They stood up and held hands. Annie shivered, pressed her lips together, her jaw working. She took a breath and said. 'No, they can't arrest me.'

Speranza said. 'If they take you, there's the danger you'll go to prison.'

'I have to get away. Get back to Finn and Katty.'

The two women looked at each other, and hugged. Annie took strength from Speranza's touch and fused it with her own energy, like a fire blown into life.

'I've got my old clothes in the bag over there. Is there a back stairs?'

'Yes, it's over to the right, at the end of the corridor,' Speranza said. 'When you're ready, I'll go down and try to delay the constables.'

Annie had quickly unbuttoned her new dress and stepped into her old skirt and blouse. She wrapped the shawl around her and reverted back into a poor country girl. She put her rosary beads into her skirt pocket and her prayer book into her bag. She kissed Speranza. 'I'll leave the rest. Look after my things.'

'Wait, Annie!' Speranza said. 'I have some money for you. She rushed to the desk and took out a five pound note out of the drawer. 'Here, take this. Get to the docks, there'll be a ferry going south to Waterford. You can get away today.'

'You've helped me so much. I'll pray for you every day of my life.' Annie opened the door, slipped out and headed for the back stairs, while Speranza took the main staircase down to the lobby to intercept the constables.

* * *

Annie opened the back door and stepped out onto the street. Suddenly, she felt her arm grabbed and pulled back behind her.

'Stop!' she shouted and tried to turn. It was a uniformed officer. He caught her other arm and held her.

'I've got her. Come and give a hand here!' he shouted.

The pain in her shoulders prevented any movement. The officer forced her arms back further and pushed her down to the ground. She bit her lip to stop from screaming.

Another officer ran down the alley beside the hotel and grabbed Annie. They dragged her to her feet and out to the police cab in front of the hotel. One of them had her by the hair and pulled a handful out.

'That'll *larn* you, bitch!' he whispered in her ear. He stank of sweat and alcohol.

She closed her eyes and felt herself pushed into the back of the cab. The door slammed and locked. She heard her name called and knew that Speranza had witnessed her arrest. Please God, she would be able to help her.

* * *

Annie sat on the hard wooden bench inside a metal cage in the windowless cab and rubbed her arms to ease the pain. She tried to slow her breathing and stop her hands from trembling. As the cage rocked back and forth on its journey to the prison she leaned forward and prayed. 'Remember, O most Gracious Virgin Mary, that never was it known that anyone who fled to thy protection, implored thy help or sought thy intercession was left unaided.' Her voice broke into a sob, but she continued, and the prayer helped to calm her mind.

The police cab stopped with a jolt, the door was opened, and Annie saw they were in front of a massive stone building with high walls all round. The constable caught her arms again and pulled her out of the cab. Pain streaked through her shoulders as they hauled her into the building. Inside, she was stripped and roughly searched. They took her knickers and bodice. Two male officers stood and watched her.

'Not much meat on her,' one said. 'She looks as if she's had a wash anyhow,' the other replied. Annie daren't speak.

A female prison officer threw a grey striped prison dress, a cap and some calico underwear at her. Annie turned away from their avid eyes and dressed herself.

They allowed Annie to keep her prayer book and rosary beads, but they took the banknote. She was pushed and pulled along a narrow corridor with metal doors on either side. One cell door was open.

They shoved her in and she fell to the floor. The door clanged as it was shut and locked. Stone walls, a small window up near the ceiling, a bucket in a corner. Annie saw a bed against one wall with just a bare, horsehair mattress and a rolled blanket. She lay down on it, her mind numb as she gazed at the ceiling. Then she remembered her prayer.

'Inspired with this confidence, I fly to thee, O Virgin of virgins, my Mother; to thee do I come; before thee I stand, sinful and sorrowful. O Mother of the Word Incarnate, despise not my petition but in thy mercy hear and answer me. Amen.'

'Da,' she finished, 'if you're in heaven, *acushla*, then now is the time to send me help.' She didn't cry, although tears wet her eyes. Help would come; from the Blessed Mother, her dead father, or from Speranza. Help would come, she was sure of it. She clung to that thought like a shipwrecked sailor clings to a broken spar, in the middle of a great ocean.

In Court

J ack was still working in the printing room when Speranza raced into the newspaper office.

'Jack! Thank God you're here. They've arrested Annie!'

Jack heard the words, then saw Speranza was breathless, her hair was coming loose from her combs and her face was flushed. 'What? What do you mean? Speranza!'

'The landlord's agent pressed charges against her, for assault! It's all my fault, I shouldn't have brought her there. I knew in my heart what the answer would be. The constable said they were taking her to Kilmainham gaol. We have to get her out of there, but I've no idea how.'

'Speranza, tell me exactly what happened will you? How did Annie get arrested, for God's sake?' Jack asked.

'Lord Ashling wasn't there, he's still in London. Jones, his agent, was horrible. He said they were all going to be evicted, the whole village, and soon.' Speranza paused. 'I'm sorry, I can't breathe.'

'Here, sit down,' Jack said, and pulled out the stool in front of the typesetting table.

Speranza sat and took a few deep breaths, then she continued. 'Annie grabbed Jones by his jacket, and shouted at him, then he tripped and fell. He must have reported it to the police. But I don't know how he found us so fast.'

'There was a constable here, half an hour ago,' Jack said. 'He spoke to Michael and then left. You don't think Michael . . . ?'

'That little rat! I'll get him sacked, so I will.' Speranza's eyes filled with tears.

Then she wiped her eyes and stood up. She smoothed her clothes, fixed her hair and pushed the pearl combs back into place. 'Crying won't get her out of there. Let's do something, Jack.'

'If Mr Gavan Duffy were here we could ask him,' Jack suggested. 'Maybe publish a story?'

'Oh, my God! I forgot he's in London! When does he get back?' Speranza asked.

'Not until next week.'

'That'll be too late. You talk to the editor, he might have some ideas. I know a solicitor who can represent her, I'll go there now.' Speranza pressed her hand against her forehead. 'Then what? I'll go to Kilmainham and try to see Annie.' She stood and held the door open.

'Yes, that's what we'll do,' she continued. 'And when Charles gets back, he's to get rid of Michael. I don't want to see him here again, or I'll be arrested for assault, too.'

* * *

Annie felt like a different person in her prison clothes. The cap felt tight on her head and the coarse fabric of the striped skirt and blouse hung around her body. The door to her cell opened and she saw her mentor, Speranza. Annie held out her hand. 'Thank you for coming.' She couldn't stop her tears. 'What have I done?'

'Annie, don't cry, I've instructed a solicitor for you. They tell me you'll be in court tomorrow morning. Oh Annie, I'm so sorry, it's all my fault.' Speranza wiped her eyes with a tiny lace handkerchief.

In spite of her troubles, Annie smiled to see the flimsy article, more suited for show than actual use, and shook her head.

'You've only been a good friend to me. I should have known they won't take pity on Irish peasants. We're only useful when we are putting money into their pockets, from the rent or our hard work. When that stops they'll have us out, or leave us to starve. I see that now. I don't know why I didn't see it before.' Annie's voice cracked and she pushed away thoughts of Katty and Finn waiting on her return.

They sat together for a while, until Speranza left, promising to come back the next day. Annie would see her in court.

* * *

Annie remembered nothing of her first night in gaol. She fell into a deep, dead sleep and early the next day she was woken and led into the courtroom and made to stand in the dock, an enclosed wooden box that reached up to her waist. The courtroom was a big place; the only thing she could compare it to was a church. Where the altar should be, there was a large cushioned chair, and the Judge sat in it. Her solicitor sat at the table in the middle of the room and faced the Judge. The rest of the place was given over to wooden pews filled with men, all there to watch the day's proceedings. Annie's was the third trial of the morning.

She looked up to the gallery and saw Speranza and Jack. They had come and they waved to her. Their presence gave her strength and hope.

The Judge wore a black gown and a white, curled wig on his head. He looked old enough to be Annie's grandfather, with eyebrows and sideburns to match the wig. Annie felt her hopes rise when she heard his Irish accent. Surely he'd understand her explanation.

The Judge then called for silence, and spoke. 'Annie Power, you're here today charged with assault against Mr Jones, the land agent for Lord Ashling. How do you plead?'

Annie's solicitor answered for her. He was a small, worried man; his body seemed lost in the layers of his black court gown. He read from the paper in front of him. 'Your Honour, Annie Power pleads not guilty. You will understand why when you hear her story.' He plopped back down on his chair clutching his paperwork.

'Well then,' said the Judge, 'Let's hear Miss Power's version of what happened in His Lordship's own home.'

Annie took a deep breath. 'Your Honour, we owe His Lordship rent on our land and our cabin, on his estate in Waterford. I went to see him to beg for a stay on the money we owe. You see, my father died just two weeks ago, and I have a younger brother and sister to look after. We've lost all our potatoes to the blight. We're going hungry and can't pay the rent.'

As Annie spoke, she felt like a child back in school, facing Miss Nagel for breaking one of her rules. She could see the judge was not impressed; he pursed his lips and squinted his eyes at her; then he started to speak.

'So, Miss Power, how did you manage to go from begging for a stay on the rent to assaulting Mr Jones?'

'I didn't assault him,' she paused. 'Well, I didn't mean to.

I got angry when he said we would be evicted - the whole village! I grabbed his jacket, that's all. Then he fell. I'm truly sorry for it.'

Annie looked at her solicitor. He had assured Annie that he would explain about Katie and Finn and she being their only guardian now. But he remained silent.

She clutched at the railings around the dock and looked up at the judge. 'My solicitor has something to say, I think,' she stammered. But the solicitor stayed in his seat, dumb.

'Miss Power,' the Judge said. 'Clearly, your solicitor is not coming to your assistance. From what you have just said, you went to his Lordship's house unannounced, and when you didn't like what you heard, you laid hands on Mr Jones. Is that correct?'

At this point, Annie's solicitor finally spoke. 'Your Honour, you can see for yourself that Annie, is a young woman trying to protect herself and her siblings from being made homeless in these terrible times. Surely you can see the stress she was under and accept her apology?'

The Judge looked at Annie. 'You were under duress, I understand that.' He adjusted his wig and cleared his throat. 'However, this is a serious charge. If everyone who had a grievance against their landlord got away with assaulting his representatives, then where would we be? Can you see that I need to make an example of you? This will deter other tenants from taking violent action in these troubled times.'

'No, please don't say that. You don't need to make an example of me,' Annie said, and looked up at the gallery towards Speranza and Jack. She looked again and saw the agent, Mr Jones, standing just inside the door, behind them.

'Wait, Your Honour,' she said. 'I can see Mr Jones is here.'

She looked up at the agent in the gallery. 'Mr Jones, forgive me, I meant no harm. Don't let them send me to prison.'

The agent looked down at her from the gallery, then he looked at the Judge and shook his head. Jack and Speranza stood there, speechless.

The Judge began to read out his verdict while prison officers stood beside Annie. She held onto the iron railings of the dock. They were cold and unyielding against her fingers, like the bars on her prison cell. She could hardly breathe as the court fell silent.

'Annie Power, I find you guilty of the charge of assault. You are hereby sentenced to be transported to New South Wales for seven years, after which time you will be free to return to Ireland.' The Judge banged his hammer down, stood and left the courtroom.

After a moment of stunned silence, Annie shouted. 'Come back! Your Honour, you can't do this. What about my brother and sister?' The door to the Judge's chambers slammed shut.

Annie looked at the solicitor who had sat down heavily in his chair. 'Say something, please,' she said. He looked away. 'I'm sorry, Miss Power.'

One of the prison guards stepped up to Annie and put iron hand-cuffs on her wrists. 'You need to come with us. You can speak to your solicitor later.'

Turning, Annie looked up and saw Jones was still there. He smirked and touched the brim of his hat, then stood and watched her being led out of the dock.

* * *

After making enquiries, Jack and Speranza were allowed in

to speak to Annie while she waited to be brought back to Kilmainham Gaol.

When she saw Speranza and Jack come into the room, she cried bitter tears. The guard stood by the door. 'You've got five minutes,' he said, then locked them in together.

Annie stood there in chains and her friends hugged her. 'I don't believe this is happening. It's a nightmare. I want to wake up.'

Jack kept her arm around Annie, while Speranza held her hands.

'I'll speak to Charles, as soon as he gets back from London. He'll know of something we can do.' Speranza said.

Annie nodded. 'Thank you. I can't be transported. I have to take care of Finn and Katty.' More tears filled her eyes and she felt them roll down her cheeks but did nothing to wipe them away.

'My dearest friend,' Jack said. 'You're their mother and father now.' Then Jack whispered, 'I'll not see you transported, Annie.'

'Let's wait until Charles gets back,' Speranza said again. 'He knows the law.'

'If he can get back in time, Speranza,' Jack replied. 'But I've an idea too. I need to think it through first. Don't despair, Annie. Pray to Our Blessed Mother for help.'

The guard opened the door. 'Your time is up.'

Jack and Speranza left, and Annie was taken back to her prison cell.

Kilmainham Gaol

At the prison, on the way back to her cell, Annie passed another, larger cell full of women. The guard told her they were all waiting to be deported. Some of the women had children with them. She thought, if it came to it, maybe Finn and Katty could come with her? No, it mustn't come to it. She wasn't going. It was all a mistake.

That night, she prayed to God and His Blessed Mother for deliverance. She repeated the prayers of the rosary; telling them on her mother's wooden beads, smooth from years of prayer, and drifted in and out of sleep.

In the early hours, she dreamed that she had finished her sentence in New South Wales and somehow had gotten home to Ireland. She'd be twenty-four by then, Finn would be nineteen and Katty, fifteen. How would they grow up without her to guide them? Would they even know her when she came back?

In her dream, she hurried along the laneway to her old home. She saw the cabin. It was a burnt out ruin. The wind howled in her ears and she called and called for Katty and Finn, but they were gone.

Banging on the cell door woke her. 'You in there,' a rough voice shouted. 'Keep the noise down, you'll wake the whole place up.'

Annie's heart hammered. Was this to be her future? Never to see her darlings again? The long night plodded through to dawn, like a slow funeral march to the grave, until low light peeped through the window.

Annie got up and used the bucket, then washed her face and hands and tidied her hair before replacing her prisoner's cap. She'd slept in the prison dress and it was wrinkled and smelled sour from others who had worn it before her. Her head ached and she felt ill, from the lack of sleep or her dream in the night; she wasn't sure which.

* * *

A warden brought in her breakfast – a bowl of gruel and a tin cup of black tea. About what she ate at home on a good day.

Later that day, Jack came to visit Annie.

'How did you get in here?' Annie asked, as they embraced.

'Speranza arranged it. She knows lots of people,' Jack said. She looked more of a man that day. Dressed in black, she wore a tailored jacket and trousers, and carried a new top hat. Her white linen shirt had a high collar that reached up past her jaw with a dark blue striped cravat elaborately knotted under her chin. Annie almost didn't know her.

They sat side by side on the prison bunk and stared at each other, while Annie took in Jack's new appearance. 'Why are you dressed like that?'

'Annie, I've a plan and you must hear me out.' Jack stood and paced the few steps across the cell.

'There's nothing you can do for me in here. I can only hope that Mr Gavan Duffy will help when he gets back from

London.' After her dream in the night, Annie had almost lost hope and her tears came fast. She wiped them away.

'Listen to me,' Jack said. 'First though, I need to tell you that the transportation ship, the King Henry, is docked here in Dublin. It sails in two days' time. The women prisoners are to be brought there tomorrow afternoon.'

'No!' Annie cried. 'Don't say that! It's too soon.'

Jack came and sat down beside Annie and whispered. 'Listen to my plan. You can see I'm still Jack. No-one knows I'm a girl, apart from you and Speranza. We can use this knowledge to get you out of here. I'll come with Speranza tomorrow, and we'll change places. You'll take my clothes and walk out as Jack, and you'll be free.'

'But . . . Jack, I don't understand. What are you saying?' Annie asked. 'How can we change places?'

'Speranza knows one of the guards. He'll turn a blind eye. As for me, I've got no family left, Annie. There's just you and Finn and Katty. You and your Da took me in when I was lost. You're my family now.'

'No, I can't let you do this,' Annie replied. 'Seven years transportation. It's madness. And we'll be found out.' Even as she spoke, Annie knew she would try anything to get back to Finn and Katty.

'It's not madness,' Jack said. 'It's the right thing for both of us. I've thought and thought about it, all night. You saved my life when you took me home with you, Annie. I want to repay my debt to you, my friend. Will you accept this repayment?'

'You'll become a criminal to help me?' Annie asked. 'You'll leave Ireland and you may never come back.' She looked into Jack's eyes and they both silently nodded.

Jack touched her hand. 'It's agreed then.'

'If we're caught, perhaps we'll both be sent to Australia. Then Speranza, you might find a way to send Katty and Finn to me.' Annie put her arms around Jack and hugged her. 'Thank you, thank you, dear friend. But how will we do it?'

Jack paced the floor of the tiny cell while she outlined the plan for the next day.

Escape

J ack and Speranza arrived at the prison for their last visit. Jack wore the same outfit she had on the previous day and she stepped aside to allow Speranza to enter the jail cell first. Annie saw that her mentor had dressed in a purple flounced dress, even madder than her usual finery, with a bright blue cloak over it. Her dark hair was braided and decorated with her favourite pearls and her eyes gleamed with excitement. She flashed a brilliant smile at the gaoler and thanked him with a silver shilling. The gaoler left and locked them in the cell together.

Speranza came over to Annie and whispered. 'Quickly!'

Annie stripped off her prison skirt and blouse, while Jack took off her clothes. Both were of similar height and thin build. The last year of hunger had seen to that. It only took a few minutes for the change to be made.

The main job was Annie's hair. It was the only thing that could obviously give her away. Speranza braided it and pinned it around Annie's head, then covered it with a black silk scarf and pulled Jack's top hat tightly down over the lot.

Jack had dressed in the prison clothes and put on Annie's prisoner's cap and she was a girl again. She hugged Annie and Speranza. 'No time for tears. God be with you and may we meet again.'

Annie hugged Jack. 'Be safe, Jack,' she whispered. '*Acushla*, we must meet again. When you get back to Ireland, come to The Nation. I'll let them know where I am. And here, Auntie Bridie's address in New York is in my prayer book.' She put the battered little book into her friend's hands.

* * *

The three women embraced again. 'This is the most risky part,' Speranza said. 'God help us.' She called through the bars of the cell door. 'Guard!'

Annie stood behind Speranza at the door and held her breath. She felt like the imposter she was, stuffed into a shirt and jacket, the cravat forced her chin up. She tipped her hat down a bit lower to shade her face, then straightened her long legs in the fitted trousers. It was the moment when they could be discovered. She steeled herself.

The guard opened the cell door. It opened outwards and Speranza stepped forward and fumbled with her purse, spilling the coins to the floor of the cell and out into the hall.

'Oh, for heaven's sake,' she said. 'What must you think of me, guard? My hands are shaking. I'm so clumsy.'

He bent down, picked up the coins, kept them, and handed one back to Speranza. He looked from her to the prisoner on the bed, now with her head in her hands, crying. Speranza pressed the last silver coin into his hand.

'Thank you, ma'am,' he whispered. Then more loudly. 'This will be your last visit. The prisoners are being transferred to the ship later today.'

Speranza took out her lace handkerchief. 'No, darling Annie.

I'll never see you again!' Speranza turned and hugged the prisoner. Her companion put his arm around Speranza's shoulder. Then the two visitors left the cell. Despite agreeing not to cry, Speranza sobbed all the way out to the front door of the gaol with her head on her companion's shoulder and stopped only when they reached her carriage.

* * *

Annie held her tears back and helped Speranza into the carriage, who then tapped on the roof for the driver to go.

The carriage drove off towards the quays, and passed the King Henry transportation ship. It was busy re-victualling for the journey to the other side of the world.

It was only when they were some distance away from the gaol that Annie shivered, then breathed the air of a free woman. She looked at Speranza opposite her, the woman who had risked her own freedom.

'You and Jack have saved my life,' she said.

Speranza smiled, in spite of her tears. 'You're a great girl. But Annie, you're still in danger, I think. You can thank me by giving my best regards to your brother and sister when you get back to Waterford. Then get them away from this godforsaken country. Yes! Let's get you away from Dublin today.'

Annie took Speranza's hand, bent down and kissed it. 'I'll never forget you and my darling Jack, never.'

Annie closed her eyes while the carriage made its way to the newspaper. She pictured her friend alone in the prison cell. Would she be discovered? Would she survive the long journey to Australia? Then, the thought Annie had pushed away for the last hours. Should Annie have done this; let her friend take her place?

* * *

Annie and Speranza arrived at D'Olier Street, jumped down from the carriage and pushed open the front door to the newspaper office. Tom Meagher was waiting for them. He heard their footsteps hammer on the floorboards in the hall and rushed out to greet them both. Then he closed the door to the street and locked it.

Annie stopped in the hallway, took off the top hat and laid it on the post table beside the door, but left the black silk scarf on. She slipped her jacket off and put it beside the hat. She looked at herself in the mirror. The few days in prison had hollowed out her cheeks even more and her green eyes, long black lashes and straight eyebrows now completely dominated her face. She smoothed her shirt over her breasts and saw Tom's reflection as he glanced at the outline of her breasts through the white shirt. She watched as his eyes moved down to the fit of her trousers around her buttocks. He seemed mesmerized by the sudden change in Annie, then he blinked, shook his head and turned away.

'I'll just be a minute,' Annie said, and broke the spell, as she rushed along the hall to the privy.

* * *

Speranza and Tom had joined John Mitchell in the leader writer's office when Annie knocked softly on the door and pushed it open.

236

She heard Tom speaking to Speranza. 'I'll go with her to Waterford and we'll pick the children up.' They both turned as Annie came into the office.

Annie smiled at Speranza and Tom. 'No, Tom, thank you for the offer, but I'll get myself home. *Go raibh maith agat.*' She thanked him again, and looked at her two friends.

Tom shook his head. 'But Annie, you still need our help.'

Speranza put her hand on Tom's arm. 'Let Annie speak.'

Annie pulled out a chair from the table and turned it towards the desk where the three of them were sitting. John Mitchell's spectacles glinted in the light through the window. Tom had his legs crossed and she sat in her chair and stretched out her own long, trouser-clad legs and crossed them at the ankles. Jack's narrow boots fitted her slim feet and the leather gleamed. She blinked at Tom and smiled, then looked into the faces of those who had helped her.

'Speranza, did you tell Mr Mitchel and Tom about Jack? That she is Jane Keating?' Speranza nodded and Annie continued.

'You, all of you, especially you, Speranza, and my dear friend, Jane, have worked a miracle. I sit here in front of you and I'm free. Thank you.'

The leader writer pointed his pen at her. 'But it's not done yet, Annie.'

She nodded briefly and continued to speak. 'You're right, Mr Mitchell, it's not done yet.' She turned to her friend. 'Speranza you promised to pay me for the poems I sent you and for helping you in Sligo. I need that money now.' She paused. 'Then I'll go home.'

Speranza shook her head. 'But, you don't understand, Annie. We've got a plan to help you. You can't just walk out the door!'

Annie looked across at her mentor and smiled. 'You're surely not planning to make me a prisoner again? Not after all the trouble you went to, getting me out of Kilmainham Gaol?'

'No, of course not. I don't mean that. But we have a good plan. Tom's going with you. He'll help you.'

'And you have my undying thanks, but I have my own plan.' Annie continued. 'I came here on a ferry from Waterford. It goes up and down the Irish Sea every day. I'll be on it this evening and I'll be back with Katty and Finn by tomorrow morning.'

Tom frowned at Annie. 'And what'll you do then? Let me help you.'

Annie looked sideways at him and smiled. 'You can help, Tom. Make me a cup of tea before I go?'

Tom laughed. 'But you're a stubborn woman!' Then he stood and went off to try his hand at making tea.

John Mitchell said. 'Tom's right, Annie. You can't stay in Waterford.'

'We'll get on a ship out of here,' Annie said. She hadn't really thought what she would do, apart from get back to Katty and Finn. Achieve that, and the rest would follow.

John Mitchel stood up from his desk. 'Then, I'll get that money you're owed.'

Speranza looked at the silk scarf tied around Annie's head. 'What happened to Katty's ribbon?' she asked.

Just then, John Mitchell came back into the room with money in his hand.

'It's in the bag I left at the hotel,' Annie said. 'It's got my clothes and daddy's pipe and my journal, too. I need it.'

'I have your money here, Annie,' the leader writer said.

'Don't worry about your bag. When Tom finally manages to make us a pot of tea, I'll send him to fetch it.'

John Mitchell put an envelope on the table in front of Annie.

'There's ten pounds in there, Annie. Payment for your work with Speranza and your poems. And some of this is an advance payment. I want you to keep on sending poems to us here at the newspaper. Write about your journey and I'll publish it.'

She picked up the thick envelope and felt the weight of paper and coins in her hand. 'Thank you, Mr Mitchell,' she said. 'I'll send you my poems and articles from wherever we finish up.'

Tom kicked at the door and was let in with a full tray of cups, saucers, milk jug, teapot, hot water jug and sugar bowl.

'Now,' Tom said. He put the tray on the table. 'Let's all sit down and have a cup of tea.'

Just as he went to pull out a chair, John Mitchell held his hand up to stop him. 'I've another job for you, Tom. Head off over to Speranza's rooms and pick up Annie's bag. As fast as you can. T

here's a good man.'

The three of them laughed at Tom's expression.

'You said you want to help!' Speranza added. She lifted the tea pot and poured. 'Ah, lovely tea. Thanks, Tom!'

* * *

An hour later, Annie stood on the doorstep of the offices of the Nation newspaper. The black top hat was firmly in place on her head. A cab waited at the kerbside. She picked up her bag, hugged Speranza and Tom, and shook hands with John Mitchell. She stepped up inside the cab and pulled the door shut and waved through the window. The cab driver raised his whip, lightly touched the flank of the horse and the cab moved off towards the quays.

Annie leaned back against the leather seat and closed her eyes. Katty and Finn were waiting for her to come home. She could almost feel them in her arms.

* * *

While Annie sat on the deck of the ferry and waited for it to leave Dublin, her friend, Jack, a woman again, was being transferred to the King Henry transportation ship.

Jack had left her prison cell and joined a group of women prisoners. There were seventy-five of them, and all bound for Port Phillip in New South Wales.

One of the guards looked closely at her. 'You're Annie Power?' he asked.

She nodded and touched her prisoner's cap. It was pulled snugly around her face.

'Are you sick?' the guard asked. He looked her up and down in the dull light of the prison corridor.

'I'm sick with sorrow for leaving Ireland,' Jack muttered in a low voice. She clutched her prayer book to her chest. 'Say a prayer for me.'

She kept her head down and turned away to follow the other women down the corridor towards the prison gates. The guard stood and looked at her as she turned the corner, then shrugged and walked away.

The King Henry was almost fully victualled for the thirteen week journey across the world. Food and water had been loaded for the convicts and the thirty crew members. There would be a stop to take on fresh water but none of those transported would set foot on land until the ship reached Australia. The weather was set fair. The next morning, the convict ship hauled up anchor and started the long journey around the globe.

Leaving Waterford

Annie lay on a wooden bench on the deck of the ferry bound for Waterford. She felt the deep rocking motion of the sea and despite the cold, slept a deep, dreamless sleep. The smell of salt water soothed her. She heard the sails flapping and sensed the seamen moving around her, but was not disturbed. She was one of just a few passengers surrounded by dozens of mail sacks for delivery to the small towns along the east coast. The boat turned into the estuary of the River Suir to begin its journey up to Waterford; her body shifted on the bench and she stirred herself. The Captain had agreed to stop for her to disembark the ferry at Passage East. It would save her a few miles walking back out the road.

The sun was just rising above the horizon when she stepped onto the quay in the village. She passed the large houses built around Parade Square for the British army officers posted at the nearby barracks. She left the village and walked off up the coast road towards Ashling. All was quiet this early in the morning.

* * *

Annie arrived after walking
their voices as she approa⌐
herself. 'Thank God.' The
and stepped into the en
back!'

She hugged them tight against
you, my darlings.' She stood and looke
both well. Marie, you've kept them safe. *Go ⌐*
Annie thanked her.

'*Céad míle fáilte!*' Marie greeted her. 'Come in and sit do
Here, put your bag down and give me that hat. Sure, what
way are you dressed at all, girl?'

Annie tried to laugh but the sound that came was more
like a sob. 'Let me kiss these two again. Thank God and his
Blessed Mother! I promised I'd come back, and here I am.'

Annie then handed over her hat and bag and sat on a stool
near the fire. She had no sooner sat down, than Katty jumped
up onto her knee, put her arms around Annie's neck and
whispered. 'Don't go away again!'

'I'm here now, *astor*', Annie said as she stroked Katty's dark
curls. 'I've brought your ribbon back. We'll do your hair later,'
she promised.

Finn sat down on the other stool. 'You didn't get to see the
Landlord then?'

'Who told you that, Finnie?'

Marie had filled a cup of water from the bucket and handed
it to Annie who took it and drank the cool water. She saw
from the grim look on her neighbour's face that she knew
something.

Finn jumped up from the stool. 'Sit here, Marie.' Then he
put his arm around Annie and leaned into her. The children's

243

uched Annie's head, still wrapped in the black

ry, but you're right,' Annie said. 'I've no good news
ou. I didn't see His Lordship. Instead, I met his agent,
hes. He wouldn't budge at all. He said there'll be no stay
he rent.'

She looked from one to the other and waited for them to
understand, but they were not surprised, they seemed to know
already.

'He's been here, your Mr Jones,' Marie said.

'What? When?'

'Yesterday,' Marie continued. 'He handed out eviction
notices to everyone here. You'll see one nailed to your door
when you go home.'

'But he told me a few weeks.' Now it was she who struggled
to understand.

'Well, he's coming back today. We're all to be out or
they'll pull the walls and roof down around us. Most of the
neighbours have gone already. You got back just in time, girl.'

Finn looked at Annie. 'I thought when he saw you, he'd let
us stay. What'll we do now?'

'Let me have another sip of this water and I'll tell you,' she
said. The soft spring water cleared the dust from her head as
well as her throat.

'So, my darlings. In short, I've had a great adventure in
Dublin and I helped Speranza and earned some money at The
Nation newspaper. Jack was there, too.'

'Sure, would she not come back with you?' Finn asked.

Annie shook her head. 'She couldn't get away. I'll tell you
another time.'

She dashed sudden tears away and pressed her lips together

then nodded to herself. 'I've decided, my darlings. We'll go to Auntie Bridie in New York.' She looked from one to the other and tried to smile. 'What do you say to that?'

Finn said. 'Yes, let's do that. We'll have an adventure too!'

Katty jumped down off her knee and hopped on to Marie's lap. 'Come with us, Marie!'

Marie smiled and shook her head. She kissed Katty, set her down on the floor and stood. '*A stor,* I'm going over to Brín in Liverpool. He sent me my fare and he's waiting for me. As soon as you go, I'm getting on a boat out of Waterford.'

Annie heard the change of tone in her neighbour's voice.

'I have their things here, clothes and books, they'll fit in your bag, Annie. I'd say that agent will be back early rather than later today. You won't want to be seeing him again, now will you?' Marie paused. 'I gave the cow to the Nolans, they'll get the last of the milk. The donkey and cart are still out the back.'

Annie looked at Marie, then at her two siblings. 'Finnie, take Katty to help you get the cart hitched up, then bring it round to the door. We're leaving, right now.'

Finn grabbed Katty's hand and, both in bare feet, they raced out to the field at the back of the cabin.

Annie pulled her blue dress and cloak out of her basket and stripped off the shirt, trousers and jacket. While she dressed, she related what had happened with the agent in Dublin. 'He didn't say anything about me?'

Marie shook her head.

'If he sees me, he'll know what I've done, and I'll be arrested again. There'll be no escape next time.'

'God preserve you, girl!' Her neighbour then picked up the bucket from the corner and threw the remains of the water over the fire. 'Now, that's my last job here. I'll never come back to Mother Ireland.' Marie swept her hand across her eyes. 'Oh, Annie, what'll become of us?'

Annie took a sovereign out of her purse and put it into Marie's hand.

'No, girl, don't give me any money. You'll need it for your journey.'

Annie folded Marie's fingers over the coin. 'Take it, Marie. You looked after my precious family. Say 'slán' to Brín for me, won't you?' she said and tears came to her eyes, for what might have been.

'I will, girl, and thank you for this. But tell me this, where'll you go to get on a ship? Not from Waterford, surely?'

'No, I can't risk going into the town. We'll head south to Dungarvan and try and leave from there.' She untied the silk scarf from her head, then began taking the pins out of her hair. 'We're blessed you didn't get rid of the donkey and cart. It'll take us there.'

Annie let her braided hair fall down past her shoulders, then wrapped her cloak round her and put the children's spare clothes into the bag, together with Jack's suit. Then she picked up the top hat.

'I'll take this and the suit with me. They'll pawn for a shilling or two, I'd say.'

The children pulled up at the door. They jumped down from the cart, ran into the cabin, slipped their boots and coats on, then stopped and looked at Annie and Marie. Annie had transformed back into herself.

'Are you ready to go?' she asked Marie. 'We'll give you a lift to the edge of town.'

'Yes, I'm ready. My bag is packed. Do you want to go back

to your cabin for a last look?'

Annie shook her head, but didn't speak while Finn picked up their bag and took it out to the cart.

Marie lowered her voice. 'I was going to bring the children with me if you hadn't come back, Annie. I told Father Corcoran to let you know where we'd be.'

Annie shivered. She'd come so close to losing her darlings. She waited as Marie put her cloak around her shoulders, tied the ribbon at the neck and pulled the hood up over her head and took a last look around what had been home for the last twenty years and blessed herself. They left together.

* * *

Finn was in charge and he shook the reins; they moved off along the laneway, then turned onto the back road up into the hills above the estate, avoiding the main road. When they had covered a couple of miles they stopped and looked down towards the big house and the cabins beyond. The agent and a gang of men on horseback were trotting along towards the cabins. They had a cart with what looked like half a tree trunk in it. They would use the length of timber to knock down the cabin walls.

The Powers stopped briefly to let Marie off on the outskirts of the town, said tearful goodbyes, then turned south to Dungarvan. Their journey was bumpy and slow and they had to keep stopping for the donkey to get a rest from hauling the three of them and the cart. Sometimes Annie and Finn would walk alongside and leave Katty drive the cart in order to lighten the load. Other times, while Finn drove, she would catch Katty's hand and the two girls raced together along the road, laughing and breathless. That day, Annie's heart was at peace. She was content to be walking strange roads and leaving her home. She had the two things that meant the most in her world, her brother and sister. She had money, and she had somewhere to go, New York, where she was sure of a welcome from her mother's sister, Bridie.

A light rain started to fall as they headed up into the Knockmealden Mountains. There was no shelter but they stretched Annie's shawl over their heads and kept on the move. Mist seemed to stand in the air, and low clouds touched the tops of stone walls around the small fields below. She gazed through the clouds, right across the valley to the far, soft rolling hillside covered in trees that were deep shades of green. Sheep grazed on hillocky fields that stretched up to where dark mountain tops loomed on the horizon.

On their journey, they passed several gangs of workers building stone walls along the sides of the road. They were mostly men, and all were drenched by the rain. The travellers kept moving for Annie wanted to reach Dungarvan before nightfall. They stopped at a small inn and ate a meal of thick barley broth with bread and butter, washed it down with a drink of creamy milk, then continued on their way. After a while the road started to descend, winding and turning, on its way towards the coastal town. As twilight began to fall, Annie saw the coastline and Dungarvan town spread out around the estuary ahead of them. Soon after, they walked across the bridge spanning the river. Annie recalled Speranza telling her the Duke of Devonshire, the same family who had given their tenants relief on their rents, had built this bridge.

The little family were stiff and tired but they halted on the bridge to look out along the river as it flowed into the wide bay and on out to the Atlantic Ocean beyond. There were plenty of small ships, and one larger one, anchored out in the deep water. Their next journey would begin out there. 'Please God,' Annie prayed.

* * *

It was almost the end of market day in the town, with a few stalls still operating in the square. Annie tied up the donkey and cart and they stood and watched crowds of people milling about. Some were fairly prosperous looking, while others appeared ragged and hungry.

'What are all these people doing here, Annie?' Finn asked.

'I don't know, *acushla*,' she replied. 'Maybe they're on the move like us. Finn, you stay with the cart, while I get us something to eat. Katty, come with me.'

Annie and Katty strolled through the market. 'There's not much left here,' Annie said. She bought a small loaf of bread and they ate it dry with a drink of water from the pump in the square. Thankfully, they had eaten well earlier in the day.

'Right so,' said Annie. 'The first thing we must do is buy our tickets to New York. Wait for me here and keep your eyes on the bag.'

She walked to a ticket office on the market square which was still open and doing brisk business. The outside walls of the office were plastered with large advertisements for passage to Liverpool, Quebec, New York and New South Wales. Annie's eyes lingered on the destination of New South Wales and thought of Jack. She breathed a prayer for her friend's safety on that long journey. She studied the advertisement for New York, read it through again to be sure, then opened the door.

The ticket office was divided in two by a wooden counter with a glass partition on top. Two clerks sat behind the screen. The public side was almost full with people waiting their turn to buy tickets. Annie joined the queue and listened to a desperate couple trying to haggle the cost of the tickets for themselves and their ten children. She saw the stony faces of the clerks. They were under orders not to budge on the ticket price.

When her turn came she asked for tickets to New York, for herself and her brother and sister.

'You're in luck, Miss, it's nearly sold out. The ship leaves tomorrow, and you'll be in New York before you know it! Ten pounds for the three of you,' the clerk said.

Annie swallowed hard. She had spent money on her ticket for the ferry back to Waterford and had given Marie one pound. 'It said on the poster that little ones travel free. My sister is only small, can she travel free?'

'Is she a babe in arms, Miss? If so, yes,' the clerk replied. He was in his early thirties, dark haired with blue eyes in a thin face. Annie saw that he wore a black topcoat, the cuffs were worn and it was over-large on his shoulders. A woollen scarf was tied around his neck and covered his shirt. The fingers of his right hand were stained with ink. Behind him she saw another man sitting at a desk, overseeing the transactions.

'The boss has held down the cost of tickets to New York, but it's up they'll be going in the next few weeks,' the clerk said.

Annie looked at him and could see he was in no position to help her, but she asked anyway.

'What can I do? We have to go to America.'

'There's a sailing for Quebec next week, on Wednesday.

You'll get tickets for all of you for five pounds,' he said.

'But I need to go to New York, to my auntie,' she explained.

'Sure, that's no problem,' the clerk replied. He pointed to a map on the wall beside him.

'Look, here's British North America with the Saint Lawrence River and Quebec. Most of the passengers who get off at Quebec walk across the border into New York State. There it is. Do you see?' The clerk pointed triumphantly to the border between the two North Americas.

'Yes, I see,' Annie said. But she only saw the distance from Quebec to New York and imagined the miles that would involve. Then she remembered that her friend, Eileen and her family, had planned to go by that route to Boston. The person behind her in the queue shuffled, waiting for her to decide or leave.

'Tickets are selling fast, Miss, so you'd better make up your mind today. We can't keep up with the demand. People are desperate to get away.'

She looked behind her. In the short time she had been in the ticket office, the door was now held open with crowds of people jostling to get in and buy their tickets.

She decided. 'We'll go to Quebec. Five pounds, you said?'

The clerk smiled and Annie took the five pound bank note from her purse and laid it on the counter. The clerk held the note up to the light to check it, nodded, then put it in the lockbox beside him and counted out three tickets.

'Names and ages please, Miss. And your occupation.'

'*Áine Ní Paor*, I'm seventeen. *Fión Paor*, is thirteen. *Caitrín Ní Paor*, is nine.' Annie replied in Irish. It was a very slight disguise of her name, but might help if anyone came looking. The clerk wrote the information in the ledger alongside the ticket numbers then stamped each ticket.

'Occupation?' he asked again.

Annie looked at him. 'What do you mean?'

'Are you a housewife, a servant? What are you?' he explained. The man behind her coughed.

'Pauper,' and 'criminal,' came to mind, but Annie replied. 'I'm a teacher.'

He smiled and wrote it down next to her name, then handed her the tickets.

'Food is included with this ticket. You'll be sailing on the Ocean Queen. The ship leaves on Wednesday. God go with you,' he said to her, then whispered in Gaelic. 'I'd be out of here myself if I had the money.'

Annie pushed her way out through the crowds in the ticket office and joined Finn and Katty waiting by the cart.

She waved the tickets in the air. 'I have them!'

* * *

The whole town was full of people on the move, and lodgings were scarce, but they got one bed in a room at an inn off from the main square. They shared the room with others waiting to emigrate. The bed itself was a worn affair with a lumpy, stained mattress, pungent blankets and a disgusting bolster to lay their heads on. In the opposite corner of the room, a family of six squeezed together on two similar beds. There was a pot under each of the beds and the smells from these added to the rank odours in the room. The nailed-shut window only made things worse. Somehow, they slept.

The next day they set about preparing for their journey. Annie found a pawn shop and got two shillings for the top hat and Jack's clothes. While there, she enquired about selling the donkey and cart.

'You'll have no luck with that, I'd say,' the owner of the pawn shop told Annie.

'The only people with money are spending it on tickets to get out of here. And no-one else has money to buy a poor auld ass, never mind a cart.'

They walked out of the pawn shop and became caught up in a large crowd of people moving through the town towards a row of shops. She saw the bakery, where she had bought bread the day before, was boarded up, and the grain merchants next door had put the shutters across their doors and windows.

Some sort of protest was under way. She looked around her and saw a young woman at the edge of the crowd.

'*Dia dhuit!* What's happening, do you know?' Annie called to her in Irish.

The woman, a slight, starved-looking creature, slowed as she passed.

'We're telling them merchants not to export the grain from hereabouts, while we're all starving. 'Tis criminal, so it is,' the woman replied, then walked on and left the three of them standing in front of a closed shop.

They watched as angry men in the crowd began to throw stones at the police officers who were trying to calm things down. Soon, Annie heard the sound of trotting horses. She found out later, that these were the British Army's Royal Dragoons. Dressed in scarlet coats crossed with white straps, black trousers with gold piping down the outside of the legs, they wore helmets of gold with black plumes. Mounted on their gleaming horses, they were a sight to behold.

The Captain of the Dragoons proceeded to read the Riot

Act. He declared the assembly to be unlawful. Then he raised his voice and shouted that if they did not disperse they would face punitive action. The angry crowd took no notice of his command to disperse and they continued to throw stones at the police and the soldiers on horseback.

A shouted order, startled Annie. 'Ready, Aim. Fire!' The Captain had ordered his men to open fire on the unarmed protesters.

It all happened so fast. She grabbed Katty and Finn and pulled them into the doorway. The smoke and sounds of the shots stunned the crowd of people, who ran for their lives. Annie heard men calling for help on the ground, they had been shot. She saw two men who were clearly dead, one had been shot through the head, the other in the chest. The mounted soldiers began to reload their weapons.

Annie grabbed Finn's hand and put her arm around Katty. 'Quick! Let's go back past the pawn shop.'

They ran back the way they had come then turned off into a side alley. They weren't the only ones; men, women and children ran with them. Some were injured from the musket shots and stumbled along.

'Don't stop, Annie,' said Finn as he felt her slow down. She looked at her two siblings and picked up speed again. They ran around the back of the square and found their lodging house. They were safe.

* * *

Over the next few days, Annie spent more of her money on food for them. The lodging house provided a bed only. They found a soup kitchen in the town which helped. Annie spent more money on a supply of dried ships' biscuits. Food was included in the ticket price, but she had gone hungry long enough. 'Never again', she promised herself.

Everywhere she went, she imagined she could see Mr Jones, the Agent, either just going round a corner or coming out of a shop ahead of her. Her heart stuttered and she gripped Katty's hand tightly, ready to run, if it really was him.

She wrote a letter to her auntie Bridie in New York to tell her they were on their way. Please God, they would arrive before the letter. Then she started on an article for The Nation newspaper about the riot and the shootings she had witnessed the previous day. She walked to the post office and made sure to pull her shawl round her head and face, for fear she would be recognised.

On their last night in Ireland, they joined crowds of people for soup and bread at a Quaker soup kitchen.

Annie had just one more task, to find a home for their donkey. She asked around the people at the soup kitchen and found a family who planned to go back home. The mother was ill and the family would wait for her to recover before getting on a later ship. Annie knew the woman would get a rest on the cart and was happy to make a gift of both the donkey and cart. Annie, Finn and Katty said goodbye to their faithful old friend. The donkey was their last tie to Ireland.

They went back to their lodgings and knelt and recited the rosary together. Finn and Katty lay down on the bed, while Annie sat on a stool and watched over her brother and sister as they slept. She prayed to the Almighty.

'Dear Lord God, help us get safely across the ocean.'

She remembered Eileen, her friend who had drowned in the Saint Lawrence River, and remained sitting by the bed until morning came. Another great test was about to begin.

Emigration

The weather that June morning was fine, with just the misty rain seen most days in the southerly parts of Ireland. Annie, Finn and Katty, joined a large group of people on the quay. Annie looked out towards the bay where the water opened out to the Atlantic Ocean.

The Ocean Queen was anchored out in deep water. Her sails were tightly furled around the spars of the three masts. A small boat pulled alongside the ship, and crewmen set about hauling up boxes, crates and barrels of supplies for the journey to Quebec. She could see the captain on deck, or she thought he was the captain. He seemed to be everywhere, checking and overseeing the work, constantly on the move. The emigrants on the quay stood in line and watched for an hour, waiting their turn. They would be the last to be loaded on board.

The light rain became more persistent and still they waited. There was hardly any talking. They could have been at mass, heads lowered, hands clasped. Smaller children ran in and out among the family groups and made Annie's surreptitious counting more difficult. She lost count at over one hundred emigrants.

Two of the ship's tenders approached the quay and tied up. Crew members climbed out. It was time to go. The crew checked tickets carefully, before the passengers were helped into the small boats with their bags and baggages. More families were loaded until the tenders were full, and sat low in the water. The crew then rowed out to the ship, embarked the passengers and returned for another group. It took more than two hours for everyone to be transferred to the Ocean Queen.

* * *

When it was their turn, Katty and Finn ran up the ladder to the ship's deck and leaned over the rail to watch Annie follow them up. The crew brought the bags up and dumped them on deck. Annie took her bag; at last they were on board. After a final check of their names and tickets, the group from the tender followed a crewman down the steep stairway to the steerage compartment.

As they descended, daylight was replaced by dimness. They arrived in a large, windowless space. The floor, walls and ceiling were constructed of timber. There were no windows, for this part of the ship was below the water-line. The dimness was accentuated by the low ceiling, which gave just enough room to walk upright, and immediately Annie felt a constriction in her throat, as if there was not enough air for everyone to breathe. Sets of bunk-beds were lined along the side walls, each with a thin horsehair mattress and woollen blanket. In the middle of the space, narrow wooden tables and benches ran the length of the room. The steerage compartment was almost full with adults and children, all ready for their journey to begin. It was quiet and the thick air trembled with anticipation.

The crewman led Annie, Finn and Katty to their allocated beds, one above and one below.

'Children share,' he said, and pointed. 'Privies are at the end of the ship, along there. We sail with the tide this afternoon. I'll come back later to collect any who want to take a last look at auld Erin.'

The crewman continued on with other passengers, assigning bunks, until all were settled. Steerage was now full. Annie's ears rang with the noise made by more than one hundred people, many of them moving and lifting boxes and bags, unpacking items needed for the journey. Some mothers shouted at their children, who spent their time climbing up and jumping off the bunks. Just like Finn, in fact.

He called from the top bunk, 'Annie, is this for me?'

'Yes, *acushla*,' she replied, 'I'll take the bottom one and share with Katty.'

She glanced across to the nearby bench and nodded to a girl sitting on her own, with a bag at her feet. She was about the same age as Annie, but smaller and slighter with the build of a child rather than a woman.

'*Dhia dhuit*,' Annie said. 'I'm Annie Power, and these two are my brother and sister, Finn and Katty.'

'*Dhia is Mhuire dhuit*,' the girl replied. 'I'm Mary Sullivan.' She had a narrow, colourless face with thin, dark hair tied back, showing her scalp beneath. She pointed to a neighbouring bunk. 'I'm sleeping there.'

After the introduction, they agreed to speak English. Annie laughed. 'We'll be needing it soon enough.' She looked at Mary's still face. 'Are you travelling alone then?'

'Yes, I am,' Mary replied. 'I have the promise of work in Boston.'

'Ah sure, we'll keep each other company on the journey, shall we? Come with us,' Annie said. 'We're going to have a look around the steerage. I could use the privy, that's for sure!'

Mary's smile brightened her face. 'And me! Let's go.'

The two girls and two children strolled towards the stern of the ship. Annie heard most of the passengers speaking in Irish. These people were most likely from Cork and further west. They were all ages; men, women and children, but she noticed quite a few young women, like Mary, travelling alone, and she wondered about the families they had left behind.

* * *

Before they arrived at the washing and privy area, they could smell it. Katty, who needed to go, coughed. 'Annie, it stinks. I can't go in there, now can I?' Annie saw her worried little face.

'I'll take a look.' Annie pushed the heavy door open and peeped around it to see a long wooden seat attached to the wall. At intervals there were holes in the seat, for people to sit on and do their business. There was a flimsy partition halfway along. It appeared there was one side for men and the other for women. Beneath the holes for sitting on, there was a great gap in the floor. Annie went closer and looked to see that the excrement was intended to fall down into the bowels of the ship. The smell was vile and she could almost taste it. Not only that, some of the excrement and a lot of the urine had missed the gap in the floor and slopped around to where Annie stood. She jumped back and shut the door.

'Jesus, Mary and Joseph,' she said and looked at her companions. 'Well! Before we even set sail!'

'By the look of that mess,' Annie continued, 'every one of the passengers had to go as soon as they boarded! It needs cleaning before we can go in there.'

Finn looked at her, his eyes wide. 'I'm not cleaning it!'

She laughed and shook her head at him. 'Not at all. We'll ask the captain. Come on, let's go and find him.'

* * *

The four of them climbed the stairs to the deck and breathed great gulps of the fresh, salty air. The ship was ready to depart with sails unfurled, catching the light breeze. Annie spotted the ship's captain standing on the deck as he, too, watched the sails.

'Wait here,' she said and moved towards him.

Sean Hennessy was a short, stocky mariner. His eyes were lined and his face tanned from exposure to the wind, black hair stuck out from under his cap and a grey-streaked beard covered most of the rest of his face.

He called out to her. 'Stop right there, Miss. No passengers are allowed on the quarter-deck.' His voice was rough and carried to the crew, some of whom turned and looked at Annie.

Annie called to him. 'Captain, I'm sorry but I need to speak to you urgently. Do you have a minute to hear me?' She heard his Waterford accent and hoped he'd give her a minute of his time. She was right.

'Make it quick then, young woman' he said, 'I've got to get this ship under way in the next half hour, or I'll miss the tide.'

'I'm here to ask you to get the privies cleaned. We can't go in there. The place is filthy. All over the floor.'

'They've been cleaned today. What are you talking about?' he asked. Annie stood her ground. 'Well, they need cleaning again,' she said. 'My little sister, nor any of us, can walk in there for the wet on the floor. And the rest of it.'

The captain looked over the rail and called a crew-member. 'Seamus, get yourself up here.' The crewman arrived and he gave Annie a hard look, if to say, what does she want?

'Go down to the steerage and sort out the mess in the privies. Then find out who's not done their job and report back to me.'

'Now girl, that'll be sorted soon,' Captain Hennessy looked closely at her. 'What's your name?'

'Annie Power. I'm from just outside Waterford. I can hear you're from that part of the country, too.'

'I am,' he said. 'Pleased to meet you, Annie. You may as well stay on deck to say your goodbye to Ireland. We'll be hauling anchor shortly.' He dismissed her and turned away before she could thank him.

Annie hurried back across the deck to her family and Mary. 'Katty, they'll be cleaned soon and then we can all go. Just hold on a little while, *astór.*' She hugged her sister, pleased with her small success.

They walked over to the ship's railing and looked up at the sails, now filled with wind. They heard the screech and clang of the anchor being hauled and the Captain's shouted orders. The ship strained against the iron chains of the anchor as it gradually loosened its hold on the sea-bed and the ship became unmoored. They were ready to leave.

'Say farewell to Ireland.' Annie stood between Katty and Finn and put an arm around each of them, as the ship slowly moved away from the land.

'I don't want to go. I want my daddy,' Katty said, and turned to hide her face in Annie's cloak. Annie hugged her sister and Finn rested his head against Annie's shoulder. Mary stood beside them and took a last, silent look at her homeland. The Power family stood together as the ship made its way out to sea. '*Slán go fóill*,' Annie whispered. Goodbye for now. Then Ireland, their home, was lost to them in the mist and clouds.

The Ocean Queen

T he hull of the Ocean Queen rose and fell with the swell of the sea. The sails were still filled with an easterly wind and after just three days of sailing, they must have been well out into the Atlantic Ocean. Annie had finally stopped falling over when the ship hit surging waves, but she had black and yellow bruises on her hands and knees. They called it 'finding your sea legs.' 'God help us all to get through the next few weeks,' she prayed.

She reached out to pick up the ship's biscuit that was her supper and felt a creeping tickle against her fingers.

'Jesus, Mary and Joseph! There's a *crathur* in my biscuit. Sure, there's lots of them creeping about!' Annie jumped up from the bench and swept the *'crathurs'* and the biscuit onto the floor.

'You have to tap them first and they all drop out,' Finn said. 'They're weevils. They won't make you sick, Annie. Look at me, I'm eating them.' Finn's face was all bones and angles as he smiled down at her from the top bunk. He and Katty ate the biscuits as if they were hardened mariners. Finn was a Power in looks and build, although his wide shoulders had no muscle on them. Annie knew that he wasn't getting enough to eat, but he never complained.

She picked up another biscuit and shook out the weevils, tiny white wriggling things, onto the floor of the ship. '*Go raibh maith agat*, Finnie,' Annie thanked him, then glanced at the weevils on the table. 'Here's a promise, my darlings. The first meal we'll eat in New York will be floury potatoes with butter and salt. Mmm, what do you think of that?'

'I want two potatoes and Finnie can have three, no, four!' Katty said.

Finn put his arm around his little sister. 'And I'll get us a drink of fresh milk to go with the potatoes and then we'll be fed for a week, so we will!' They laughed together at their wonderful plan.

Annie chewed carefully on the hard biscuit and recalled the food eaten at home in Waterford, before the Hunger started. Freshly baked oat cakes, hot from the griddle, with creamy milk, still warm from the cow for breakfast. Dinner was always a pot of steaming, boiled potatoes set down in the middle of the small table. Her mouth watered and she could almost feel the heat as she picked one up and burst the skin open to show the creamy-white flesh of the potato. If they were cooked just right, then the flesh would be dry and 'floury', just waiting for a touch of butter and salt. Most days, their meal was varied with the addition of scallions, sharp and crunchy, the oniony smell mingling with the steaming earthiness of the potatoes.

Here on the ship, however, food seemed to be in short supply. There was a bowl of thin porridge in the morning, a dinner of watery soup with some hard bread and a supper of those ships biscuits with nothing else.

Annie was thankful she had bought some extra dried bread and biscuits in Dungarvan. They didn't go too hungry, but other whole families had nothing extra, just the ship's food. Annie could hear many as they complained about the state of the food. Their new friend, Mary, sat with them at dinner times, yet she had no appetite for the thin gruel. She was done after a few spoonfuls, and refused Annie's offer of some of their bread.

'We've been hungry for nearly a year now, Annie. Sure, you know that yourself. I thought it was at an end when I set foot on this ship. But it still goes on.' Mary said. She kept her voice low so that Finn and Katty wouldn't hear. 'As if we're sentenced to a slow death, they're giving just enough food to keep a bit of life in us.' Mary's eyes were large in her face and full of dark shadows. She looked like the ghost of a woman.

* * *

By the second week of their journey, Annie was bored, and saw that most of the children were feeling the same. Hailing from west Waterford, Cork and some from further west, many of the children spoke only Gaelic. So, as she had done at school back home in Ashling, she gathered a few of the smaller children together and started to teach them to speak English. This was one thing they would need when they arrived in America.

The children, ten of them, sat together on the wooden floor in steerage. The grating in the ceiling was opened to let in some air and light and this dispelled some of the claustrophobic stuffiness and smells.

One of them, young Cormac, looked up at her, his fair curls and whole body bouncing with anticipation. He was small and bare-foot, as all the little ones were, and many of the adults, too. He was still dressed in his woollen baby dress, not yet breeched. That would come when he reached the age of seven.

'Cormac, you sit there next to Ailis. Caitlin, Roisin and Clodagh, come and sit next to me.'

The girls were a couple of years older than Cormac and their woollen dresses were ankle length, faded and ragged around the hem and the neck. None of them had a change of clothes for this journey, and their dresses were dirty, along with everything else about them.

Ailis and Clodagh wriggled and whispered. Annie smiled at their good humour. They were always hungry, only half washed, hair full of lice, yet they saw this journey and this little school as a great adventure.

'Today,' she said in Irish, 'we're going to learn some things about North America and we'll speak in English so we can get some practice. And, I found a new song we can learn too. Who likes to sing?'

At that moment, two little boys arrived.

'Ah, Gerry and Colm, you're here, good. I thought you were lost.'

'Annie, we're sorry to be late,' Gerry said as they sat down, heads bent. Annie looked at their faces.

'Are those tears I see on your faces? Tell me, what's happened to make you cry?'

Gerry told their tale. 'We went to look for some more water for mammy. She's still sick, so it might make her better. We asked the sailor and he hit me and then he squeezed Colm's arm and bent it and he told us to get away out of it.'

Colm held his arm up for her to inspect the bruising coming through on his bones. His face was streaked with grubby tears, a sad little six-year old.

'Sure, you're a brave boy, Colm. Here, let me kiss it better for you, and you too, Gerry,' Annie kissed them both.

'He's a bold man to do that to you,' she said. 'I'll go and speak to the captain after the lesson.' Annie sat the two boys near her and continued the lesson.

'My lovely scholars,' she said. 'We've work to do and songs to sing. Now then, who can tell me the name of the capital city of North America?'

The small group of children and their teacher had fun arguing about the English pronunciation of the names of the American cities they were heading to, with their families. Annie finished the day's lesson by translating Gaelic lullabies and songs the children already knew, into English. They all sang together in Irish and then followed her English translations.

* * *

Later that day, Annie knocked on the captain's cabin door. She had sat in a corner of the deck and watched and waited until he left the quarterdeck, then followed him, like a cat after a mouse. A stout, black mouse.

'Miss Power is it? *Dia dhuit.* Come in,' he said. 'I heard you singing with your little ones today. You're doing a good job there. So, tell me what brings you here? Not the privies again, surely?'

'*Dia is Mhuire dhuit,* Captain. No, the privies are emptied and we have clean water, so thank you,' she replied.

Annie stood in front of a map table beside a window, and she glanced out at the surging ocean. At that moment, a large wave caused the ship to heave and she put her hand on the table to steady herself. She straightened up and then looked at him.

'I've come to talk to you about one of your seamen. This morning he hurt two of my little scholars. He shouted at them and hit young Gerry and bruised little Colm's arm.' Annie paused, then added, 'Colm's just six and Gerry's eight, they're brothers.'

'Well, what were they doing then? They must have been up to something. I can't have steerage passengers roaming the ship. Although you seem to be able to get anywhere you please.' He chuckled to himself at his clever joke.

'They were looking for some water for their poor mother, who is in her bed, unable to move with sea-sickness.' Annie blinked away tears as she spoke. 'I ask you, Captain, don't we have enough trouble without our children suffering at the hands of a bully?'

The Captain stood and walked over to join her at the map table. 'You're right, Annie. I didn't mean to make fun of your troubles. Do you know the name of the seaman?'

'They told me someone called him Fintan.' She swallowed hard, her breath was ragged.

'Come and sit down here for a minute while you compose yourself.' He pulled a chair out for her. 'Here.'

She sat and smiled at his kindness. 'Thank you. These poor little ones, they're in such a sorry state already.'

'It won't happen again. I'll see to it, and that's a promise,' he said. 'Now then, tell me about your scholars. What are you teaching them?' He sat back at his desk.

Annie took a breath and began to speak. 'You know they're mostly from the south and west, so they don't have much

English?'

He nodded, and she continued. 'They'll need the English when we get to America, so we practice every day, just for a couple of hours in the mornings.' She smiled. 'I even have some adults join us. As well, it makes the journey more bearable for everyone, me included.'

'Sure, that's great work you're doing, Annie. Listen, will you tell Gerry and Colm that I'm sorry for this? I have children of my own back home in Waterford, and I'd hate anyone to raise a hand to them.'

Annie smiled at him. 'Why don't you call in to the school in the week and tell them yourself? The crew let us on deck if the day is fine, or you know where to find us in steerage, if it rains.'

'I'll do that, Annie. Now I'd better get off and find Fintan. I'll see what he has to say for himself.' He stood and offered his hand across the desk to Annie. They shook hands.

* * *

The captain was true to his word. A few days later, he stopped by the little school on deck and listened to the children singing their songs with Finn and Katty. Older children and adults were practicing their numbers with Annie.

The lessons were just ending and Annie pointed to the brothers. He sat down on the deck and spoke to the two boys. Colm held his arm out to show his fading bruises. The captain shook his head. 'But aren't you the brave boys. And how's your mother? Annie tells me she was sick.'

'She's better now,' Gerry replied. 'Mary brought her water and biscuits.'

'That's good to hear, Gerry. When you get back, tell her the Captain was asking after her, won't you?'

'We'll go and tell her right now. Is that alright, Annie?'

Annie nodded and smiled. The two boys ran off to tell their mother they had spoken to the ship's captain, and Finn and Katty ran with them. It was as a good a time as any for a race.

The captain turned to Annie. 'And tell me this, Annie. How do you know so much about teaching?'

'I was a pupil at Miss Nagel's school in Ashling, where we lived,' Annie told him. 'She came out from Waterford every day to teach the children on the estate. I was one of her first pupils. And when I turned fourteen, and it was time to leave, she asked me to stay on and help her with the teaching. I did, and I loved it.'

Annie turned her gaze away and looked up at the masts standing tall in the sky above her, then continued. 'Earlier this year, some of the children stopped attending. Their parents had no money to pay for the teaching. Miss Nagel then couldn't pay the rent on the barn, our school, so His Lordship took it back. We tried everything, but that was the end of it.'

There were no tears as she spoke, but she felt a deep sadness in her heart when she recalled that meeting with the children and their parents, her neighbours. Annie pushed her shoulders back and lifted her chin. She turned back to look at him.

'There you have it, Captain. Now, tell me, will you help with my little school here?'

He smiled. 'I can let you have some slates and pencils for writing practice. I have a supply for myself and the watch crew. Can you use them?'

'*Go raibh maith agat.*' She thanked him and smiled and felt a little of the darkness inside her lift. 'I'll set myself the task of making sure all my pupils can write their own name in English by the end of this journey.'

They shook hands again and the captain promised to send her slates and slate pencils that day. She hurried off to tell Katty, Finn and Mary her good news.

The Atlantic Ocean

B y the end of the third week at sea, the privies were a stinking mess again, and the water barrels were either empty, or half-full of stale, dirty water.

The ship's crew were seen less and less in steerage, as the air grew more stinking from the smells of unwashed people and their excrement. As well, the noise, especially at night, was a torment. Annie cuddled Katty and listened to the coughs, snores, shouts and drunken arguments. God alone knew where they got the drink from, but only the children seemed able to sleep through the night.

* * *

Early one morning, Mary brought Annie a cup of water and sat on the edge of her bunk. 'There's not much water left, Annie, I hope those crew will bring fresh barrels down soon.'

Annie thanked her and sat up to sip at the tepid, stale water. She scratched at her head. 'Dear God, I'm eaten alive with lice, they're all over me. Wait for a minute will you, while I go to the privy? I dread going there.' She pulled her shawl round her and headed off.

Mary sat with the children until Annie came back from the

aft end of the ship and motioned to Mary.

'Come over here,' she said. They both sat down by the long table in the middle of the room, away from where the children slept. 'There's uproar down that end of the ship. There must be about forty people complaining about the filth and the mess in the privies, not to mention the rotten water in the barrels.'

'Again! But sure, what can we do?' Mary asked.

'We'll go and talk to them, that's what we'll do.' Annie replied. 'I'll tell Finnie we won't be long.' She climbed the ladder to the top bunk and roused Finn, whispered to him, then kissed him, and came back down to Mary.

'Right, let's be quick. I don't want to leave them alone too long.' The two women made their way past rows of bunks with bags and baggage piled at the sides of the room. It was early with many still asleep, but some beds were empty.

Annie heard the shouts as they got nearer to the stern of the ship and then saw a crew member forced back against the side of the ship, clearly the object of the noisy crowd of men and women.

She recognised the crewman. It was Fintan, the one who had hit Colm and Gerry. She looked at him with a grim smile. Well deserved, you coward, she thought.

Annie jumped up onto a bench.

'*Dia daoibh, a chairdre.*' Annie had to shout to be heard over the angry voices and hoped her Irish greeting to friends would be heard.

'Friends, tell me, what is this? Is it the water? Is it the privies?' She spoke in Irish and looked at the men and women. Every one of these people had the look of pinched starvation in their faces, with grey-tinged skin and hollow cheeks.

Several of the crowd turned and saw the girl on the bench was one of their own. An older woman answered.

'Sure, girl, we'll all die if this doesn't improve,' the woman said. 'The water is filthy, the privies overflow daily. They seem to think because we don't speak English we can live like pigs.' The woman was in her forties, dressed in black and by her accent from the Midlands or thereabouts. 'Who are you, anyway?'

'My name is Annie Power. I'm from Waterford and my friend here is Mary Sullivan from Cork. I'm travelling with my brother and sister.'

The crewman saw the crowd had quietened and looked at Annie. He narrowed his eyes. Mary reached her hand up to hold Annie's hand.

Annie called out again, her voice gathering strength. 'We must speak to the captain. I spoke to him last week, he's a Waterford man. I'm sure he'll sort this out.'

'So why isn't he here then?' An angry voice came back at Annie.

'I don't know why, but we must tell him. What do you say some of us go up on deck and find him?' she asked.

'I'll come,' said the older woman, 'but the rest of you need to settle down a bit or we'll all be thrown overboard.'

A young man stepped forward. 'I'll come too,' he said. He was better dressed than most, in a woollen tailcoat and knee breeches with a dark green waistcoat, and the high-crowned hat typical of the west of Ireland. He held a small clay pipe in one hand.

'*Go raibh maith agat,*' Annie thanked them both and spoke to the crewman. 'Come on with us, we're going to find the captain. Or do you want to stay here?'

He joined them and they left together.

* * *

The four passengers and the crewman walked back through steerage and up the stairs to the deck. Outside, the wind whistled through the rigging, all the sails were full and the ship moved fast across the surface of the sea. It was still early and the sky was not yet fully bright. Annie turned to see the rising sun on the horizon behind the ship. She took a deep breath of the clean salty air and breathed out her prayer. 'Remember, O most gracious Virgin Mary.'

The crewman went on ahead to call the captain and while they waited, the two passengers introduced themselves to Annie and Mary. The older woman said, 'I'm Philomena Burke, from Cahir. I'm travelling with my grandchildren. Their father's meeting us in Quebec.'

The women then turned to look at the young man. He smiled. 'I'm John O'Connor from Dungarvan. I'm going to join my cousin in Boston, he came this way last year.' He paused, then nodded as if a decision was made, and continued to speak. 'Sure, he had an awful journey. Almost fifty people on the ship died during the crossing. I heard they threw the bodies over the side of the ship, and that included a priest!'

'I heard about that ship,' Mary said. 'Was it the Saint Andrew?'

John nodded again.

'What was the cause of the deaths?' Annie asked.

'Cabin fever,' John said.

Mary added, 'It's caused by impure air, so they say.'

Annie thought of Katty and Finn breathing in deadly air.

'My God, we can't have that on this ship. What can we do?'

'We're doing something right now, girl. And it's you're the brave one,' Philomena said. 'Now we need to sort out this fine captain. Is this him?'

It was. He walked along the gangway and stopped in front of the deputation. 'Right, people. What's going on here? My crewman said he was assaulted when he went to clean out the privies.'

The crewman had caught up with them and pointed at Annie. 'She was inciting them to riot, Sir.'

'Away about your business, Fintan. I'll deal with this now.' The captain opened the door to his cabin and held it for them to walk in. He sat at his desk and faced them, his back to the glass-fronted bow of the ship.

'Now, tell me your names and your problem.'

Annie introduced her new friends and they stood in front of the captain's desk. The ship was moving fast through the ocean and Annie leaned against the hull to keep her balance. She glanced through the window and saw only pale sky and dark ocean. When would they get to journey's end?

Annie heard Philomena speak.

'Captain, Sir, we've been on this ship for three weeks now and we're living on stale water and short rations, we've only seen half the food we were promised with our tickets. And what's worse, those privies are filthy all the time. Are you surprised that people are getting angry, I ask you? The next thing is, they'll be getting sick from the foul air we're breathing down there.'

Before the captain could reply, John added. 'Annie didn't encourage anyone to riot, Sir. She and Mary came to find out what the trouble was. She asked if some of us would come and

277

speak to you. You'll see for yourself, most of the passengers have been half-starved for months before boarding this ship. They're angry, but they've not got much of a fight in them.'

Annie looked at Philomena and John. They spoke up well for themselves. She was in good company.

'We're frightened we'll finish up like the passengers on the Saint Andrew last year,' Annie said. 'You must have heard about that ship, Captain?'

The captain sighed. 'Yes, I do know of the Saint Andrew, Annie. God rest them poor souls. But you've no need to be concerned on this ship. I've done this crossing many times, and with no deaths. There's been some sickness, but every one of my passengers arrived in Quebec.' He looked at each of them. 'Philomena, you asked about the food you were promised with your ticket?'

Philomena nodded. 'My own stock of food is running low, Sir, and most of my neighbours with children are down to the rations we get from the crew. We'll not survive another three weeks on those.'

I don't understand this. You should be getting three meals a day. There's plenty of provisions on board. I'll find out what's going on there.' He continued. 'I know the crew sometimes get too busy up on deck to do the cleaning every day. What do you say we get some volunteers to help out?'

John raised his hand and said, 'I'll get a few men together and we'll help the crew with the water and the privies.'

'Good man.'

Philomena spoke up again. 'Sir, there's a few with sea-sickness who are still not well. I can organise a corner in steerage and look after them. I have some experience of nursing.'

'That's great, Philomena. I'll let the crew know you're setting up an infirmary for the sick, and that John is going to help out with the cleaning.'

'I'll help you, Philomena,' Mary said. 'And Captain,' she added. 'Do you know that noxious air can cause fever?'

'I had heard that, Mary. I'll see the grating to steerage is opened first thing every morning, weather permitting of course. I'll get the crew onto this straight away and make sure the water barrels are checked.'

Captain Hennessy led the way to his cabin door and shook hands with each of them. 'I think we have a plan of action. Let's get started, and we'll talk again.'

* * *

They made their way back to the lower deck. On their arrival they were greeted by a waiting crowd of passengers. Annie explained their plan and John, Mary and Philomena began to recruit volunteers for their jobs. Before she left, Annie thanked each of them.

'*Go raibh maith agat*, Philomena, Mary and John. I pray to God this will better our situation. I'll continue with my little school, but now I must get back to Katty and Finn. They'll think I've fallen overboard!'

* * *

Annie breathed easier on returning to her brother and sister. Finn and Katty were on the bench waiting for her and she put her arms around them.

'Just a few more weeks, darlings, then we'll be in Quebec

and nearly there.' Annie said.

She told them about the meeting with the ship's captain, then took her rosary beads out of her pocket. They knelt to say their morning rosary and offered it up for a safe passage, as they did every morning.

The Storm

A storm was coming. The ship had slowed in its progress over recent days as it ploughed through heavy seas and the tops of waves began to break, showing white against the dark green ocean. Deep troughs appeared as the sea strained against the increasing power of the north wind. The sky darkened and the morning sun was overcast by a mountain of heavy black clouds.

Barefoot sailors ran down the steps into the steerage to batten down the hatches. They checked all boxes and passenger trunks were safely stowed under bunks or seats. The doors to the privy were locked and, as they left, the crew locked the doors to steerage behind them.

Annie and her brother and sister sat on the floor beside the walls of the hull and waited. She heard shouted orders to the crew on deck and the creak of sails as they were hauled down and lashed to the masts. Then silence. The light was dim in steerage, with only the sound of a crying baby being hushed by its mother. Annie took out her rosary beads and noticed others had done the same.

She prayed with Finn and Katty, until they were shocked by a crash of thunder right above the ship. She felt the sound reverberate through the walls of the ship. This was

281

immediately followed by the flash and crackle of lightning. She smelt burning air, and the steerage compartment lit up for an instant. Some of the passengers screamed. Then silence again, as if everyone on the ship held their breath.

The Ocean Queen seemed to falter in its motion. Then, suddenly, from moving up and down the ship rolled right over almost onto its side. Sea water flew in through the sides and joints of the ship's planks, spraying everyone with freezing salt water. Many passengers were thrown from their bunks to the floor. Screams rang through the hull again. Annie held on tight to Finn and Katty. They were drenched by the water coming from all sides. Bags and boxes, anything that was not tied down, including small children, were thrown into the air and crashed down.

Annie had her back to the wall of the hull and as the ship heaved and rolled, she rolled with it and ended up on her back looking across at the deck. It was now vertical. The ship remained suspended almost upside down. It seemed as if time stopped, there was silence and the three Powers clung on to each other. Annie prayed out loud. 'Remember, Oh most Blessed Virgin Mary,' but she couldn't continue as the ship seemed to bounce, and Annie's head banged off the wall of the hull, which was now the floor. She put her hand up to her head and let go of Finn who slid away on the wet surface. He managed to crawl back and held on to the leg of the bunk. Katty clung on to Annie and kept her eyes shut.

Slowly the ship rolled back and righted itself. Annie heard more shouts of alarm. Adults tried to hush the cries of their terrified children. Many became sick from the constant jarring motions of the ship and the air was soon filled with the sour smell of vomit.

The ship creaked as if about to burst, and rolled and wallowed on the ocean, hammered by wind, waves, thunder and lightning. Annie finished her prayer. Was this the end? If she was going to drown that night, then she would join her mother and father in heaven.

As the hours passed, Katty and Finn retched and threw up in the corner of the hull and crept back to the safety of Annie's arms. Annie sang the lullaby their mother had sung to her as a child; of the fairy who had returned a stolen child to its mother. The sweetness of the Gaelic words and the familiar tune comforted the children, and counteracted the howling wind and the crashing and banging from the deck.

After some time, the movement of the ship eased a little, and Katty and Finn slept. Annie sat, exhausted and battered, and kept watch through the night until morning came. If she were to drown, then she would be awake and meet death face to face, like her father did.

* * *

The eye of the storm moved across their ship, then resumed its hammering and harrowing of the ocean and anything on it.

By late the next morning, the tempest had eased and the crew worked to repair damaged sails and spars. Once that was done, they fed the starving passengers, who had not eaten for a day and a night. The crew then hauled up the sails, caught the stiff breeze and the ship continued on its journey. Annie found some dry clothes in her bag, and the three of them soon felt warmer. She spread out their sodden blankets and clothes on the bench to dry.

Soon after, the Captain came round to check on his passengers. There was no ship's surgeon, so he inspected the injured, and conferred with Philomena and Mary. They had bandaged up the bruised limbs and the heads of those passengers who had been thrown off their bunks in the height of the storm.

As he passed through steerage, Annie called to him. 'Captain, are we safe now? I thought we would sink last night.'

'To be sure, it was a mighty battle there for a while, Annie. But we're well out of it now. Are you and your brother and sister unharmed?'

'I've a pain in my head from when I banged it off the floor, no, the wall. But yes, we're unharmed.'

'No school today then, girl. Have a rest for yourself. We've lots of repairs to do today. I'll make sure you can start up tomorrow.' He tipped his cap to Annie, and continued his rounds.

John O'Connor, and some of his fellow passengers, worked all morning with the crew to clean up the mess in steerage and replenish the water. By evening, things were almost back to normal and most of the passengers had recovered from the storm.

The next day, as the captain had promised, Annie had a dry space on deck to resume her lessons with the little band of scholars. They had been frightened, but were mostly unharmed. She racked her memory to find tales with happy outcomes and get some smiles from her class. Finn and Katty joined in and by the end of the first morning they finished with a song, while Finn played the tin whistle.

Ship fever

Two days after the storm ended, Annie walked through to the corner of steerage where Philomena and Mary had the bunks for those suffering from sea-sickness. '*Dia daoibh, a chairde*,' she greeted her friends. She looked around at the people in bunks. 'I see you have even more with the sea-sickness.'

'It's not all sea-sickness, Annie,' Mary said. 'I fear the storm shook loose a fever on to us. We have two very sick people here. Come and see, they're burning up.'

Philomena knelt beside a sick couple lying on a lower bunk to offer them a drink to cool them. The old man and woman clung together in their misery.

'T'is the fever,' Philomena confirmed. The storm had indeed shaken it loose.

Mary walked back with Annie and they sat at the table to eat some dinner with Katty and Finn.

'Annie, how much longer do we have on this ship?' Mary asked.

'I don't rightly know, my friend. A week or two? I think we lost time over the last few days with the storm. I'll ask one of the crew, and tell you when I find out.'

They finished their broth and wiped the bowls with the

last of their bread. Then they sipped a cup of water from the barrel. Finn and Katty gathered up the bowls and brought them over to the crew member at the serving table.

'I'd drink a cup of tea, that's for sure,' said Mary after tasting the water. 'Did you ever smoke a pipe, Annie?'

Any sort of fire below decks was forbidden, but passengers could enjoy their pipes when out on deck.

'No, not me, but my Da did. He loved his pipe,' Annie replied. 'He was always looking for a halfpenny to buy a bit of tobacco. Sometimes he'd just sit there and puff on the empty pipe.' Annie smiled at the memory. 'Why do you ask?'

'I used to smoke a pipe, a small clay one. I loved the taste and the smoke in my throat after the dinner,' Mary said. 'I heard the smoke protects you from the fever. Did you ever hear that?'

'No, but we'll be fine,' Annie replied. 'We've come this far. With God's help we'll not be much longer at sea.'

If Mary was troubled, then Philomena was even more so. She had come to find Annie and Mary. She motioned the two of them to move away from the children.

'We must tell the captain,' she said to them, her face looked grim. 'There's been two more come along, the last while. They're getting sick and have the runs. It's definitely ship fever. I've seen the same thing in the infirmary in Cashel, and it kills people.'

'My Da died of a fever,' Annie said. 'He got better, then he got sick again and died in a week.' Annie swallowed hard and stopped speaking.

'You go and tell the captain, Annie. Sure, bring him to see for himself, why don't you?' Philomena said. 'Mary, we need to get back to them poor souls.'

* * *

Annie hurried to tell the captain. He grabbed his hat and rushed down to the infirmary with her. There were indeed two very sick passengers, an old woman and her even older husband. They lay together, eyes closed and barely moved. Heat rose off them in a cloud of vapour.

Philomena lifted the old man's shirt. His skin was pale and hairless; there wasn't an ounce of fat on his body and his belly was covered in tiny red spots. She replaced his shirt and looked at the Captain. He nodded and turned away, motioning the women to come with him.

'And there's two more just come to tell me they have the same thing, Captain. For now, they're not too bad. God willing, it'll be just these few that get it,' Philomena said.

'We've another ten days of sailing before we get to the Saint Lawrence River,' the Captain replied. 'I'll put more sail on to get there as fast as we can. Philomena, get the other two over to this side of the ship and keep the rest of the passengers away. You and Mary are doing good work. If you need any help, let me know and I'll send a crewman down.'

The Captain bid them goodbye and returned to the upper deck. Soon after, the ship gathered speed.

* * *

Philomena and Mary did their best to ease the suffering of the old couple but it was to no avail, they died that night. Ship fever had washed on board in the storm.

The couple were buried the next morning. The Captain recited some prayers, and the emigrants stood in silent witness. Annie closed her eyes when she saw the bodies wrapped together in sail cloth and tied with rope. Then she forced herself to watch, as the dead were lifted onto a plank balanced over the ship's rail. Their bodies slid down the tilted plank and into the water. The ship ploughed on across the ocean and the old couple were soon left far behind.

In the evening of the same day, when the children were asleep in their bunk, Annie sat at the table with Mary.

'I have something to ask you, Mary,' she said in a low voice. 'Will you see that Katty and Finn get to New York if anything happens to me? I've written down Bridie's address. Here.' She held out a piece of paper. 'And there's some money here in my belt.' Annie touched her waist. 'I have a great fear that they'll be left on their own. Finn is a big boy now, sure he'll turn fourteen in September, but he'd never get himself and Katty to New York on his own.'

Mary hugged Annie and took the slip of paper. 'We'll get there, don't be afraid.'

Annie was relieved, knowing she had a friend on board.

Mary Sullivan

In spite of the fever on board, Annie continued with the morning school sessions for her scholars. Whenever she could, she brought them up on deck. The air turned colder as they sailed further west. It was now into August. They had been at sea for almost two months.

The children shivered in their thin dresses and shirts and breeches, so Annie decided they'd warm up with a dance. Finn fetched his tin whistle and played a jig. The dancers' bare feet skipped around the deck, hair flew as they moved to the music. Their laughter carried as far as the Captain's deck and up to some of the crew high in the rigging. John and Mary came up out of steerage and jumped into the dance. They caught Annie's hands, as Finn started to play a reel. Annie remembered the leaving party for Eileen, almost a year ago. How she and her friend had danced, the night before the family left for Boston, and their great hopes for the future.

The days passed, and the Ocean Queen sailed nearer to their destination. Fever still affected some on the ship, mainly among the older passengers, but there had been no further deaths, and those who had the fever were well looked after by Philomena and Mary. One day, the Captain announced that the ship was on the last leg of its journey. In just a few more days, they would turn into the Gulf of Saint Lawrence, then on to Quebec in British North America, and the end of their great journey.

* * *

The very next day, Mary fell ill. Philomena sent word to Annie to come to the infirmary. Annie left her pupils and hurried towards the rear of the ship where she saw her friend lying on a bunk. Her eyes were closed.

'Mary, what's happened to you?' Annie sat beside her friend and took her hand and felt the feverish heat burning through Mary's skin. Annie's whole body shuddered with dread.

Mary raised her head up from the pillow. 'I think I have the ship fever, Annie. My head is so painful, I can't open my eyes.'

Annie hugged her tightly. 'No *astor*, not you. You're just tired. Lie down again and I'll wash your face to cool you down.'

Annie managed to keep her voice steady as she sat and washed Mary's sweating face. Mary relaxed into a deep sleep as her face and body cooled. Annie stood and stretched the aches out of her back, then bent over her sleeping friend and kissed her cheek.

'I have to go to the school, but I'll come back later,' she whispered. Philomena looked at Annie, but neither spoke. Philomena just raised her hand as Annie left.

Annie's little scholars were still on deck when she returned to her class.

'Annie, where have you been for so long?' Katty asked.

'I'm sorry, sweetheart, I've been to see Mary. She's got a fever.'

'Oh, Annie, is she poorly?' Katty's forehead wrinkled.

'A little bit. I'll go back later to see her,' Annie sat down on the deck floor. 'Now then, tell me what you've been up to while I was away, my little scholars.'

Finn spoke up. 'We've done some arithmetic and everyone has practised their English, but we're a bit tired now, Annie.'

'You've worked hard all morning. Well done, everyone,' Annie said. 'So, then we'll have a tune on the tin whistle. Finnie, you're our musician. I hope you're not too tired to play a couple of reels for us?'

Finn was never too tired to play his beloved tin whistle. They sat and listened to the music. Some of the children's parents joined them, and when Finn stopped playing, one of the parents began to sing in a sweet tenor voice.

Annie spent the afternoon with Mary. She had improved a little and they chatted about Mary's job in Boston. She was to be a domestic in a boarding house. 'I'll go back to Ireland, Annie,' she said. 'I'll save every dollar I can, and when this blight is finished, I'll go back home.'

That evening, Annie, Finn and Katty joined the queue for their supper. The Captain, still true to his word, had been sending down four large boilers of soup. They waited with their bowls and the oniony smell of the soup made their mouths water. Annie waved to the Captain as he passed through the steerage deck on his rounds. He smiled and waved back at her and her siblings.

After supper and prayers, Annie tucked her little sister into the lower bunk they shared. Finn was close. He had made some friends on the ship and they chatted together at the table nearby.

'I'm going to sit with Mary for a while. Katty, you need to

be asleep by the time I get back.' Annie loved to look at her sister's dark curls spread out on the hard mattress. 'Stay well, my darling,' she prayed.

On her way to the small infirmary, Annie saw other children were settled in for the night and steerage had quietened a little after the noise and movement of the day. She took a deep breath, then went to join her friend.

* * *

Mary was sitting on the side of her bed and reached over to kiss Annie as she sat beside her.

'You're looking much better, thank God,' Annie said.

'I'm on the mend already,' Mary replied. 'I'll take it easy for a day or two, Annie, but I feel much better.'

Annie's dread lifted somewhat, but she remembered how her father had improved and then suddenly relapsed. It was no help to say this to Mary, so she stayed quiet. There were others lying in bunks around them, unwell and feverish.

'Ah Annie, I can't wait to get off this ship,' Mary said. 'I want to start my new life. But I'm sorry we'll have to say goodbye, cara.'

Annie smiled. 'You haven't seen the last of me, Mary Sullivan! We can travel part of the way together. Then I'll write to you as soon as we get to New York. Boston's not too far away for a visit, now is it?'

Annie kissed Mary's cheek and felt the fever-heat still there, just under the skin. She stood and picked up a bowl. 'I'll get some water and you can have a wash. Have you eaten today, my friend?'

'No. I've slept most of the day,' Mary replied. 'I'm not

hungry, Annie, but I need the privy.'

Annie helped Mary to walk along to the privy, yet once back at her bunk, Mary had very little energy left. Annie wrung out the cloth and helped Mary to wash her hands and face.

When that was done, Annie said, 'Mary, I have to go back to the children. I'll come back in the morning. If you need me for anything send someone to call me, won't you?'

'I will to be sure,' Mary replied. 'Now go and get some rest yourself. God bless.' Mary turned on her side and closed her eyes.

* * *

Annie made her way back to the front of the steerage; the light was dim; only a few drinkers sat and chatted in low voices. The emigrants were in their last week of travel, and were all weary of this confinement in what felt like a constantly moving coffin.

Both children were asleep when she got back. Finn on the top bunk, and Katty, Annie's little shadow, lay on the lower bunk. Annie lay down and put her arm around her sister's small body. She said a prayer for Mary, and, exhausted, was soon asleep herself.

* * *

She woke early the next morning, left Finn and Katty asleep, and went back to check on Mary. Philomena met her a little distance from the infirmary and put her hand on Annie's arm.

'I was just on my way to call you,' Philomena said. 'The fever is back. She's burning up, sure God love her.'

Annie closed her eyes and touched her hand to her heart. 'I'll go to her.'

Philomena's eyes overflowed with tears, and she stood aside to let Annie pass.

Annie saw at once that Philomena was right. Mary was lying on the bunk and had pulled away the blanket. Annie could see the sweat had run down her neck and chest. Mary had been sick at some point and her white shift was stained with green and black bile.

Annie knelt beside her friend. 'Mary, darling. It's me, Annie.'

Mary's eyes fluttered, but did not open fully. Her face was flushed and contorted with pain. 'Annie,' she whispered.

Annie pulled the blanket away from Mary's body and picked up a bowl of water and a cloth from beside the bunk. The water spilled over the side of the bowl, but Annie took no notice and squeezed the cloth out. She wiped the sweat away from Mary's face and dried her skin.

'I'll cool you down with this flannel. That'll make you better,' Annie said. The words echoed in her mind. The very same words she had said to her father. 'Just a few more days, Mary. We'll get off this ship. Just think! We'll be in America!'

Annie rinsed the cloth out and wiped Mary's sweat away again and again. She fetched more water and continued until she lost track of time. She was in a dream, on a moving ship between two worlds. At times she saw her father's face and he smiled at her. 'Look after Finn and Katty, won't you, my girl?' he said. Annie nodded and blessed herself then continued to try and cool Mary's fever.

Later, at some point, Philomena caught Annie's hand and held it tight in hers. The movement jolted Annie out of the dream.

'Annie, stop now. It's over. Let her be.' Philomena pulled the blanket up over Mary's still face and body. Then she put her arm around Annie's shoulders. They both wept for their friend.

* * *

The next morning, Annie, Finn and Katty stood on deck as the captain read out the prayers for those buried at sea. She looked at the faces of the people around her; at Philomena, with her grandchildren by her side, and John, who was holding his hat in both hands, his head bent. Annie recalled how he had danced with Mary that evening on deck. She had seen the sweet understanding between them and her heart ached for the never-ending sorrow heaped on her countrymen and women.

Passengers and crew stood silently, as the remains of Mary Sullivan, wrapped in canvas, slid overboard. She was the last of her family.

After the funeral, Annie sat at the long table in steerage and wrote a poem for Mary.

I should have stayed at home and starved,
died in my bed with a soft grave to lie in
near my cabin in the green hills by the river.
There'd be a priest to pray over me.
But no, not me. I wanted to live!
I came here, across this great ocean,
and now, I lie buried alone in deep water.

* * *

The journey had been judged a success. Only six people, including Mary, had died on the crossing. The ship was now just three days out of the Gulf of Saint Lawrence. Almost there.

Quebec, British North America

The Ocean Queen sailed past Newfoundland. Steerage passengers were allowed on deck to watch as they passed Prince Edward Island in the Gulf of Saint Lawrence. Just two more days, and they would set foot in British North America. Most of those on board had no intention of staying in this part of the world. British rule brought more reminders of the landlords who had left them to starve back home. They were done with that, America beckoned.

Annie stood on deck. She breathed in the cool air and looked at the land and the wide sky, almost white with low clouds. She pulled Katty and Finn close to her.

'We're nearly there, my darlings. We dock in two days. Please God, we'll see Aunt Bridie soon.'

She continued to look at the strange landscape and bitter tears filled her eyes. They were only here because her father had died. He would never have left Ireland. Poor Eileen too, must have stood here with her parents and looked out at these mountains, not knowing how their journey would end. And Mary, she almost made it here.

Annie felt the warmth of Finn's hand on hers, then he reached up to wipe away her tears. She kissed his face. 'Finnie,' she whispered.

She walked back with Finn and Katty to the steerage deck. She felt strangely chilled, probably from standing on deck for too long, but when she touched her face, it was hot, despite the cold in the rest of her body. She put a blanket around her and sat on the bunk for a few minutes to get the heat in her, but her body still felt cold and she started to shiver. She turned to face the wall and pulled open the front of her dress. Dread coursed through her, when she saw the dull red spots on her chest and stomach. Ship fever. It could only be that. She lay down in a daze.

* * *

Since the old couple and Mary died from this disease, there had been three more deaths from ship fever; two steerage passengers and a crew member. But many more were ill.

She heard Katty called Finn. 'Come and see Annie, she's lying down.'

Annie tried to think. What to do? She whispered to Finn. 'Run and tell Philomena I'm sick. Come back to me and mind Katty. Don't leave my side.'

Despite Annie's muddled words, Finn understood. Philomena came and checked on Annie. Finn insisted they would look after their sister. The two children stayed with Annie as she became delirious with the fever. Katty held her hand and Finn gave her water to drink. They both knelt beside the bunk and prayed for her to get better. Philomena came back later and helped Annie change her shift and wash her face and hands.

Annie drifted in and out of consciousness through the night

and all of the next day. The ship continued its journey and sailed along the Saint Lawrence River to Grosse Isle, an island just a few miles north of Quebec.

In Annie's mind she was back at home in Ashling. She spoke to her Da about the potatoes, how good they looked, fresh out of the ground, and how the next day they had turned black and putrid, and she saw again her father's tears of frustration. They both knew the family couldn't last another winter without their food crop.

* * *

The Ocean Queen docked at Grosse Isle. Emigrants were to be inspected and the sick would be quarantined there on the island. The other passengers would stay on board, and continue their journey to Quebec.

The Captain came down to the steerage to check on the passengers. He saw Annie lying down. Finn and Katty sat nearby on a bench.

'Annie, are you on the mend, girl?' he asked.

Annie nodded. 'I am Captain,' she replied. Annie's voice was hoarse. Her eyes were swollen in her gaunt face. But she had the strength to sit up. She swung her legs over the side of the bunk and held on to the sides with both hands. The tendons in her hands and feet gleamed like pale twigs.

The Captain leaned in close to her and felt her flushed face. 'You're still poorly.'

Katty came over and sat next to Annie. 'She's nearly better now, Captain. Aren't you Annie?'

Finn held up his tin whistle. 'I've been playing for Annie. I think it woke her up!'

'You've a great little crew there. Annie, we're docked in Grosse Isle for the passengers to be inspected. Those who are sick will be taken off here and sent to quarantine on the island. Then we'll continue on to Quebec.' He paused. 'What's it to be?'

Annie took a deep breath. 'I can walk. Finn and Katty will help me.'

'The Medical Officer has already moved some off the ship,' the captain said. 'Your friend John was one of them. He's been sick for the last two days, like you.'

He pointed to the black clad Medical Officer talking to a family just a few yards away from Annie.

'I'll say the same thing to you as I said to that family. You need to convince him that you're well enough to go on to Quebec.'

Annie pulled her blouse on and buttoned it. Her fingers trembled, but she got the job done.

'Another word of advice for you, Annie,' he said. 'They have quarantine sheds in Quebec, too. Do your best to avoid them, and in Montreal. You won't want to be separated from your brother and sister, now will you?'

She looked at him, understood there was some kind of warning, and shook her head.

'We won't be separated,' she said. Tears filled her eyes and trickled down her face. 'I'm sorry.' She wiped her face and brushed her hair back.

'Now,' the Captain continued. 'When the Medical Officer has completed his checks, we'll weigh anchor and we'll be in Quebec in a couple of hours. I've heard that you can travel free of charge from there to Montreal. After that, you'll need money to get to New York. It's a long journey mind,' he said.

'And if you get stopped by border guards, you'll be sent straight back here to Quebec.'

The Captain held out a large envelope to Annie. 'Take this. I've written some directions down for you,' he said. 'Travel on the water, where you can. I'd say you're in no fit state to be walking hundreds of miles, are you now? The Captain smiled briefly. 'Head south to Lake Ontario. There's a map in here'.

Annie took the envelope from him. 'I'll take your advice, Captain,' she said. 'We're so thankful to be here. And thank you for this, I'll not forget you.'

The Captain left to join the Medical Officer who continued his checks on passengers. Those who were sick with the fever would be transferred to the quarantine sheds on the island.

* * *

Annie finished getting dressed. She had kept her money-belt round her waist, and was relieved to find it still intact, although there was not much in it. She had never been this thin. Her hip and rib bones almost pushed through her skin. Her eyes felt too large for her face, and she could feel the bones in her skull and eye sockets. Katty and Finn stood by their bag and waited.

'Are you all better now, Annie?' Katty asked. She knelt and helped Annie pull her stockings on, then held Annie's shoes for her to slip on.

'I'm all better, *astór*,' Annie said. 'Thank God. We'll just wait for the Medical Officer.'

Annie's legs buckled as she stood, her vision blurred and she fought the dizziness in her head. She put her arm around Finn's shoulder and kissed him, then she saw the Medical

Officer coming towards their bunk and straightened up.

'Now then, Captain, are these the last of the passengers?' the Medical Officer asked.

'Yes, Doctor,' the Captain replied. 'As you can see they're well, and eager to continue their journey in Quebec.'

The doctor motioned Katty to come and stand before him and he felt her forehead and her neck. Then he did the same for Finn. It took him only a moment to pass the children. He looked at Annie. 'Have you been sick with the fever, miss?' he asked her.

Annie shook her head. 'No, just a bit of sea-sickness, doctor. I'll be fine when I get on land.'

The doctor looked at Finn and Katty, then back to Annie. He pressed his lips together and appeared to make a decision.

'Welcome to British North America,' the doctor said. He turned to the Captain. 'I'm finished now, sir. I'll head back to the quarantine hospital, if you'll arrange for me to be transferred?'

The two men left, and Annie sat down. She put her arms out and Finn and Katty sat one on either side of her. They hugged each other, then Annie blessed herself.

'Come on, help me up on deck, you two. I need to see land!' Annie said.

Finn held their bag in one hand and put his other arm around her waist. They left the steerage compartment that had been their shelter for the last two months. Soon, they would set foot on land, in Quebec.

* * *

The three of them stood on deck and waited for the ship

to move away. They looked across at the quarantine island, Grosse Isle. Green water tumbled with white-topped waves and ran fast between the shores of the island and the mainland.

Finn and Katty sat with their backs to the bulwark of the deck, while Annie leaned against the ship's railing and looked across the quay towards a large shed. She squinted to read the sign on the wall of the shed. "No Admittance – Quarantine!"

To the side of the shed, she saw an open pit, a great hole dug into the earth.

'What is it? A grave?' she whispered to herself.

Annie watched as a nun, dressed in a grey habit, came out of the shed. She carried a small bundle, wrapped in a blanket, in her arms. The nun knelt at the edge of the pit, unwrapped the blanket and rolled a child's body into the open grave, then blessed herself. The child was only small, younger than Katty. Annie couldn't make out if it was a boy or a girl. Annie caught her breath and put her hand to her heart. That child was someone's darling. Where were her mother and father?

Annie spoke the words of the poem she had written for Mary.

> 'Have you come all this way to die here and be buried,
> with no Priest to say a prayer for your souls?
> Ah, my poor brothers and sisters.'

She made the sign of the cross and said a prayer for the dead child and the others in that open pit.

Annie made a promise to herself, that neither she, nor her sister or brother, would be rolled into a pit for a grave.

The last of the sick were moved off the ship and the Ocean Queen hauled anchor and continued her journey to Quebec.

Crossing the border

nnie, Finn and Katty, ate their last meal on the deck of the Ocean Queen and looked out at this strange new land. On either side of the river, tree-covered hills rose to the sky. The sky itself seemed bigger than anything she remembered from home. Not just wider but higher, with white clouds scudding across the blue beyond. Annie shaded her eyes from the glare of the sun reflected off the clouds.

She remembered the package from Captain Hennessy and opened it. Inside the package, there were two letters, a map, and five silver shillings. She read the first letter to her siblings.

Dear Annie, here's a map and directions that will get you, Katty and Finn, safely to New York. Don't stay in Quebec, go straight to Montreal.

From there, take a steamer ship along the Saint Lawrence River, and head for Lake Ontario. Disembark at Kingston. You will still be in British North America. At Kingston, hire a boat to take you to Oswego. Once there, you will have crossed the border into America, Annie.

From Oswego, get a canal barge to Albany, then continue on down the Hudson River to New York.

I have enclosed a few shillings to help you with the fares. You worked hard on the journey across and, in my opinion, you have earned this. I also enclose a letter of recommendation. It may help you find a job when you get to New York.

God bless you. If you were my daughter, I would be proud of you.

Captain Sean Hennessy

Annie folded the stiff parchment letter and smoothed her hand over his signature. 'Thank you, Captain,' she whispered.

Together with Finn and Katty, she studied the map that would take them to New York. It was a rough sketch, but she could see Montreal, then Kingston on Lake Ontario. And the Captain had pencilled in the border between the British controlled part of North America and free North America.

She tucked the letter into her journal, then opened the smaller letter. This was written in Captain Hennessy's best copperplate handwriting, on embossed paper. At the top of the page was printed the name of the ship, Ocean Queen, and its home port of Liverpool. She read the beautiful words about herself, "a teacher dedicated to the welfare of her young pupils", "a credit to the teaching profession". Annie folded the letter carefully and stored it in her journal with the first letter. 'I'll not forget this,' she promised herself. 'I'll repay this good deed as soon as I am able.'

She looked around her at the other Irish immigrants sitting on the deck of the ship. Some were the children she had taught. All had dreams for a new life, free from hunger and sickness. She prayed for them to have good fortune in their new life.

* * *

The ship arrived in Quebec late in the afternoon. The immigrants disembarked onto a crowded pier. Still not fully recovered from the fever, Annie's senses were overwhelmed by the noise and crowds of people milling around the streets and alleyways that surrounded the dock. She was pushed and shoved out of the way by rough hands and, after one push, nearly fell into the stinking gutter. Finn and Katty held on tight to her and they followed signs to a ticket office.

The roadway was crammed with mule-pulled carts, hand-pushed carts, horses carrying their riders on urgent business and hundreds of people on foot. She covered her mouth with her hand to stop the smells of horse dung, smoke and that mousy smell she recognised from back at home. It had killed her father and seemed to be everywhere.

'Hurry,' she said. 'I want us to get out of here as soon as we can.'

They went as fast as Annie's legs would allow, along the road towards a large building with a banner across the top of the door - Steamer Tickets to Montreal!

Once inside the building, they joined another queue of immigrants. She checked her money, not much left, and was thankful for Captain Hennessy's gift. They were soon in possession of tickets to Montreal. Annie was even more thankful to find Captain Hennessy had been right. The tickets to Montreal were free.

* * *

Still moving swiftly, as if being pursued, Annie and her siblings rushed back along the quayside to board the River Rose, a flat-bottomed steamship that was already teaming with people.

306

They found space to sit on the deck and waited for the steamer to begin the overnight journey to Montreal.

Katty's head appeared to be on a swivel as she looked at everyone and everything on the crowded vessel. 'Annie, I can see some people who were on the ship with us from Ireland.' Katty jumped up and pointed. 'Look! There's John.'

She took off across the deck and was joined by Finn. They both called out, 'John, John! Come and see Annie, she's all better.'

John turned and smiled when he saw the two Power children heading his way. Then he looked across and saw Annie. He walked over to her with Katty and Finn.

'I thought you didn't make it, Annie,' John said. 'I was sick myself, and they disembarked me into the fever shed in Grosse Isle. When I saw the condition of the others in there, I got out and jumped on a ferry to Quebec.'

'I had Katty and Finn looking after me,' Annie said. 'Are you better, now?'

John's lovely jacket and waistcoat were worn and stained. His hat was crumpled, but his eyes shone as he nodded. 'Yes, I'm well enough, Annie. The fever has eased. I tell you, a good feed wouldn't go astray on me, but that'll come when I get to Boston. And it won't be long now.'

As they spoke, the steamship set off upriver to Montreal. It was now late August and the evening showed the promise of autumn. They looked over the side of the steamer and saw lines of ships waiting to unload their emigrant passengers into Quebec. The Ocean Queen had arrived just ahead of all the rest.

Finn asked if he and Katty could go for a look around the ferry. Annie nodded her assent.

'Come on, Katty,' Finn said. 'I'll race you to the end of the ferry and back.'

'This is the first time in days I have seen them smile,' Annie said. 'And it's so good to see you, John.'

'It's good to see familiar faces. I know you're heading for New York, and I'm going to Boston. But can we travel part of the way together? I need some company and I can think of none better than you, Finn and Katty. What do you say?' John waited for Annie's reply.

'Captain Hennessy gave me a map with directions,' Annie said. 'We'll be travelling on the water and you're welcome to join us.'

They settled down to overnight on the steamer. In the early part of the evening, Finn played his tin whistle while Katty danced. The familiar music of home soon drew other children who joined in the dancing. Later, they lay on deck and slept through till morning.

* * *

The River Rose docked early in Montreal. This port was huge, and was filled with ships of all sizes. As they waited to disembark, Annie saw her first ever canoe flitting across the water. It was long and narrow and the rower slipped the canoe between the three and four-masted ships at anchor. These great ships were either unloading imports from English manufactories, so John informed her, or taking on exports of furs, wheat and timber bound for England and her other colonies. She watched as around fifty horses trotted onto one of the ships. Annie looked at John. 'Where are they bound for?' John's expression told her that he had no idea either and they laughed.

If they thought they had left the fever behind them in Grosse Isle, they were mistaken. The fever travelled with them, and as they walked down the gangway, Annie saw lines of people, clearly ill, just sitting alongside the pier.

'Those poor people. Is there no-one to take care of them?' It appeared not.

Instead, Annie heard shouted orders from one of the crew of the River Rose. 'When you disembark, everyone needs to report to the immigrant sheds, over that way near Wellington Bridge.'

'I'm done with reporting,' Annie said. 'Let's get out of here.'

* * *

John bought some fresh water and bread and fruit from a trader on the quay. They took it with them, walked away from the quay, and sat beside a warehouse overlooking the river. They watched the busy port in action; great ships coming and going, hundreds of men working on the docks and hucksters selling dreams to immigrants like Annie.

While they ate, Finn saw a notice board on the side of one of the warehouses, it was full of posters looking for information. Finn stood for a while and read a few, until one in particular, caught his eye. He looked over to Annie and Katty, and then he reached up and took the poster down from the board and brought it back to Annie and showed it to her. It was a newspaper advertisement. Annie read it.

The *Montreal Transcript*, 11 August 1846:

"Information wanted of Abraham Taylor, aged 12 years, Samuel Taylor, 10 years, and George Taylor, 8 years old, from county Leitrim, Ireland. Were landed in Quebec about 5 weeks ago, their mother having been detained at Grosse Isle. Any information respecting them would be thankfully received by their brother, William Taylor, at this office."

'Annie, do you think those boys will be found by their brother?' Finn's eyes filled with tears.

'I don't know, Finn. Five weeks is a long time in this crowded place. I hope they'll be found, and I hope their mother is better now. Come here to me,' Annie said. She pulled Finn into her arms in a tight hug and tried to still a shiver that ran through her body. She took in a deep breath. 'We're together, and nearly there. With God's help we'll get to New York.' She wiped away Finn's tears. 'Now then, put the poster back on the board, and come and we'll say a decade of the rosary for those boys to be found. What do you say?'

Finn nodded and walked back to the board, and pinned the poster back up. Then he came back to Annie, Katty and John. They had finished their meal and knelt together on the stony ground.

Annie took out her rosary beads, blessed herself and started to recite the Hail Mary. Finn, Katty and John joined in to complete the prayers. 'Holy Mary, Mother of God, pray for us sinners, now and at the hour of our death. Amen.'

They finished the decade of the rosary, and Annie prayed, 'Dear Blessed Mother, thank you for helping us to arrive safely. Have pity on those brothers, and reunite them with their family.'

* * *

Their next task was to find a steamer for the onward part of their journey. Their steamship out of Montreal sailed at noon for Kingston, on Lake Ontario. The great Saint Lawrence river spread out ahead of them, and the sun was high in the sky and sent its light skimming across the tops of the waves, as if to speed their journey.

'Annie, I can't wait to see New York and Auntie Bridie. Are we nearly there?' Katty asked.

Annie smiled. 'Darling, we've a way to go yet. Tomorrow morning we'll get to Kingston, please God, and then we'll cross Lake Ontario into North America. After that, we'll travel to New York and Auntie Bridie. She's waiting for us.'

The day passed slowly as the ferry cruised south, past hundreds of islands, large and small, scattered through the river. At this point Annie could just about see each bank in the distance as the river widened on its passage towards Lake Ontario, flowing past tiny islands and coves. She observed a small village on the river's edge. These were no turf cabins, they were houses and mostly built of timber. Some had thatched roofs, others were roofed with shingles, and some even had rooms upstairs. To walk into that house, go upstairs and look out of the window and see this ferry full of immigrants steaming along the river. 'What is it like to live that life?' she asked herself. In a house with a stairs and comfortable beds and chairs, enough food to eat. She shook her head.

The steamer passed the small village and continued its journey south-west to Lake Ontario. The sun in the big sky above shone on the faces of her immigrant companions. Although most were half-starved and dressed in second or third-hand clothes, Annie saw her own hope reflected in their faces. Almost there, thank God and his blessed Mother.

311

Annie was still weak after the fever and tears came easily. She wiped her eyes, stood and looked over the crowded deck to find Finn and Katty. There they were, playing with a group of children, watched over by John. As she watched, John looked across, saw her and lifted his hand in greeting, and she smiled.

* * *

As night fell, Annie settled Katty and Finn beside her and sang their favourite lullaby. Even Finn smiled when he heard her sing.

'I'm too big for you to sing me to sleep,' Finn said.

'You're still my little brother. I'll sing you to sleep any time I please,' she replied, and smoothed his dark curls back from his forehead. If only their Da could be with them. They should have left when Eileen and her family left last year. She shook her head at the thought. It might have been the Power family who drowned in the Saint Lawrence River, along with their friends, the Butlers.

Annie slept for an hour or two, then sat and watched the luminous half-moon and the stars glittering in the night sky. There seemed to be more stars here than she remembered back at home. Later, dawn lightened the river and the ferry began to change course on its approach to Lake Ontario. The ferry slowed and turned towards a large town ahead on the north side of the river estuary. They had reached Kingston. Annie joined other passengers as they rushed to the side of the ferry to watch the town approach.

They docked. Annie picked up her bag, and together, they stepped onto the quay.

* * *

Annie checked her map. 'Captain Hennessy said we need to get a boat around the lake to Oswego. That'll bring us into North America,' she said. 'We need to get some food first though. I'm starving.'

They strolled along the quay towards some shops and bought a bottle of tea, and some bread and cheese and ham.

Finn spotted a low wall and they sat on that to eat their breakfast. For Annie, the taste of American food was a revelation. She was used to home-made cheese, but had not eaten ham for many months and the tender cooked meat strengthened and cheered her. It didn't take much to fill her stomach, and after a few mouthfuls she was satisfied.

'Right, is everyone ready?' Annie asked. 'Now we can go and find our crossing into North America.'

There was a busy trade in passage across the lake. No ticket offices, just haggling with boat owners. Their boat was a fishing boat by the smell of it, and they crammed in with others and set off around the lake. The lake water was calm and reflected the blue sky. Annie saw more small settlements built around the lake. The fishing boat worked its way to the North American side of the lake and they docked in Oswego in the early afternoon.

Oswego was a small village, and no-one questioned them or checked their papers. From there, the canal connected right through to the Hudson River and then south into the heart of New York. Annie held on tight to her map. They bought more tickets, this time, one way to New York city. Their boat, the Oswego Chief, would take them to Syracuse, and from there on to Albany. They were on the last stretch of their journey.

* * *

The days of that journey east were like a wonderful dream for Annie. The newly built canal ran through wooded countryside. In some places the canal was more like a river until they arrived at lock gates and had to wait their turn to move through the locks. Traffic was immense. Many of the boats carried cargo rather than passengers. The Oswego Chief had a mixture of both passengers and huge loads of grain destined for New York city and perhaps further afield. Would that they could send some to Ireland, she prayed.

Their steamship stopped at Albany where John took his leave of them.

'You've got my address, Annie?' he asked and he hugged Katty and Finn.

'I have it in my journal,' Annie replied. Then she stepped forward and embraced him. 'God go with you, John.'

'And I have your address safe here,' John said, and put his hand on his breast pocket. 'I'm only sorry poor Mary couldn't be with us.' He picked up his bag and they watched him walk along the gangplank and on to the quay. He turned and waved, before merging with the crowds on the quay.

John would take a train to Boston. Annie and her siblings would stay on board the steamship until their final destination, New York

New York

The siblings slept outside on the deck of the ship for the last three nights of their journey. Annie learned that their steamship, the Oswego Chief, was one hundred and sixty-five feet long and newly built of wood and iron. It looked more like a barge, flat bottomed to travel the Hudson River, with two masts for the sails and a stout chimney for the engine that turned the covered paddle wheels. It was just one of many ships that sailed and steamed along the Hudson.

The days were cold, almost freezing and they huddled together for warmth on deck as they travelled through the American countryside. A crew member pointed out the Catskill Mountains in the distance, filled with dense green forests.

They had brought food with them and ate sparingly. Annie saw Katty and Finn become more and more excited as the steamship drew closer to New York city. For the last hour of their journey, there were so many ships that the river was almost hidden from view. Finally, their ship eased in beside the docks, and the steam engine shut down.

Annie stood at the ship's railings with Katty and Finn; they and the rest of the passengers were lined up along the railings of the ship to get a first glimpse of New York. The area around the docks was full of sheds and stone warehouses built along the quays to store the grain, timber and other goods that came into the city. Not much further beyond the warehouses, Annie saw more steam rising, this time from the nearby railway station.

They saw hundreds of people moving around the quays and docks. Many were sailors and even more were just like Annie and her siblings, newly arrived migrants. Annie noticed quite a number of men waiting at the end of their gangplank for the passengers to disembark, and thought they must be waiting to meet relatives.

* * *

They hugged each other, and Annie began to relax. All this way, and finally here. Thank God! They walked down the gangway and set foot in New York.

They had just the final short journey to their aunt's apartment. They followed their fellow passengers along the pier to leave the docks, then Annie saw a sign for a privy just a few yards away.

'Wait here, Finn, and mind the bag, I'll only be a minute,' Annie said, and handed him the bag. 'Katty, wait with Finn.' She went into the shed and crouched over the wooden seat. The stench in the shed meant she only took a few moments.

When Annie came outside the shed, she saw the pier had filled up with another ship load of disembarked emigrants, who pushed and jostled past her.

She couldn't see her brother and sister through the crowds of people and she froze for a second. 'Oh, my God! Where are you, Finn and Katty?' She blew a breath out. 'Oh, there he is, Finn!' she called.

He was by a wall at the end of the pier with the bag at his feet, but alone. Finn looked up at the sound of his name, saw Annie and waved her over to him.

'Where's Katty?' she called, then yelled, 'Katty, where are you?' Annie's heart almost stopped in her chest. Where was her little sister? She raced along the pier, pushed her way through to Finn, who said. 'She was just here, a second ago.'

A flash of colour caught her eye. Yellow or gold. Katty's ribbon? Was that Katty calling?

'Someone's taken her!' Annie screamed. 'That way.'

The sister and brother raced down a side-street and away from the pier. They saw Katty up ahead, as she struggled to get away from the man who held her. Annie recognised him as one of those standing at the end of the gangway. He was bearded and ragged; his skinny arm was wrapped around her sister's waist as he tried to force her to run.

Annie shouted. 'Katty, Katty. We're coming! Help! Stop him! He's taking my sister.'

People stopped and gawped as Annie and Finn raced along the alley. Two young men joined them, and they began to catch up with the bearded man.

Annie heard Katty scream again, and saw the man turn down a side alley. He now had Katty by the hand and dragged her along with him, but they were almost on him. He looked back at them and saw he would be caught.

'Let her go, let her go!' Annie shouted and reached out for her sister's hand.

The man pushed Katty away, she fell to the ground and he continued to run. Finn and the two young men chased after him but he turned a corner and vanished into a narrow

317

alleyway.

Annie stopped, bent down and pulled her sister into her arms. She felt Katty's heart beat like a *bodhran* against her own. 'Katty, sweetheart, I have you. Did he hurt you, darling?'

Katty shook her head, and kept her face turned into Annie's chest. Annie felt her sister's heartbeat begin to slow a little and held her tight. They both trembled.

Finn came back to Annie with the two men who had helped. 'We couldn't catch him.'

Annie shook her head. 'No matter. And thank you for your help,' she said to the men. They shook hands with Finn and went on their way.

Annie put her hand out and pulled Finn to her. 'She's safe,' and she felt great tears pour from her eyes and harsh sobs escaped as she tried to catch her breath, until finally, she was able to compose herself. Katty still had her arms around Annie's neck and Annie urged her to stand, then she picked her little sister up and carried her.

* * *

Passers-by continued on their way with barely a glance at the three siblings on their way back to the pier. Finn retrieved their bag, which, by some miracle, was where he had dropped it. Annie's whole body shook with fear, her head pounded and she had to swallow hard not to be sick. They sat together on a low wall near to the ship they had just disembarked.

'Sweetheart, tell me what happened,' Annie said.

'I'm sorry, Annie, I was just looking at the boats. The man called me over and he said Da had sent him. I told him my Da wasn't here, but he grabbed my hand and pulled me around the corner.' Katty's face was streaked with tears, her hair was all tangled. Annie noticed a bruise on her arm where the man had pulled her. 'I shouted for you, did you hear me?' Katty asked.

'We did, sweetheart, and we came and got you. He was a bad man. He's gone now.' Annie smoothed her sister's hair back from her face and fixed her ribbon, then kissed both face and ribbon.

Finn put his arm around Katty. 'I nearly caught him, Katty. And if I had, he was in big trouble, I swear.'

'We need to get out of here now, before anything else happens,' Annie said. 'Let's go. We'll get a cab up to Auntie Bridie's.'

Annie took one of Captain Hennessy's shillings out of her money belt and they walked together to a line of horse drawn cabs waiting at the end of the pier.

'How much to go to Saint Patrick's Cathedral?' she asked the first cab driver.

'Just two dollars to you, Miss.'

Annie held up her hand and showed him the silver shilling. 'That's all I have.'

The cab driver pulled a face at her offer and turned away. Annie picked her bag up and they moved on to the next cab with Finn and Katty close by her side. She held up the silver coin to the driver, who jumped down and opened the door to the cab.

'Saint Patrick's? In you get, Miss.'

They had their ride and it didn't take long. Annie was used to busy streets after her stay in Dublin, but this was of a totally different magnitude. They were hemmed in by tall buildings and crushed by crowds of people. The cab jolted along congested, muddy streets and stopped outside a great Cathedral. It seemed to Annie that every single person she heard, spoke a language that she didn't understand. She held on tight to Katty, who had begun to look around her, and they turned on to Prince Street. In her letter, Aunt Bridie had said she lived in the apartment block on the corner.

* * *

The three Powers stood silently on the street outside the brownstone apartment building. There was a steep flight of stone steps leading up to the front door. Annie's heart was too full to speak, after all these weeks and miles to reach safety for herself and her siblings. Then she and Finn and Katty ran up the steps and knocked hard on the door. As they waited, Annie whispered 'Thank you, Jane.' Her friend had sacrificed herself so Annie could save herself and her brother and sister.

The door opened and a woman stood there. Annie recognised her mother's sister straight away. Bridie opened her arms to her nieces and nephew. The first words she spoke were the Irish welcome. *'Cead Mille Failte.'*

Annie had succeeded. They had reached their safe haven.

Epilogue. July 1846

The transportation ship for New South Wales sailed on south through the Atlantic Ocean. Jane Keating readied herself for the new life ahead of her. She wasn't afraid of what was to come. Anything was better than slowly starving to death in Ireland. At night, she dreamed of Annie, Finn and Katty, and hoped they'd make it safely to their aunt in New York. She knew she had done the right thing in taking Annie's place on the convict ship, and was sure that she would meet Annie again. Seven years wasn't that long. She made a vow. We'll meet in New York, my friend.

About the Author

I was born in England, of Irish emigrant parents. I have always had a deep interest in Irish history, particularly in relation to British colonialism and the Irish Diaspora. I began researching and writing this novel some years ago.

I recently completed a Master's Degree in Creative Writing with the Open University.

Together with writing novels, I blog about 19th and 20th century Irish history, emigration, women, writers, poets, art, and politics.

I hope that you have enjoyed reading this book and I will be grateful if you can post a review on www.Amazon.com/
  Thank you.
  Bridget Walsh